ANYONE BUT YOU

OLIVIA SPRING

Boldwood

First published in Great Britain in 2025 by Boldwood Books Ltd.

Cover Design by Rachel Lawston

Cover Images: Rachel Lawston

A CIP catalogue record for this book is available from the British Library.

Paperback ISBN 978-1-83633-023-3

Large Print ISBN 978-1-83633-022-6

Hardback ISBN 978-1-83633-021-9

Trade Paperback ISBN 978-1-80656-027-1

Ebook ISBN 978-1-83633-024-0

Kindle ISBN 978-1-83633-025-7

Audio CD ISBN 978-1-83633-016-5

MP3 CD ISBN 978-1-83633-017-2

Digital audio download ISBN 978-1-83633-020-2

This book is printed on certified sustainable paper. Boldwood Books is dedicated to putting sustainability at the heart of our business. For more information please visit https://www.boldwoodbooks.com/about-us/sustainability/

Boldwood Books Ltd, 23 Bowerdean Street, London, SW6 3TN

www.boldwoodbooks.com

To anyone who is looking for true love. Sometimes it can happen with the most unexpected person when you least expect it.

ANYONE BUT YOU PLAYLIST

Love Yourself – Justin Bieber
What's My Name – Rihanna ft. Drake
Attention – Charlie Puth
Hollywood – Madonna
Lost Angeles – The Aces
Holding Out for a Hero – Bonnie Tyler
Dark Horse – Katy Perry
Nice To Each Other – Olivia Dean
Stargazing – Myles Smith
All The Stars – Kendrick Lamar and SZA
A Sky Full of Stars – Coldplay
Waiting for a Star to Fall – Boy Meets Girl
Stars – Simply Red
Kiss Me – Ed Sheeran
Good in Bed – Dua Lipa
Downtown – SWV
Malibu – Kim Petras
Malibu – Miley Cyrus
Smile – Gorgon City ft. Elderbrook
If You Could See Me Now – The Script
Wannabe – Spice Girls
Never Gonna Give You Up – Rick Astley

1

HALLE

'I'm sorry to have to tell you this, Halle, but you're in serious danger.' My best friend Vanessa's face fell.

'Danger?' I frowned, holding my beef taco in mid-air. 'Of what?'

'Of your poor vagina being resealed due to lack of activity!' she cackled, before draining her glass of red wine and slamming it on the table triumphantly like she'd just told the best joke ever.

'Not funny and *harsh*.' I rolled my eyes before sliding the last taco bite into my mouth. It was delicious and I resented the fact that her stupid comment had delayed me from finishing it by at least ten valuable seconds.

'But it's *true*! That guy at the bar has been giving you serious *let me rock your world* vibes all night and you've ignored him. *Again*.'

'For good reason! Every time we come to this bar, he's cosying up to a different woman. He's got player written all over him.'

'That doesn't have to be a bad thing. You could do with a good roll in the hay. You know I love you, but just because you're waiting for your knight in shining armour to ride in and sweep you off your feet, doesn't mean you can't *ride* someone else in the meantime! Safely, of course. Seriously, Hal,' she ran her hand through her sleek, jet-black shoulder-length hair, 'it's been two years since you've had a shag. Just go over there, tell him you want to bang and take him home.'

'Are you insane?' I gasped. 'He could be a murderer. And I don't even know if he fancies me!'

'Firstly, Harvey, the owner, told me that's his best friend's son, so if he does anything, I'll know where to hunt him down. And secondly, *of course* he fancies you! You're gorgeous. Your parents knew exactly what they were doing when they named you Halle – you're the spitting image of Halle Berry. You could easily pass for her younger sister. Your chocolate curls are popping, your gorgeous brown skin is glowing, your nails are flawless as always, and that pink lip gloss you're rocking suits you. Is it new?'

'No...' I eyed her suspiciously. She wasn't usually so effusive with the compliments. She must really want me to get back out there. 'Er... thanks.'

'Just speaking the truth, babe. Anyway, I've lost count of the times bar guy's checked you out since we've been coming here. He *definitely* likes you. Plus, you're a Brit living in New York. All you have to do is say *hello* and he'll get an instant boner from your accent.'

'That's such a cliché,' I scoffed.

'Works for me!' She grinned. 'The other day, there was a hot policeman cordoning off an area downtown, so I went over, put on my best Liz Hurley accent and said, "Oh, my goodness, officer. What an *earth* has happened here?" And you know the first thing he said?'

'What?'

'Well, after he told me someone had been attacked, which obvs was terrible, he said, "Hey! Nice accent." Trust me. These

American guys are putty in our hands. Moving to New York was the best thing we ever did. You need to take advantage of it more. It's a dating hotbed.'

'For *you* maybe.'

When I was growing up and watching TV shows set in New York, I used to think it was the dating metropolis. But the reality was that ever since I'd moved here six years ago it'd been more *sexless* than *Sex and the City*.

'It could be for you too. If you were more open-minded.'

'You're not talking about threesomes again, are you?' I narrowed my eyes.

'No! It's hard enough getting you to get *one* man into bed, never mind two. I mean, being open-minded to dating opportunities. I know you've got your reasons, so I understand why you're worried, but at some point, you have to try again.'

'I *am* open-minded!' I protested. 'I signed up to that Love Hotel place.'

'Correction: *I* signed you up for your birthday.'

'And I'm going to pay you back every single cent for that deposit because that was *way* too generous of you. Might take me approximately twenty-five years, but I'll find the cash eventually.'

I still couldn't believe Vanessa had done that for me. The deposit was over fifteen hundred dollars, but Vanessa said when she kept hearing me talk about how cool it sounded, she wanted to help.

The Love Hotel was a luxury resort where you were guaranteed to find your Mr Right. They had locations in Europe and they'd announced that they were opening up a branch in the US soon. I didn't know exactly where yet, but in the unlikely event that I got selected (places were like gold dust), I'd be up for going.

'I'm happily single and childfree and I have a great job, so I have money to spend. We've been best friends for practically our whole lives! So if I can't spoil you once in a while, what's the point?'

Our dads both grew up together in New York and fell in love with British women when they moved to London and although Vanessa was a few years older than me, I'd known her since birth.

'Well, I appreciate it.'

'I know. So, when was the last time you checked your emails to see if the hotel had been in touch?'

'Er...' My cheeks heated. 'Maybe a few days ago,' I lied.

If I was being honest, it'd been at least a week. When Vanessa first applied almost three months ago, I *did* check every few days, but after six weeks of disappointment it didn't feel healthy to obsess over it, so I stopped.

Anyway, emails were always depressing. I didn't need that kind of negativity in my life.

'A few *days*?' Vanessa gasped. 'I check my emails at least ten times an hour.'

'You're a lawyer. Emails are important to you. I work in a juice bar. It's not like I have customers emailing to order their morning green juice.'

'Give me your phone!' she ordered, thrusting her hand in front of me. There was no point in arguing, so I handed it over.

'I should never have...' Just as I was about say I regretted giving her my password, an advert flashed up on the TV opposite us that made my stomach churn.

'What's wrong?' Vanessa asked, before following my gaze. 'Oh, shit.'

Plastered all over the screen was my ex, Brett's, annoying face. He was cosying up with his gorgeous supermodel wife in their huge mansion with their perfect one-year-old daughter, promoting the latest season of their reality show.

Most people worried about bumping into their ex at the supermarket, but for me, things were more complicated. Brett was a famous rockstar and although I didn't do social media, barely a day went by without me seeing him plastered on a billboard, hearing his songs blasting on the radio or seeing his perfect life advertised on the promos for his reality show.

Don't get me wrong, I was totally over him. The arsehole broke my heart and I knew I was better off without him. But I just wished I didn't have to see him again.

They say that everything in life is either a lesson or a blessing. In his case, it was both. Although it didn't feel like it when it happened, breaking up was definitely a blessing. And the lesson I learnt was to never date anyone famous again. Just the thought of it made my blood run cold.

'It's fine!' I insisted. 'I need a drink. Want another?'

'You paid for dinner and drinks last time!' Vanessa protested. 'It's my turn.'

'I'm buying *you* a drink,' I insisted. Even though technically I couldn't afford it, Vanessa was always so generous, so I wanted to treat her for a change. 'And I'm going to talk to Bar Bro. You're right. I should have some fun.' I pushed my chair back, stood up and strutted to the bar. 'Another red wine for Vanessa, please, Harvey,' I said, then turned to the guy who'd been giving me the eye. 'Wanna get some air?'

My heart pounded. This was so *not* me. I didn't ask random guys if they *wanted to get some air*, but there was a first time for everything.

'Sure, honey,' he grinned, sliding off his stool, before following me.

'Your drink's on the way,' I said to Vanessa. 'We're stepping outside.'

'I was wondering how long it'd take you to make a move,'

Bar Bro said as he led me down the alleyway at the side of the
bar then gently eased me against the wall. 'If you're looking for
a good time, you've come to the right place. I can't wait to slip
and slide inside your ocean, baby girl. I'm gonna give it to you
so good. One ride on my jumbo jet and you'll be begging for
more.'

My eyes popped. His *jumbo jet*?

I'd never shied away from sexy talk but calling his cock a
jumbo jet was a first. I supposed there was nothing wrong with a
bit of confidence. And this was just supposed to be a bit of fun.
What this guy chose to call his dick wasn't important.

'Maybe we could just, er... kiss?' I said with a weak smile.

If he thought he was going to fuck me down an alleyway, he
could think again.

Although Vanessa was right about it being a while since I'd
been intimate, I still wasn't ready to sleep with anyone. Especially not with a man who was clearly a player. Not after what
happened before.

Just as I was considering whether I should explain to Bar Bro
that I had no intention of riding his *jumbo jet*, he gripped the
back of my head then pushed his mouth on mine.

It took approximately one second for me to realise that
letting this guy kiss me was a very, very bad idea.

He'd said he wanted to *slide inside my ocean*. But the only
wetness happening right now wasn't from between my legs. It
was from the excessive amount of his saliva I felt dribbling down
my chin.

Ugh.

This guy was plunging his tongue in my mouth like he was
trying to unblock a toilet and the sloshing sound he was making
in the process was gross.

My first instinct was to push him away, wipe my mouth and

run for the hills, but I didn't want to be cruel. Maybe he just needed time to warm up.

But as the kiss continued, I felt like I was being sucked into a cyclone. He was slobbering all over me like an overenthusiastic dog.

Just when I thought it couldn't get any worse, he burped.

Yep. Mid-snog.

As the taste of raw onions and stale beer flooded my mouth and invaded my nostrils, I fought the urge not to gag.

I'd tried, but I just couldn't do it.

I jerked away, desperate to run to the bathroom and guzzle a pint of industrial-strength mouthwash.

'Best kiss you've ever had, right?' Bar Bro said proudly, a satisfied grin plastered over his face.

'I... I have to go,' I said before sprinting inside the bar and straight over to Vanessa. 'We need to go. Right *now!*'

'What?' Vanessa said. I gestured with my eyes to the door where Bar Bro was walking in. 'Oh... okay.' She grabbed her stuff. Once we were safely inside a yellow taxi, I breathed out a sigh of relief.

'Remind me never to attempt to pick up a random guy again,' I said, thinking that going to the Love Hotel was looking even more appealing.

Obviously, they wouldn't vet guests for their kissing or dirty talk skills (imagine if someone had that job!), but the calibre of men had to be better than that guy. I'd contact them again first thing on Monday to see if they had an update.

Vanessa was right. It was time for me to get back on the horse. But I wanted to find someone decent. Picking up strangers wasn't my thing. Neither were dating apps. Getting the professionals to weed out all the weirdos was the best way forward. It was time for a fresh start.

'I take it from the way we ran off like murderers fleeing a crime scene, your experience with Bar Bro wasn't good?'

'That's an understatement! Forget calling him Bar Bro. I've renamed him *Burp Bro*. That was the most traumatic first kiss of my life. And considering my first boyfriend's tongue almost got stuck in my braces, that's saying something.'

When I told Vanessa what happened, she winced.

'That's gross! Sorry, babe. I wish I could say that your bad dating experiences were over, but... What the fuck?' Vanessa's jaw suddenly dropped.

'What's up?'

'I've got good news and bad news.' She sighed as she looked down at my phone. With everything that had happened, I'd forgotten that I'd given it to her.

'Yeah?'

'So... the good news is that you had a place at the Love Hotel in California.'

'Oh my God!' I squealed, causing the cab driver to jump. 'That's amazing. I was happy to go before, but thanks to Burp Bro, I'm ecstatic! I know how hard it is to get a place there, so I realise how lucky I am. I'm ready, Vanessa! I'm gonna take my dating life more seriously. I was just thinking that I'd email them on Monday morning to follow up. I'm so glad that now I don't have to!'

Talk about great timing. This was brilliant news.

'I mean, I know it's in California, which isn't ideal, especially if it's anywhere near LA or Beverly Hills,' I continued rambling. I used to always want to go there. But I'd avoided it like the plague, because it was where my ex was. 'But it'll be fine. Hard, definitely, but fine. Wait...' I frowned again. 'Why aren't you excited?' Considering she encouraged me to apply and paid the massive deposit, I thought she'd be relieved that it wouldn't go to waste.

'Hold on. You said that there was bad news. Is the bad part the fact that it's near Brett's house or something?'

'No,' Vanessa said solemnly and took a deep breath. 'The good news is that you *had* a place.'

'You mean *have*, right?'

Vanessa shook her head.

'You *had* a place, but to secure it, you were supposed to confirm and pay the balance: last week.'

'Wait, what?' My brain scrambled.

'They sent the original email weeks ago, Halle. You said you checked a few days ago!'

'I must've got my dates mixed up... Maybe it went to junk,' I said, trying to hide my embarrassment.

'It was in your inbox. And they sent multiple emails. And said they'd tried calling several times... didn't you see the missed calls or voicemails?'

I swallowed hard as I remembered a period when I got a series of calls that I didn't answer. I'd seen voicemails too but I'd ignored them.

'They were from an unknown number. I... you know that's triggering for me.'

My chest tightened as a fresh wave of memories came flooding back. To the majority of the population, avoiding calls from people who weren't in your contacts might seem OTT, but when you'd been through what I had, it was justified.

'Maybe if I call them and explain...'

'The last email said if you didn't reply within forty-eight hours you'd forfeit your place and the deposit. Permanently. And that was sent a week ago...'

She held up the phone so I could see the text written in very clear bold red writing. And I felt sick.

So that was that then.

Looked like my days of picking up randos in bars weren't over.

I had the opportunity to meet someone half decent and I'd wasted it. Along with Vanessa's money.

Thousands of people dreamt of securing a place at the Love Hotel.

And I'd got one, but I'd blown it.

Shit.

2

JAKE

'Got a minute?' Roger asked as I swiped a freshly toasted bagel off the kitchen counter. 'We need to talk.'

'Whoa.' I held up my hands defensively as I took in his serious expression. 'Sounds like you want to break up with me!'

'This is serious, Jake.' He blew out a frustrated breath and I realised that he wasn't joking. I'd known Roger since high school and I could count on one hand the number of serious chats we'd had.

'I was just on my way out. Got a meeting with Wilma.'

'Good. Great. Cool.' He shuffled awkwardly on the spot. 'I'm glad you're meeting your agent because... Cathy's busting my balls. She... We need to know how much longer you're planning on sleeping on our couch. It's been more than two months and...'

'I know.' My chest tightened. 'I'm sorry. I'm working on it. Things haven't been easy, but I'm trying.'

'I get that, man. It's just that...'

'I hear you. And I'm really grateful for everything you've done. Listen, Wilma said there's some stuff in the pipeline. I'll be out of your hair soon. Promise.'

'Can you give me a timeline?' Roger asked.

I knew that if it was up to him, he'd let me stay for however long I needed, but his wife Cathy wasn't so sympathetic. It was obvious from the way she glared at me that I'd overstayed my welcome. Although now that I thought about it, she glared at me before I'd begged them to sleep on their couch because I had nowhere else to go.

'Soon. I should know more after this meeting. Did Cathy get the money I left for her yesterday?'

'She did, thanks.'

'It's every spare cent I earned working at Pollo Pops. I tried asking for my job back there again a few days ago, but the boss said I was too much of a distraction. Said he wanted customers to come to buy fried chicken, not to take photos of me.'

'I know. That sucks. But I guess I can't blame them. It's not every day you see a celebrity serving chicken wings at a fast-food joint.'

'*Ex*-celebrity,' I corrected, then shuddered. 'Ugh. I can't even believe I used the "c" word. I never liked calling myself that – even when my music was successful. And it definitely doesn't apply to me now. *Has-been* is more accurate.'

'Come on, man. Don't be so hard on yourself. You've got talent. You've been successful once and you'll do it again.'

My stomach twisted. It was nice that he still believed in me. Especially when I didn't believe in myself. But what I'd said was true. I was a washed-up ex-singer who couldn't even keep a job in a fast-food joint in LA and was about to be out on the streets if my best friend's wife got her way.

As much as I wasn't Cathy's biggest fan, I couldn't disagree with her. I *had* overstayed my welcome. She was right to want to have her apartment back to herself without her husband's loser of a friend hanging around like a bad smell.

Yep. I'd officially hit rock bottom.

'Thanks. I'll be out of your hair in a few weeks. A month, tops,' I said, plucking random dates out of the air.

'I appreciate that.' His shoulders relaxed. 'But only if you find somewhere. I need to know that you're okay.'

'I'll be fine.' I slapped him on the back affectionately. 'I made you a bagel.' I pointed to it on the counter. 'Better run.'

'Thanks! Good luck with the meeting.'

'Appreciate it.'

I left the kitchen, grabbed my jacket, then caught the bus to Wilma's office.

'Jakey boy!' Wilma said when I stepped into her office then sat down.

I hated when she called me that. Wilma was only in her mid-fifties, but it made her sound like she was an old lady talking to a child. Her bleached blonde hair was slicked back and her bright pink lipstick stood out against her tanned skin.

On the plus side, she sounded more upbeat than usual and after my chat with Roger earlier, I hoped that meant she had good news.

'Hey.'

'So.' She leant forward. 'I called you in because one of the great opportunities I put you forward for a few months back has just been confirmed.'

'Yeah?' I sat up straighter. This sounded promising. I knew she'd put me forward to judge some TV reality singing contest and although I wasn't keen on those shows, I was desperate, so I'd do it in a heartbeat.

At least I'd be able to guide the kids and hopefully help them from getting sucked in and spat out of the industry like I had.

'Yeah! You've got a place at the Love Hotel!'

'Huh?' I frowned. I remembered filling out the dumb application in her office a few months ago because she told me they were looking for 'stars' who were single. At the time I thought it was weird because it had nothing to do with music, but I'd gone along with it because I had bigger things on my mind to think about. Like the fact that I'd just had to sell my home and had nowhere to go.

'The Love Hotel,' she repeated. 'It's opening soon and they've invited you to be one of their first celebrity guests. The buzz around it is crazy. Forget the elite dating apps. *This* is the hottest place to be for singles!'

'How will staying in a hotel for single people get me out of my situation and help me make music again?' My frown deepened.

'It's all about *exposure*. We need to reinvent your image. No one wants you right now. I've tried every reality show under the sun and no one's biting.'

I wasn't sorry about that. The idea of appearing on one made my skin crawl. But I wasn't gonna lie. The fact that *they* didn't even think *I* was worth inviting stung a little. Things must be even worse than I thought.

'Maybe if you hadn't persuaded me to do that stupid BUTT-RRR advert, my career wouldn't be in the toilet right now.'

'It was supposed to be cool!'

'Well, it wasn't. If I had a cent for every time someone sung it to me when I walked down the street, my money troubles would be over.'

About eight months ago, she'd persuaded me to appear in an ad for a new brand called BUTT-RRR where I sung cringey lines like 'I want to spread you like butter on my warm toast', whilst thrusting my hips back and forth.

It went viral for all the wrong reasons and unsurprisingly, it got banned. The critics had a field day, citing it as a prime example of just how far I'd fallen.

'That's because the jingle was catchy!'

'It killed my credibility. I even got fired from a freaking Pollo Pops because people wouldn't stop coming in to take pictures!'

Wilma blew out a breath. She knew I was right. It was one of the worst decisions I'd ever made.

'You could always do those personalised video messages. People would love to hear you do the whole jingle.'

'No! I'm trying to distance myself from that. Not lean into it.'

I just wanted to make music again.

Not the shit the record company forced me to sing when I was in the band.

And not the shitty spreadable butter jingle that ruined my career.

I wanted to make the music *I'd* written. The music that reflected my personality. That came from my *soul*.

But I had bills to pay. And I had to find a place to live. I needed money. Fast.

And the thing about having debts was that it fucked with your creativity.

I hadn't written a single song in years.

If I could find that creativity again, then maybe I could try and release my own music independently. But that wasn't gonna happen anytime soon because every time I sat down to write, I was crippled with anxiety.

All I could think about was all the shit I'd been through these past few years and what I'd lost. Then I'd worry about how hard it'd be to get enough people to listen to it to have a chance of even beginning to make a living from music again. And how crushing it'd be if people hated it.

So it was easier not to try at all. But the bills didn't go away, which was why I was having this shitty conversation.

'Explain what the plan is with going to this hotel.' I blew out a defeated breath.

'You go there and create an online diary documenting *everything*. Take photos of you arriving. Videos of you choosing your outfit. Talk about how nervous and excited you are about meeting your match. That shit will make you super relatable. Everyone knows how hard it is getting out there again. And because of your reputation for being a womaniser, it'll show the public that you have real feelings and that you're serious about finding true love.'

'But I'm not,' I protested. 'The last thing I need right now is a relationship.'

I hadn't dated seriously in years and I couldn't even remember the last time I'd hooked up. That was the other thing about having financial problems and not having a permanent roof over your head. It wasn't exactly an aphrodisiac.

'Semantics.' She waved her hand away dismissively. 'You're not going to the hotel to *actually* find love. You're going there to revive your career.'

My face crumpled.

'That makes no sense.'

'Stay with me, Jakey boy! I haven't finished explaining. As I was saying, you document *everything*. Take photos of the woman they match you with, your first kiss... get *all* that shit on camera.'

'Wait, what?' I frowned so hard I probably left permanent lines on my forehead. 'You want me to film the woman too? Wasn't there an NDA? And we're not gonna kiss! I won't even be attracted to her.'

'Again, semantics! You're allowed to take photos of your

match. Just not other guests without their permission. And it doesn't matter if you're not attracted to her. You just have to *pretend* you are.' She rolled her eyes.

'You're getting me confused. I'm an *artist*. A *musician*. I sing. I don't act.'

'The point is,' she replied, ignoring my very important objection, 'the public will be invested. They'll be glued to their screens. They'll want to follow your story. They'll want to watch you two fall in love. And do you know what that means?'

'Enlighten me,' I huffed, thinking I didn't like the sound of this idea at all.

'The more people that are invested in your story, the more followers you'll get. And the more interest you'll have from the reality shows.'

'But I don't want to do a fucking reality show!' I shouted. 'I don't want to be filmed eating kangaroo testicles. I don't want to go on a dancing show or be locked in a house with other Z-list celebrities. I want to make *music!*'

'Ah, but that's the genius part,' she smiled. 'If you do this right, you won't have to go on other people's reality shows. They'll give you your own! People will want to know what happens *after* you leave the hotel. Just picture it: they'll follow you and the love of your life as you start a new life together. It'll show the public everything: you two moving in together, getting engaged...'

'What the fuck?' My nostrils flared.

'You wouldn't go through with it, *obviously*.' She rolled her eyes again. 'The point is, whilst they're documenting your romance, we'll show you working on your music. And then *boom!* With all the extra exposure you'll get from social media, the reality show and your blossoming romance, the public will forget about the whole BUTT-RRR thing and be itching to hear your love songs. It's genius, right?'

'It's batshit crazy!' I shook my head.

'Why?'

'Because you know I fucking hate social media. I'm a private person.'

'Says the guy who's been pictured sucking face with *hundreds* of women.'

'But *I* didn't take those photos. That was an invasion of my privacy. And that's the point. I don't want to share my private life any more.'

'Well, you're fresh out of options. If megastar musicians like Bruno Mars, The Weeknd and Ed Sheeran have to do social media, then so do you! Behind-the-scenes access sells.'

'Even if it does, doing something like this would be immoral. The woman I'd be matched with will be there to find love, so going there knowing I have no intention of having a real relationship is dishonest. I don't want to lead anyone on.'

Having one-night stands was one thing. I always made it crystal clear from the start that it was just a hook-up. But going to a hotel where the objective was to meet your soulmate just to revive my career left a bad taste in my mouth.

'When I submitted your application, I said you were looking to date another celebrity, so it'll be fine. Whatever you do will benefit *both* of your careers and once we know who it is, I can speak to their agent to make sure we're all on the same page and work together to make the partnership mutually beneficial.'

'Still doesn't seem right.'

'This is LA, baby! This shit happens all the time. If you want to get back in the game, you need to do whatever it takes. And it's not like I'm asking you to do anything difficult. All you have to do is take some photos and videos whilst spending two weeks in an all-inclusive luxury hotel. People would kill for an opportunity like this. You should be kissing my feet, not acting like a spoilt brat who's just been told he can't have ice cream at a birthday party.'

Ouch.

In the grand scheme of things, maybe it wouldn't be such a hardship. For starters, as grateful as I was to have a roof over my head at Roger's apartment, it would be nice to sleep in a decent bed again, even if it was just for two weeks.

As much as I hated everything about this idea, I wasn't in a position to pick and choose. I was lucky that Wilma was even representing me. Most people dropped me when my career tanked. Including my so-called industry friends.

And knowing that I'd be matched with another celebrity, no doubt another has-been like me, made me feel a bit better about things. At least they'd understand the way things worked and know this was just purely a business arrangement, not anything romantic.

As much as I hated posting on social media, right now this was the only opportunity I could see to get me back on my feet again.

If two weeks at a hotel was my ticket to saving my career and securing my future, then as much as I didn't want to, it looked like I didn't have a choice.

'When did you say that I'd need to go there?'

'In three weeks.'

That was sooner than I thought. But soon was good.

I'd promised Roger I'd be out of his hair in a month, so I'd be able to keep my word and get to stay somewhere nice for two weeks, rent free.

Wilma was trying to help, so I needed to do my part. Although the idea still sounded dumb as fuck, I had to give it a chance.

'Okay,' I said, ignoring the crushing feeling in the pit of my stomach. 'I'll do it.'

3

HALLE

Usually, I wasn't one for believing in miracles. But as my chauffeur-driven Rolls-Royce pulled into the grounds of the Love Hotel in California, which was based near fancy Malibu, I was convinced they were real.

Less than a month ago I was freaking out about the fact that my aversion to emails and answering phone calls had led me to miss out on my big chance to secure a place at this world-renowned matchmaking hotel. And now, I was here.

It hadn't been easy though. Ironically, *I'd* spent the weekend bombarding *them* with emails, begging them to give me another chance. Then on Monday morning I'd called head office to apologise for not responding sooner.

Just when I was about to offer to name my firstborn child after whoever took pity on me and gave me a place, they confirmed that I was in.

I'd screamed down the phone louder than an excited hyena, but thankfully the lady on the other end understood my enthusiasm. And now that I was here, I could see my elation was totally justified.

As the driver cruised down the enormous driveway, my eyes popped. The word 'luxury' didn't even begin to cover this place.

The huge white stone building looked like a modern palace. It was flanked with lush palm trees and in front of the hotel was an impressive circular water fountain which had a white marble statue of a couple kissing under a gold umbrella, so it looked like they were locking lips in the rain. The woman even had her foot popped – just like that iconic scene in *The Princess Diaries. So romantic.*

The car stopped, the suited and booted chauffeur got out and opened the door. As I slid off the backseat and stepped outside, the sunshine instantly warmed my skin.

I closed my eyes and inhaled the delicious salty sea air, thinking it was a billion times better than the smell of rubbish, pollution and stale piss that hit me when I left my apartment building this morning.

Just as I was marvelling at how blue the sky looked and taking in a glimpse of the beach and the ocean I spotted in the distance, I saw a woman in a branded Love Hotel uniform, with long, curly pink ombré hair, light brown skin and a wide smile walking towards me.

'Halle?' she asked and I instantly noticed that she had a British accent.

'That's me!' I replied.

'Welcome to the Love Hotel, California! I'm Sammie, your Love Alchemist.'

'My *what*?'

'Your *Love Alchemist*, which is basically a silly way of saying I'm the person responsible for helping you and your match fall in love. Oops, I didn't mean "silly". I take the hotel's job titles *very* seriously. They're just a bit weird, that's all. Not weird. *Different.*

Interesting. Shit. I'm making a right pig's ear of this welcome! And now I just swore!' She slapped her forehead. 'Sorry. I'm a bit nervous. I'm new to the job. That doesn't mean I'm not good at it though, because I *totally* am. Not that I'm being big-headed. I was just trying to reassure that you're in good hands.'

'You're fine!' I laughed. 'It's lovely to meet you, Sammie.' I stretched out my hand. She went to shake it, then paused.

'Wow! Your nails are stunning!' She dipped her head to admire them.

Pride bloomed in my chest. I'd painted my thumbs, forefingers and little fingers a vibrant orange shade and the two fingers in the middle were a nude shade with a cute orange daisy design in the centre.

'Thanks! So you're British? That's a nice surprise.'

'Yeah, there's a few of us here. Jasmine, one of the Love Empresses, is from London like me.'

'*Love Empress*? You're right. The job titles here are weird!' I laughed and her face fell. 'But in a totally *interesting* and very cool way.'

'Phew! Thank God you're nice. I don't want to get reported to management for slagging off the job titles with one of my first guests! Let me get you checked in.'

Sammie led me through the grand reception. It had immaculate black and white chequered flooring, a grand sweeping gold staircase, plush white sofas and an enormous colourful floral display nestled on a large white marble table.

Soothing acoustic music played softly in the background, which instantly made my shoulders loosen and the ginormous windows along the back wall boasted floor-to-ceiling panoramic ocean views.

Wow.

This place was the closest I'd ever been to paradise. I couldn't wait to get outside and sink my feet into the gorgeous golden sand.

'So,' Sammie said, 'are you excited about meeting your match?'

'Yep! I hardly slept last night. I can't wait to find out who it is.'

'He hasn't arrived so I haven't met him yet, but I know you'll be blown away.'

'Really?' My eyes widened with anticipation.

'Yeah! Everyone is... No, I'd better not say any more for now. But a lot of people would *kill* to be set up with him.'

'Oh, wow! No pressure for me then.'

'You've got nothing to worry about, hon! You're freaking gorgeous. *He's* lucky to be matched with *you* too.'

'Thanks. Let's hope he agrees.'

Once I'd completed check-in, Sammie gave me the grand tour of the resort. It was so big that we did it on one of those golf cart buggies.

Apparently, the management had spent ages searching for the right plot of land. They wanted an amazing secluded beach location that was close to popular locations like Malibu and Los Angeles, but that'd give them the space they needed to create a dream resort which offered both privacy and luxury.

There were two large swimming pools, three restaurants, a huge spa and the beach had some of the softest-looking sand I'd ever seen. It was straight out of a high-end travel magazine.

Considering how plush the surroundings were, I shouldn't have been shocked when I saw how incredible my huge room was. It had white solid oak furniture, a sea blue, grey and white colour scheme and a ginormous king-size bed with expensive-looking crisp white bed linen and gold-trimmed pillows. I couldn't wait to sink into that mattress tonight.

Modern beach-inspired art adorned the walls. The bathroom had a massive rainfall walk-in shower. There was even a remote-controlled toilet. Wow. Even flushing the loo was fancy here.

And when I opened my grand balcony doors I was treated to stunning unobstructed ocean views. No wonder it cost so much to come here.

Once I'd showered, I started to get dressed. I was meeting my match at eight-thirty, which was in less than an hour.

Vanessa had asked me to call once I was ready. So after doing my hair and make-up, which took longer than expected, and sliding into a knee-length orange patterned summer dress to match my nails, I hit the video call button.

'Hey!' she said as she appeared on the screen. 'Loving the eye make-up and your hair is on fleek!'

'Thanks, but you know no one says *on fleek* any more, right?'

'No?' She frowned. 'What are the cool kids saying these days then?'

'You'd have to ask one of them. I'm thirty-four, so I have no idea.'

'You're a baby! I'm forty-one and still consider myself young, so compared to me, you're fresh out the womb! Anyway, you look amazing! How you feeling? What's it like there? And when do you meet your Mr Right?'

'My stomach's churning so much it could turn milk into butter! As for this place, it's off the scale.'

I described the surroundings to Vanessa and she oohed and aaahed before asking me to send her photos.

'You know I don't do the whole pictures thing. I prefer to be in the moment.'

'Being in the moment is all well and good if you've got a photographic memory. But how are you going to remember what food you ate if you don't take pictures? Or how beautiful the sunset was?'

Vanessa was one of those people that took a dozen photos of her dessert before she took a single mouthful. No judgement because once upon a time, before the shit hit the fan, I did too. But not any more.

'Everyone's become a slave to their phone. They're obsessed with taking and posting photos without giving a second thought to the consequences...' My stomach tightened as a painful memory shot into my head.

'I hear you. Sorry. I'm just so used to taking photos that sometimes I forget about what you went through.'

'It's okay. I overreacted. I know you're just curious to see what the hotel and food are like, so it's not the same. Photos probably won't come out well on my phone, but I'll try and take a few.'

A couple of years ago I'd traded my phone in for the most basic mobile I could find which was the complete opposite to Vanessa's which had all the bells and whistles.

'Thanks. So when will you meet your mystery guy?'

'In...' I glanced at my watch. 'Shit. In seven minutes. I'd better go.'

'I'm so excited for you, hon! Have fun and remember to take precautions.'

'I'm not having sex on the first date! I'm not here for a fling! I'm here to find my forever guy. The whole point is to get to know him as a person over the next two weeks. We'll have the rest of our lives to explore each other's bodies.'

'If you say so. From what I've heard, when you get matched it's instant fireworks so if the mood strikes, don't fight it. Please tell me that you've cleared out the weeds down there?'

'The weeds?'

'You haven't had any action for years, so you don't want the poor guy to waste valuable time trying to hack through a bush to reach your promised land.'

'My *promised land*?' I chuckled.

'Yes. Please tell me you've pruned your pussy?'

'Did anyone ever tell you have a way with words?'

'What can I say? It's a gift!' she cackled.

'FYI, lots of women choose not to shave these days.'

'Sorry! I didn't mean to body shame. You're right. To rock or not rock the bush is a personal choice.'

'Exactly. But fear not, the *gardening* has been done.'

'Cool. I'll let you get to your date. Break a leg!'

As I headed to the restaurant, my heart thundered in my chest. It'd been ages since I'd had a first date and so much was riding on this.

Normally, the most you'd have to lose would be your time, the cost of your travel and a drink. But I'd used all my savings to pay the balance to come here. Vanessa had invested in this trip too. I couldn't afford for anything to go wrong.

I took a deep breath.

It'll be fine.

The experts know what they're doing.

'Good evening,' a hostess with a southern American accent said as I stepped through the huge glass restaurant doors. 'May I take your name, please?'

'It's Halle. Halle Remington.'

'Oh, yes, here we are.' She pointed to my name on the iPad screen. 'Nice to meet you, Halle. You're looking gorgeous! Your date's a very lucky man. And you're sure in for a treat with him! He's not here yet but we're all *so* excited.'

'Great!' I said, thinking that everyone seemed very enthusiastic. He must be *really* good-looking. Or maybe he had a cool job like working in an animal shelter. That'd be right up my street.

Anything would be better than my ex. Once he got his record deal, all he ever spoke about was how many followers he had on social media or the pretentious parties he loved going to.

My pulse raced. I was so nervous. Even though I'd just checked myself in my room, the urge to make sure I didn't have lipstick on my teeth was suddenly overpowering.

'Do I have time to use the ladies'?'

'Sure, honey. It's just down the hall on your right.'

'Thanks. Back in a mo.'

When I got to the bathroom, thankfully everything was fine. I went for a quick wee, washed my hands, then gave myself a final once-over in the mirror before heading back out to the restaurant.

When I arrived, a crowd of people had gathered by the bar. I hoped someone hadn't fainted. I quickened my pace, eager to see what was going on. The hostess approached me just before I reached the crowd.

'Halle! Hi! Your date's arrived!'

'Great! Is he at the table?'

'If only!' She laughed and I frowned. 'He wasn't able to make it that far. Looks like I wasn't the only person who was excited to meet him.'

'Huh?' My face creased.

'Your date is... well, I don't want to ruin the surprise. Come with me, honey,' she said, leading me towards the swarm of guests. 'Sorry, everyone. I need to steal him away. His date is here. And remember the hotel rules and the NDA you all signed. No photos, please,' she said sternly.

A collective disappointed groan echoed around me.

Now I was really confused. I remembered that we had to sign an NDA saying that we wouldn't take pictures of other guests without their express permission or post anything about them online, which I thought sounded OTT, but I understood that it was to respect everyone's privacy. And obviously it didn't bother me because I wasn't interested in photos or social media. But what made her say that now, about my date?

My mind raced, then the most likely reason hit me.

If she'd told them not to take photos, that must mean that...

Oh, God.

No, no, no.

Please, no.

As the crowd dispersed and I saw who was in front of me, my stomach tensed and the blood drained from my face.

'Halle, I'm so thrilled to introduce you to your date, the one and only Jake Myers, although I'm sure there's not a woman on the earth who doesn't know who he is and want him to *BUTT-RRR them up.* Am I right?'

She chuckled, obviously thinking it was hilarious to reference that stupid ad jingle he did, but I wasn't laughing.

At all.

Dread and disappointment washed over me.

'He's...' I wanted to say the word 'famous' but nothing came out.

I couldn't believe they'd set me up with *him.*

One of the main things I'd asked for on my questionnaire was *not* to be matched with anyone high profile.

That was a definite no-no. A deal breaker. The reddest of red flags.

After what I'd been through with my ex, the last thing I wanted was to date another singer.

And Jake wasn't just any singer. He had a reputation for being a notorious womaniser.

My ex liked sleeping with groupies (as I found out the hard way), but Jake Myers made him look like a boy scout.

I was a good person.

I was kind to others.

I always gave my seat up on public transport to those who needed it more. So why was I being punished like this?

I didn't know what the hell the hotel was thinking matching me with Jake, but I had no intention of sticking around to find out.

4

JAKE

You've got to be fucking kidding me.

This was my match?

If I was looking for a real date, she'd definitely tick my boxes. She was tall, had a killer body, sparkly chocolate-brown eyes, brown skin and shoulder-length curly hair, which was a kind of cinnamon shade with flashes of golden highlights.

And her nails were fire. They matched that pretty orange dress that she was wearing which clung to her long, toned legs and every delicious curve.

Yep. The way she looked definitely wasn't the problem.

But the deal was that I'd get matched with someone used to being in the public eye.

I was supposed to be set up with someone with the same objective as me: to get exposure to revive their career. So considering I had no idea who she was, it didn't matter that she was as fine as hell, because she didn't fit the brief.

'This way, please,' the server said, signalling for us to follow her to the table.

'After you,' I said, allowing Halle to pass me. Not because I wanted to check out her butt. Like I said, my presence at this hotel was for purely professional reasons.

I blew out a breath, trying to calm myself down.

Maybe I was overreacting.

Just because *I* didn't recognise this Halle woman, it didn't mean that she wasn't famous.

She could be a reality TV star or a social media influencer.

It was fine.

I needed to chill.

Once we started talking over dinner, everything would become clear.

'Allow me,' I said, pulling out her chair. Just because this wasn't a real date didn't mean I was gonna forget to use basic manners.

'Thanks,' she said flatly with her gaze fixed to the crisp white tablecloth.

She seemed... pissed off.

Not that I wanted to toot my own horn, but normally when women saw me, they'd act all gushy and flirty. But this Halle woman looked at me like I'd just bathed in dog shit.

Maybe she just wasn't a fan of my music. Or maybe like most people, she hated that goddamn commercial I did.

'You're welcome,' I said, settling into the white leather chair.

I'd been to a lot of fancy hotels in my time, but I had to admit that this one was up there with the best of them. It had a minimalist style, y'know, white walls and flooring, but the blue and gold accents and quirky beach art made it feel luxurious without feeling too snooty.

We were seated right next to floor-to-ceiling sliding glass patio doors which gave us impressive panoramic views of the ocean. Watching the waves crashing against the shore was one of my favourite things to do. I couldn't wait to get out on the beach tomorrow.

Roger had offered to drop me here and the traffic was crazy, so I'd arrived later than planned. I'd had to rush to check in, shower, dress and get to the restaurant on time, which meant I hadn't had a chance to take a look around the resort, but there'd be time for that tomorrow.

'You're British?' I said, breaking the silence.

'Ten out of ten for observation,' she replied, still avoiding my gaze.

Ooof. She was a prickly one.

That was okay. I was out of practice, but if I dug deep enough, I could still find the charm that used to get the ladies eating out of my hand.

'Thanks for the compliment!' I replied. 'What part of London are you from?'

'Why do you assume that I'm from London? There are other places in the UK, you know. Just because *you* lived there before doesn't mean that every person from Britain is from there too.' She rolled her eyes.

'Hmm, so you know I lived in London. Interesting...' I smiled.

'It's public knowledge. Unfortunately, I already know a lot about you.'

'Is that right?' I smirked. 'Care to share?'

'Not particularly.' She crossed her arms over her chest and I noticed, not for the first time, how good it looked in that dress.

'Unbelievable!' She shook her head. I hoped she hadn't seen me checking her out.

'Thanks, sweetheart. Careful. With all these compliments you keep giving me, I'll get a big head,' I joked.

'I wasn't calling *you* unbelievable. Well, I was but not in the way you're thinking. Forget it.' She huffed as the table fell silent again.

Damn. This was gonna be a lot harder than I thought.

As I scanned the room, thinking of something to say to relieve the awkwardness between us, I saw a couple posing for photos, then remembered that I was supposed to be taking pictures too.

My whole body stiffened. All I wanted to do was to try and enjoy this dinner and work out the strategy with Halle to help us make the most of this arrangement, but instead I'd have to take a billion photos of my food and fuck knows what else.

Reluctantly, I slid my hand in my pocket and put my cell phone on the table. If it wasn't right there in front of me, I'd forget. Seemed kind of rude, but Halle was in the same business, so she'd understand why it was important.

When I looked at the screen I saw two missed calls from Wilma. Shit.

Just as I was about to pick up the menu, my cell rang again and Wilma's name flashed up.

Halle's eyes darted to the screen and she glared at me before looking away. I hit the ignore button, then picked up the menu.

My cell buzzed again.

'Do you want to get that?' Halle snapped.

I looked down at it, weighing up my options. If I ignored it, I'd piss Wilma off.

She probably just wanted to check I'd arrived safely and confirm I was taking photos. All I needed was to quickly reassure her and she'd stay off my back.

'Yeah...' I said. 'I probably should. Sorry. This will only take a minute.'

I stood up, slipped outside, then answered the call.

'Aren't you there?' Wilma bellowed.

'Yeah. I'm in the middle of dinner with my date. Not that she's my real... never mind.'

'So why haven't you posted anything yet?'

'I was running late. I didn't have time. I'll do it, okay. Just give me a chance.'

'You'd better. There's a lot riding on this. I had to pay upfront to secure your place at the hotel, so you owe me. If you want to save your career and make sure I get a return on my investment, you need to follow what I say to the letter.'

I swallowed hard.

I'd agreed to do this because I thought it was a way to get my career back on track without selling my soul.

But as Wilma reeled off her list of requirements for what felt like the hundredth time, I realised it was too late.

I'd already sold out. Big time.

5

HALLE

So fucking rude.

Who not only takes their phone out on a first date but then also interrupts it to answer a call from another woman?

Jake Myers. That's who.

I saw the way he winced when her name flashed up on the screen like he'd been caught out.

I knew it wasn't his mum because from what I'd read, they'd fallen out. I hadn't seen anything about his sister in a while, so they probably didn't speak any more either. Not that I kept tabs on his life or anything. Like I said to him, a lot about his life was public knowledge and the co-workers I used to have gossiped about celebs like it was a national sport.

If it was anyone else, I wouldn't jump to conclusions, but Jake's reputation preceded him. He wasn't known as Hollywood's bad boy whore for nothing.

When I'd asked if he needed to take the call, I was expecting him to say no. I mean, would it have hurt him to turn it off or at least put it on silent?

By taking that call and leaving me alone at the table, he'd

made his priorities very clear: his phone or rather his fuckbuddy was more important than me.

What was he even doing at a place like this? A strip club was more his scene than a hotel designed to help you find your one true love.

And why was *I* still here? I should find my Love Alchemist woman, Sammie, and ask for a refund, like I'd told myself I'd do when I got introduced to Jake. But then I saw the food some couples were eating and I was starving, so decided I should at least get a meal out of this shit show before I left.

Just as I was contemplating my next move, Jake came back.

'Sorry about that.' He pulled out his chair and sat down.

'Everything okay?' I asked, wanting to give him the benefit of the doubt. Maybe it was his granny calling because she was sick or there was some kind of emergency. I wanted to at least be sympathetic.

'Yeah.'

'So no major emergency then?' I asked, giving him the opportunity to get himself off the hook.

'No.' He shrugged. In other words, he left me alone at the table for something that could've waited. Yep. Just like I said before: *rude.*

Once the waitress took our orders and our drinks had been delivered, Jake pulled out his phone.

'We should take some pictures,' he said.

'Of what?' I frowned, before sipping my prosecco which tasted amazing.

'Everything?'

'Why?'

'For...' He took a glug of beer then fidgeted with his napkin. 'Instagram and stuff.'

I rolled my eyes so hard they almost tumbled out of my sockets.

They say you shouldn't jump to conclusions, but so far, everything I'd seen had reinforced all the stuff I'd heard about Jake.

He'd had women swarming around him at the bar.

He'd had a woman call him repeatedly before we'd even ordered our starters.

And now, instead of trying to get to know me, he just wanted to take selfies 'for the 'gram'.

This was exactly why I didn't want to date another celebrity. They were always so full of themselves.

Jake started snapping away, taking photos of the sea views from our window, pictures of the restaurant and then he turned to face me. Nice of him to remember that I was even here.

'I suppose we should take a selfie,' he said, a wave of something flickering across his face.

He was probably worried that I didn't fit his social media 'aesthetic' which was true. I'd seen the kind of women he dated.

Whenever I walked past those gossip magazines in the supermarket, Jake was often splashed across the cover with his latest squeeze who was normally a gorgeous model, actress or singer. So I knew from experience that being pictured with someone like me wasn't going to fit his image.

Then again, since that terrible butter jingle came out, I didn't think he'd been seen out in public as much as he used to.

I knew full well that I shouldn't listen to gossip, but I'd overheard someone in the juice bar say that he'd disappeared because he went to rehab to treat his sex addiction or something.

Ordinarily, I wouldn't care. Live and let live. It was his life. But now this was personal. Now it mattered, because I'd dropped a shitload of money to be here and arrived to discover that the so-called love gurus had decided that a playboy was my perfect match.

What a joke.

'As tempting as that sounds, I'd rather lick a pig's arse,' I said firmly.

'If that's what you're into, I'm sure that could be arranged.' He flashed a cheeky smile.

God. Why did he have to have a nice smile? All perfect white teeth and soft-looking full lips.

Arsehole.

'Obviously I'm not into that, I was just... Never mind. The point is, *no*, I don't want to take a selfie.'

'What?' He frowned like I'd just sprouted five heads.

'Listen, I know you're probably used to people begging to take photos with you and I'm sorry to bruise your ego, but I'm not interested.'

His jaw dropped so hard he was lucky it didn't shatter on the table.

'But I'll tag you. I can even invite you to be a...' He paused like he was searching for the word. '*Collaborator*! So when I post, I can invite you and when you accept it'll show up on your feed thing too.'

'I'm not on social media,' I said flatly. 'So I have no interest in *collaborating* or having any photos with you showing up on my *feed thing*.'

'Wait. You *don't* want to take a selfie and you're *not* on social media?'

'That's exactly what I said. You're slowly starting to get the hang of this listening thing, well done!' I deadpanned.

Jake sat there in silence, his face contorting in a million different directions.

'So why did you come here?' he asked.

My eyeballs trebled in size as I tried to take in the ridiculousness of his question.

'You're seriously asking me what made me pay a fortune to come to a place called the Love Hotel? Er, this is probably going to blow your mind, but I came here to... newsflash... find *love*.'

'Good one!' Jake chuckled. 'Delivered like a true pro.' He nodded his approval, whilst I crossed my arms across my chest as my expression turned to stone. The silence stretched for several beats before what I'd just said finally started to penetrate his tiny brain. 'Wait. You're being *serious*?'

'Of course I'm being serious!' I snapped.

'Shit,' he muttered. 'So... you're not... what do you do for work?'

'I work in a juice bar. In New York.'

'But are you an aspiring singer?'

'No.'

'Actress?'

'No.'

'Just to be clear, you're *not* working in a juice bar whilst you do auditions or wait for your big break?'

'No!'

Well, that might not be entirely true. I'd always wanted to make a proper go of becoming a freelance nail technician, but I didn't think that was the kind of 'big break' he was referring to.

My mind drifted as I thought about how amazing it'd be if I could follow that dream, but then I dismissed it. There was no point. That was never gonna happen.

'Fuck.' His gaze dropped to the table.

'Why? Is that why you're here? Are you hoping to meet an aspiring singer or actress?'

'I was... I just... We should order more drinks.' He wiped the sweat from his brow.

This was weird. Now he seemed nervous. Whenever I'd seen him in interviews, he'd always seemed confident. And when we'd first sat down, he was full of cocky comebacks. But his body language had suddenly changed.

Maybe that woman had given him an earful when she found out he wasn't free for a booty call.

'Good idea,' I said.

As Jake studied the drinks menu, I caught myself scanning his face.

I'd met a few celebrities in my time, thanks to the ex who won't be named, and sometimes they didn't look how I'd imagined them in real life.

All that retouching in magazines made them look so flawless. But in reality, celebs were still people with scars and breakouts, just like us.

Well, that wasn't strictly true. I'd never seen a celeb with a breakout because they probably had facials that cost hundreds of dollars every week to prevent them.

Anyway, the point was, they didn't always look as perfect as we were led to believe.

But as much as it pained me to admit it, Jake was as ridiculously handsome as he looked on those billboards, TV adverts and music videos.

He was tall with thick dark brown hair, tanned skin, hazel eyes and a muscular body that belonged on the cover of a fitness magazine.

If he was a regular person with a normal career like me and I discovered that a man that looked like him was my date, I'd be doing cartwheels and backflips. But looks weren't everything. And if I wasn't already put off by his reputation, after spending less than half an hour in his company, I knew with absolute certainty that he was not the man for me.

Which was a problem. I didn't pay to be matched with a walking red flag.

I had to voice my concerns, right? Even if they couldn't give me a refund, surely they could arrange an alternative match instead?

Either way, I was not going to waste two weeks of my life with a narcissist who was more interested in taking photos than getting to know me.

No way.

I'd decided: once I'd finished dinner, I'd find Sammie and get this resolved.

She might think he was a catch, but I was ready to toss him right back into the Pacific Ocean.

Yep. A replacement was the best course of action. Here's hoping the next man they had lined up was better than the first.

6

JAKE

I'd been on a lot of awkward first dates in my thirty-six years on this earth, but this was one of the worst I'd ever had.

We'd been here less than an hour and it was already a shit show.

The conversation sucked.

Not that you could even call it that because a conversation involved both parties talking.

Whenever I tried to ask a question, Halle either glared or gave monosyllabic answers. And that was before we got to the fact that she wasn't even remotely in the public eye and, most critically, didn't want to be.

Ordinarily, meeting someone who had zero interest in fame would be a breath of fresh air, especially after what happened to me before. I hated the whole 'celebrity scene'. I'd spent a lot of years wishing that people would see me as a person instead of someone who could get them into parties or give them a leg up in the industry. But in this case, Halle not wanting to raise her profile was a disaster.

Wilma assured me that I'd be matched with someone who

had the same agenda. In other words, someone who *hadn't* come here to fall in love.

I'd made it crystal clear from the start that I didn't want to lead anyone on. And despite that I'd been matched with someone who was looking for a damn happily-ever-after.

What the hell was I supposed to do now?

I couldn't exactly tell Halle that I was only here because I was desperate to get my career back on track and had no interest in her romantically. She'd think I was a jerk. And she'd be right.

I told Wilma that this was a shitty idea.

I was supposed to be taking photos to help secure some corny reality show. But Halle made it clear that she wasn't down for taking pictures with me. Hell, she wasn't even on social media.

These days, finding someone who wasn't surgically attached to their cell phone was like discovering a unicorn. I thought I was the only one who hated that BS, so once again, ordinarily, I'd find her aversion to it refreshing. But for the purposes of pimping the shit out of this hotel stay, this was a bust.

My cell vibrated in my pocket. When I slid it out, there was a message.

WILMA

Where are the photos, Jakey boy?

Post something NOW!!

I groaned and shoved it back in my pocket. It was already rude for me to leave the table, so I wasn't gonna start posting during dinner. Wilma would need to wait until I'd finished.

When the server placed my steak and fries on the table, I couldn't wait to devour it. I was starving. But then I remembered that I was supposed to be documenting everything.

I held my phone up in the air, plastered on a fake smile, then took a shot of me licking my lips whilst staring at the plate with the ocean views behind me.

So fucking corny.

'Unbelievable,' Halle sighed.

'Don't like taking photos of your food?' I asked.

'I prefer to eat it,' she said.

'Me t—' I was about to agree with her, then remembered I was the one who'd just taken a cheesy food pic, so I'd look like a hypocrite. *I* knew I was, but Halle didn't need to know that too.

Not that it mattered, considering it was clear that for whatever reason Halle was not my biggest fan.

'How's your salad?' I asked, changing the topic.

'Delicious. Why? Want to take a photo of that too, to *post on the 'gram*?'

'You got a problem with me?'

'I… it doesn't matter,' she sighed again. 'Let's just eat.'

'Look, I don't know what I've done to offend you, but like it or not, we're here for two weeks together. And things will be a lot less painful if we can at least try to have a civil conversation and get to know each other.'

'Not necessarily,' she mumbled, which was confusing. 'So what do you want to talk about?' she huffed. 'Yourself?'

'Why? Am I your favourite subject?' I smirked, deciding that I might as well try and have some fun. 'I can tell by how you've been flirting with me all night that you're a fan. Bet you've been to all my concerts and you had a poster of me by your bed that you used to kiss every night. Am I right?'

Halle's face fell and her cheeks flushed.

'Of course not!' she protested.

'Ah! No, I get it. You didn't just have *one* poster. You covered your bedroom walls with *hundreds* of posters of me.'

'*As if!*' Her face hardened.

'Actually, I think you're coming on so strong right now that maybe I should call security. You're borderline *obsessed* with me!' I laughed.

'The only one obsessed with you is *you*. Your ego's so big that I'm surprised there's room for anyone else in this restaurant!'

'Just trying to lighten the mood, sweetheart. You're sitting there, glaring at me like I'd just asked you to lick my butt hole on the first date.'

'Gross.'

'Hey! Kink shaming isn't okay.'

'Neither is talking about licking arseholes at the dinner table.'

'Says the woman who spoke about licking a pig's butt earlier.'

'I didn't say I wanted to do that! I said I'd rather lick it than take a selfie with you, that's different.'

'Uh-huh. If you say so, sweetheart.'

Halle rolled her eyes disapprovingly, then fixated her gaze on her southern fried chicken and fries.

'So, do you live in LA?' I asked, still determined to keep the conversation going.

'No. New York.'

'Cool. How long you lived there?'

'Six years.'

Jesus. This was like getting blood out of a stone.

'Anytime you want to elaborate on your answers would be good. And if you *really* want to go crazy, maybe you could ask me some questions too so that we could have a real conversation.'

She sighed, then paused for a few beats.

'My dad's originally from New York and after he separated from Mum, he moved back when I was in my mid-twenties. My best friend, Vanessa, had also landed a big job at a law firm in the city by then too, so I used to visit as often as I could. And during one of my trips, I met someone and I ended up staying.'

'*Met someone*? Like a boyfriend?'

'Yes.'

'Care to elaborate?'

'No. Listen, I appreciate you making an effort to make conversation, but I'm tired. It's been a long day.' She swallowed the last piece of chicken, then pushed her knife and fork together in the centre of her plate.

'Got it. We done here?'

'Yep. Enjoy the rest of your evening.' She stood up, pushed her chair back then left.

Well, that went well.

I'd only spent a couple of hours with her and it was more painful than surgery without anaesthetic.

If I couldn't even get through dinner with her, how the hell was I gonna survive two weeks?

And more importantly, how would I convince her to go along with Wilma's plan?

7

HALLE

As my alarm sounded, I groaned. Partly because this bed was so comfortable, I hated the thought of having to leave it, but mainly because I knew it meant that I had to face an entire day with Jake. Getting through that dinner was hard enough.

This wasn't how it was supposed to be.

I thought that I'd be spending my days gazing into the beautiful eyes of my match, skipping along the beach hand in hand and being ridiculously loved up. Not sitting at a table glaring at him like I had last night.

Okay, if I was being totally honest, on a purely superficial level, when I was glaring, I noticed that his eyes actually were annoyingly beautiful. They were a greenish-brown golden shade and all sparkly. And of course, he had long lashes. Ugh.

When he'd made that joke about me having a poster of him on my bedroom wall, I wanted the ground to swallow me up because I'm embarrassed to admit that there may have been a point that I... fancied Jake.

And shamefully, I *did* have a poster of him on my bedroom wall. A fact that he must *never* know.

Jake used to be in a boyband, The Real-Lists, and they were huge. So in my defence, it was probably easier to find a teenage girl who *didn't* have a poster of them on their wall.

And I was young and stupid back then so it was different. Now I knew better.

Been there, done that, worn the T-shirt, got zero interest in dating a popstar ever again, thank you very much.

That was why I was so grumpy last night. Normally, I was a softie and although I wasn't the life and soul of the party, I could hold a decent conversation. But when I saw Jake, my walls instantly went up. When everything imploded with my ex, it nearly destroyed me and I couldn't risk getting hurt like that again.

After I'd left the restaurant last night, I wanted to call Vanessa to talk it through. Then I remembered that New York was three hours ahead and I didn't want to wake her up, so I'd left her a voice note explaining what had happened and asked her to call me whenever she was free.

In the meantime, I'd speak to Sammie and ask for a different match. Their database must be huge and everyone on the dating scene wanted to come to this hotel, so hopefully it'd be straightforward.

Once I'd showered, I headed to the restaurant for breakfast.

'Morning!' Sammie said as I walked in. She was standing next to a good-looking guy with olive skin.

'Hi,' I said.

'How'd you sleep? And how was your dinner last night? So cool that you've been matched with Jake Myers!'

My stomach twisted. Sammie made it sound like I'd been paired with LA's most eligible bachelor. More like Mr Community Dick.

'I slept really well, thanks.'

'The mattresses and pillows are so comfy, right? When I stayed at the Love Hotel, I was tempted to buy an extra suitcase just to steal the pillows!' She laughed, then her face fell as she realised what she'd just said. 'Not that I'm encouraging you to do that, of course.'

'Don't worry! The pillows are safe. I didn't realise that you stayed at the Love Hotel too?'

'Yep. The Italian one. That's where I met the love of my life!' She turned and smiled at the man beside her. 'This is my other half, Romeo. He's also a Love Alchemist here.'

'Oh!' My eyes widened. 'Hi, Romeo. I'm Halle.' I stretched out my hand.

'Nice to meet you.' He smiled and shook my hand.

'It's so cool that you guys met there and now you're working together. I'd love to hear more.'

Sammie and Romeo looked at each other and grinned.

'It's a long story... Best to save that for another day.' She flashed Romeo a knowing smile which immediately piqued my interest. 'So? You didn't tell me how it went with Jake.'

'Er... actually, if you've got a second, I wondered if we could have a chat about it.'

'Course! Honey, can you cover for me?' she asked Romeo.

'Sure,' he replied.

'Let's go for a walk,' Sammie said, heading through the doors and down towards the beach. 'So, what's up?'

'Jake's not a good match for me.'

'What?' Sammie's eyes widened. 'Why?'

'I know you think that it's cool that he's famous and stuff, but when I completed the questionnaire, one of the things I specifically asked for was *not* to be matched with anyone high profile.'

'Oh...' Sammie's face fell. 'Well, doesn't the fact that he's not as mega famous as he used to be help?'

'No. It's more about the traits that famous people have whether they're at the top of the charts or not. The arrogance and self-absorption. The obsession with fame and maintaining their profile. Sometimes when they're worried about losing their fame it's even worse.'

'Sounds like you're speaking from experience?'

'Unfortunately, yes. I used to date Brett Burch.'

'Oh, wow. The guy with the reality show who's married to that supermodel?'

'The very one.' My stomach tightened.

'And I'm guessing it wasn't a good break-up?'

'Correct.'

'I'm so sorry. I know Jake doesn't exactly have the reputation of a choir boy, but people change and not all celebs are the same, right? I mean, I haven't met many, but it wouldn't be fair to judge Jake because of the sins your ex committed. The hotel's procedures are very thorough, I mean, they're not always perfect...' Her voice trailed off. 'Sometimes people seem like a good match on paper, but when they meet it just doesn't work out.' Sammie paused for a few beats, like there was more she wanted to say, but for some reason she couldn't. 'But you can't throw in the towel without at least giving it a good try.'

'I'm not so sure...' I blew out a breath.

'Let me ask you some questions,' Sammie said. 'First up, are you attracted to Jake, physically?'

'Well, obviously he's an attractive man,' I shrugged, trying to sound casual. If I told her that I'd had a crush on him since I was a teenager and still thought that he was ridiculously good-looking, that wouldn't help my case. And the fact that I found him very attractive was irrelevant. I was looking for love, not eye candy.

'And how was the date last night? Did he ask you questions about yourself or did he just talk about himself all night?'

'He left the table literally minutes after we'd sat down to take a call from another woman!'

'Okay, that's not ideal, but maybe it was important. And just because it was a woman, it doesn't have to mean anything. It could've been his sister, his aunt or a work call.'

'Yeah,' I sighed. I knew she was right and I hated how paranoid I sounded, but I challenge anyone to go through what I had and not have trust issues.

'So? Did he ask you questions about yourself?'

'He did,' I admitted. 'He tried to, anyway, but I... I wasn't feeling very chatty.'

Shame washed over me. If I was being honest, I probably wasn't the best date yesterday. I should've made more of an effort.

But I was scared. I barely made it through hell last time.

'I get it.' Sammie nodded sympathetically. 'You had your defences up. You were in fight mode because you'd been hurt by a famous guy before and you're worried about history repeating itself, right?'

'Exactly,' I said, relieved that she understood.

'Well, the good news is, you're here for two weeks, so you've still got plenty of time to get to know each other. Although it might not seem like it right now, you two have been matched for a reason. And if you keep your guard up, you'll never be able to tell for sure if you have a connection. I know it won't be easy, but try and lower your defences a little? Start fresh today. We've got our briefing in an hour and I reckon our first couples activity will help break the ice a bit.'

'What is it?'

'It's a surprise.' She grinned. 'Have breakfast, then meet by the Palm Pool. Jake waited for you for breakfast, but then had to leave to take some photos, but he gave me his number to pass on.' She handed me a piece of paper. 'He said to call if you want company. Otherwise, he'll see you at the briefing.'

'Oh. Okay.' I slid the paper in my handbag then glanced at my watch. He must've come down early.

Maybe I'd judged him too harshly about the whole taking photos thing. If he'd left breakfast to take more, perhaps it was a serious hobby and he wanted to take some professional shots of the scenery.

But when I looked over at the beach, I caught Jake posing for selfies, like he did at dinner.

Everyone was free to do whatever they wanted. But I knew I couldn't be with someone who was more interested in having a relationship with their phone than spending time with me. I didn't want to have to fight for their attention.

I know Sammie said that not all people were the same, but so far, Jake's behaviour was feeling way too familiar.

Nope.

I'd prefer to be matched with literally anyone but him.

Right now, there wasn't a single thing that convinced me that Jake was boyfriend material.

And it'd take a major miracle to prove otherwise.

8

HALLE

I was seated on one of the many plush white sun loungers by the giant love-heart-shaped pool, waiting for the first briefing to start.

Just like the rest of the hotel, everything screamed luxury and attention to detail. I'd noticed that even some of the daybeds were heart-shaped too. The designers had clearly made an effort to make sure the surroundings were romantic.

Shame there'd be no romance between me and my match.

Although it felt good to air my concerns to Sammie, I still had my reservations about Jake. And I wasn't going to change my mind.

Just as I was about to start mentally counting all the things I didn't like about him, I spotted Jake striding towards the pool.

As I took in the sight of his broad shoulders and muscular arms in the white T-shirt he was wearing, my breath caught in my throat. He might be an arrogant arsehole, but I couldn't deny that he was an extremely good-looking one. Gah.

Anyway. It didn't matter. His personality sucked.

'Hey, Smiley!' He flashed his Colgate grin. He'd definitely had his teeth done. There was no way his own could be that perfect.

Jake sat down on the plush daybed beside me and I tried to ignore the delicious masculine scent that surrounded me. It smelt like an expensive aftershave called Eau de Sexy Man.

Shame that it was *him* wearing it.

I snapped out of my trance. I should *not* be thinking about how great he smelt or how good his arms looked in that T-shirt. We weren't going to be matched for long. Soon the hotel would realise it was a mistake to put us together and find me a suitable replacement.

When I finally shifted my thoughts away from Jake's unfairly attractive appearance, I realised what he just called me and frowned.

'My name is Halle: H-A-L-L-E. Want me to write it down to help you remember?' I said sarcastically.

'I'm aware of your name, sweetheart, but considering how much your face always lights up whenever you see me, I thought *Smiley* suited you better.'

'It doesn't light up!' I narrowed my eyes.

'See! There it is!' he laughed.

'I'm not smiling, I'm *glaring*!'

'Really?' He rested his finger on his chin. 'Nah... that's definitely the look of love. Deny it all you want but mark my words, you'll be flashing me a smile that's bigger than Julia Roberts's before you know it.'

'You're so...'

'Amazing? Handsome? Funny? Jeez. Thanks for all the compliments.' He smirked and my glare deepened. Just as I was searching for a response to make it clear that I definitely would *not* use any of those adjectives (well, the handsome one was accurate, but I wasn't about to tell him that), Sammie started talking.

'Morning, everyone! Welcome to the Love Hotel California! How are you all feeling today?'

'Awesome!' a guy with a shaved head called out from one of the sun loungers closest to where Sammie was standing.

'Excited!' shouted a woman with long, wavy blonde hair.

'Loving the enthusiasm!' Sammie replied. 'I'm here to explain how everything's gonna work, so you know what to expect. During the first week you'll be doing a different activity every day with your match, but it'll be in a group setting. For example, tomorrow we'll be going on our first excursion outside of the hotel. Then during the second week you'll be responsible for organising your own couples activities, where it'll be just the two of you. Sound good?'

'Yeah!' multiple guests chorused whilst my mouth clamped shut.

I was tempted to jump up and say that it sounded like a nightmare, but I resisted. A whole week of doing things just with Jake? No, thanks.

Then I remembered it wasn't an issue. I told Sammie that I'd try and make things work, but let's be honest: it was unlikely that I'd survive more than a day with him.

'Great!'

As Sammie started talking about various daily 'Love Tasks' we'd also need to complete, like taking photos together for a 'Memory Book' and choosing five songs a day that described how we felt about our match to help create a playlist, I nearly threw up.

The only songs that came to mind right now when I thought about Jake were 'You're So Vain' by Carly Simon, 'Love Yourself' by Justin Bieber and 'Me, Myself and I' by G-Eazy and Bebe Rexha.

Actually, maybe the playlist wouldn't be as hard as I thought. But the photos together was a hard pass.

'Looks like you'll get to take photos with me after all,' Jake whispered in my ear and I tried to ignore the double assault on my senses as his sweet, warm breath tickled my ear and neck and the scent of him flooded my nostrils.

'Nope,' I said flatly, as I turned to shoot him another of my glares.

This was crazy. I swear I'd dished out more dirty looks in the past twenty-four hours than I had my whole life.

I hated the way my stomach flipped as I took in the sight of him. His face was less than a metre away and I could see the stubble on his skin. It looked...

I shook my head like I was trying to shake the stupidity out of my brain. It didn't matter how good his stubble looked. Or that his hazel eyes were a lighter shade of greeny-brown today. Or how soft his lips seemed.

Totally irrelevant.

'We'll see,' he smirked and I wanted to scream *it's never going to happen*. God, I hated how cocky he was.

'So we're going to dive straight into your first activity. Because you're still getting to know your match, I thought we'd do some icebreakers, starting with a little roleplay!'

'Oooh, hello!' someone called out suggestively and the group erupted into laughter.

'No! Not *that* kind of roleplay, you filthy lot!' Sammie cackled. 'This roleplay won't be anything X-rated. Seeing as we're in California and Hollywood is the home of films, or *movies*, and the Love Hotel is all about romance, we're going to focus on romantic movies.'

'Yeah, baby!' a woman with porcelain skin and striking long red hair cheered.

'So,' Sammie continued, 'I'd like you and your partner to write down the name of one romantic movie and an iconic scene from it. We'll put your suggestions in a hat, you'll pick one out that another couple has suggested, then you'll act out at least sixty seconds from that scene.'

'What?' I gasped a little too loudly.

'You'll be acting out a romantic scene,' Sammie repeated. 'Don't worry, we're not expecting anyone to start snogging, sorry, *making out*. I know you only met yesterday. Although I'm sure we've all done a *lot* more than kiss someone we've known for less time than that!' Sammie cackled again. 'Right? Or is it just me?'

'Not just you!' a guy with shoulder-length black hair and white skin called out.

'Phew! Thankfully, those days are over for all of us. Now you're here, you're sure to find deep, meaningful *luurve!*'

Jake snort-laughed and I shot him a disapproving look.

See. That was exactly why I wasn't enthusiastic about being paired up with him. I knew that he wasn't taking this seriously.

He'd probably been paid shitloads of money just to come here to raise the hotel's profile. The hotel probably wanted to sell the whole 'come to this resort and you'll get matched with someone famous' bollocks.

Except this wasn't a joke for me. I could've done a lot with the money I spent coming here. I genuinely wanted to find someone special.

'How will we know the lines to say?' a woman with deep brown skin and braids called out.

'Don't worry. When we did our trials for this activity, most couples picked the same films so we already have a list of the fifty most romantic scenes. I'll give you an iPad with a mini script and you'll be able to watch the clips to help you fine-tune your performance.'

'Great!' the woman replied.

'You'll have an hour to prepare, then each couple will perform on the stage over there.' Sammie pointed to a platform that had been set up on the beach. 'And the winning couple will get a special prize.'

'Oooh!' the redhead called out again.

'Oh, and as part of your prep, I'd also like you to introduce your match to the group. So tell us their name and three things that you've learned about them so far. That'll help everyone in the group get to know each other better too. Any questions?'

'How long do we have to come up with the film and scene idea?' a black guy with low-cut salt-and-pepper hair asked.

'Let's say fifteen minutes. If you need longer, just let me know.'

'Okay.' He nodded.

'Any other questions?' Sammie said. I wanted to ask if I could sit the activity out completely, but I knew she wouldn't agree. 'No? Okay, great! Pens and paper are on the tables beside you. Good luck!'

Ordinarily, I'd like this kind of thing. Even though my own love life was crap, that didn't stop me from enjoying a good romcom, whether it was a book or a film. They gave me hope. Helped me to believe that one day I'd find my Mr Right. I was hoping that coming to this hotel would be my ticket to happiness, but it was just another reminder that fairytale endings didn't exist.

Anyway, I was getting side-tracked. I needed to focus on the task.

'So, come on then.' I faced Jake. 'Tell me your favourite romance films.'

'Don't have any.' He reached in his short pockets, pulled out his sunglasses then put them on.

'Don't believe you.' I raised a suspicious eyebrow. 'A lot of your songs are romantic, so that had to come from somewhere.'

As soon as that sentence flew from my lips, my internal organs shrivelled up like dried raisins. I shouldn't have said that. Now he'd know that I listened to his music and as I'd already realised, the guy had a giant ego. He didn't need me to stroke it.

'A *lot* of my songs, huh?' He cocked his head and a smile tugged at his lips. 'To know that they're romantic, you would've had to have listened to them. I *knew* you liked my music!' he gloated.

I walked right into that one.

'I don't have to like them to be aware of them. When all the radio stations are playing them, it's hard to escape. They get stuck in your head like those annoying earworms.'

'Hmm-mm.' He looked at me with suspicion. I was a rubbish liar so I shouldn't be surprised that he didn't believe me.

The truth was I *did* like his music, but I wasn't going to tell him that.

'Anyway, you probably didn't write those songs, so it'd make sense that you're a cynic when it comes to romance.'

'I wrote *all* of my songs,' he corrected. 'The solo releases anyway. When I was in the band, we had to do whatever we were told.'

'Oh,' I said, thinking that sounded awful. I wanted to know more, but seeing as this match was temporary, I didn't have the right to ask him personal questions.

'Yeah...' His voice trailed off. 'I used to watch those kinds of films, but then...' He paused again. 'Sammie said they had popular films on the list, so we should choose a classic.'

'We could go for *Bridget Jones*,' I suggested. 'Like when Colin Firth's character says he loves Bridget just the way she is.'

'Maybe.'

'Or the line in Jerry Maguire.'

'Where Cuba Gooding Jr. says "show me the money!"?' Jake laughed.

'No! When Tom Cruise says "you complete me" and Renee Zellweger's character says "you had me at hello".'

'I hear you, but is Jerry Maguire really a romance or a sports comedy drama movie with some romance? It'd be better to choose something that's more of a traditional romcom. Like a Hugh Grant film.'

'Like *Love Actually*? Or *Notting Hill*?'

'Yeah.'

'See! I *knew* you liked romcoms!' I stifled a smile as I repeated what he'd said before about me liking his music. Jake didn't reply. 'Okay. What quotes should we use? Anything come to mind?'

Seeing as he'd suggested a Hugh Grant romcom, I wanted to see how much he really knew about them.

'We could use the quote from the bookstore scene where Julia Roberts talked about being a woman standing in front of a man, wanting him to love her.' He shrugged like it was no big deal.

My jaw dropped.

Most guys I'd dated wouldn't even be able to name a single romcom, but Jake not only seemed familiar with them, he was able to quote from them too. And the line he'd picked was exactly the one that I would've chosen.

Yeah, he hadn't got it word for word. I think it was a *girl* standing in front of a *boy* and she was *asking him* rather than *wanting him* to love her, but it was close enough.

I was borderline impressed.

'What?' He pulled off his sunglasses and frowned. Then I realised that my jaw must still be on the floor. 'Didn't expect me

to quote from one of the most famous scenes in romantic cine-
matic history?'

'Honestly?' I said. 'No. But like you said, it is pretty iconic.
Let's run with it.'

I picked up a sheet of paper and wrote the quote down, then
folded it up. I'd take it over to Sammie in a minute.

'Cool. Now it's time for the best part of this activity.'

'What? Is it time for me to leave you already?' I grinned,
thinking that'd definitely be something to smile about.

'Ouch.' He clutched his stomach and I tried to ignore how the
fabric of his T-shirt clung to his abs. 'Harsh.'

'I was joking.' *Sort of.* Actually, I was deadly serious. Just
because Jake knew about romcoms, it didn't change anything. He
still was *not* my perfect match.

Far from it.

'Wow.' Jake gasped dramatically. 'She *jokes*? I thought your
personality permanently operated on one setting: glaring.'

'Haha, very funny.'

'It's true! All you've done since dinner is glare at me.'

'Whatever happened to calling me Smiley?'

'Touché. But seriously though, why do you hate me so much?
Did I refuse to give you an autograph after you camped out
overnight to come to one of my shows?'

'Not everything's about *you*!' I rolled my eyes.

'No?' His jaw dropped with mock surprise. 'All these years
everyone lied to me!' He laughed. 'So what is it then?'

'Doesn't matter.' I waved my hand dismissively. 'What's your
favourite part of the task?'

'Sammie said we have to introduce each other to the group
and tell them three things about each other. I've already got
yours locked down: one, she hates me, two, she hates smiling and
three, she's from New York. Nailed it, right?'

'The smiling part is incorrect. I smile a lot. But only when I'm around people that make me happy.'

'Damn, girl. You're firing so many shots at me I'm gonna need stitches to patch up all these holes! So what have you learnt about me?'

'That's easy: one, you love yourself, two, you're a musician and three, you're a closet romcom lover.'

'Wrong on all counts. Once upon a time those observations might've been true, but not any more.' His gaze dropped to the ground. 'Except the romcom one. When I liked them, there was nothing closeted about it. I had no problem telling people I enjoyed watching them. I owned that shit. I'm gonna take this to Sammie.'

As he plucked the piece of paper off the table then strode over to Sammie, shock rolled through me.

When I'd said those things about Jake, I'd expected him to deny them.

Obviously, he wasn't going to admit that he loved himself. But hearing him say that it might've been true 'once upon a time' suggested that he didn't love himself any more. Especially as I noticed there was a sadness in his eyes when he said it, which was swiftly followed by him avoiding my gaze.

And surely he didn't mean that he wasn't still a musician? Yeah, it'd been a long time since he'd released any new songs, but you didn't just stop being a musician when you took some time out. Surely it was in your blood forever?

I knew I shouldn't care, but I'd be lying if I said I wasn't intrigued. I wanted to know why he didn't make music any more.

He'd said that he used to love romcoms too, but I got the impression that he wasn't into romance any more. And if that was the case, then I wondered not for the first time what the hell he was doing here, at the Love Hotel.

9

JAKE

As I got off the daybed and walked towards Sammie to give her the piece of paper with our movie quote, I wondered what the fuck was wrong with me.

Halle made a stupid statement about me then all of a sudden, my chest tightened. It was like something she said triggered me.

It wasn't the romcom stuff. Like I'd said, I used to like them. I found them calming. It was reassuring to know there'd always be a happy ending.

And it wasn't hard for me to remember the scene in *Notting Hill* because I instantly related to Julia Roberts's character. I'd lost count of the number of times I just wanted someone to accept me for being me.

Not Jake the rockstar. The celebrity. The Hollywood bad boy. Just the guy from a small town in Kansas who enjoyed having a good time with his friends, like most people.

It sounded corny, but watching that film made me feel seen. Like I wasn't alone. That one day I'd find my person. But when reality hit and my heart got crushed, there was no way I could keep watching them.

That was one of the reasons I'd stopped writing songs too. What was the point of writing about love when you realised happy endings didn't really exist?

A lot of writers channelled heartbreak into their music. But for me, even though getting the words onto the page was cathartic, when I tried to sing them, the pain was too much.

And so I stopped. Then when... when something fucking awful happened, I knew there was no way I could. Soon a few months turned into years. I couldn't blame my label for dropping me.

Which is why Halle's comment about me being a musician was wrong. She'd used the wrong tense.

I wasn't a musician. I *used* to be one. All I was now was a washed-up has-been. And that was exactly why her third observation was also incorrect. I sure as shit didn't love myself right now. Most days I could barely stomach looking at my own reflection.

My cell vibrated in my pocket.

I didn't even need to look to know that it was Wilma, chasing again for more photos and content.

Yep. My life sucked.

'Here you go.' I handed Sammie our quote.

'Thanks!' she said as she unfolded the paper. 'Oooh, nice one! Pick a quote from the hat before I put your one in.'

'What did we get?' Halle appeared next to me as I rummaged around the hat then plucked out a piece of folded paper.

'Here.' I handed it to Halle. 'You do the honours.'

She unravelled the paper excitedly, but when she opened it, her face fell.

'No way.' She grimaced. 'Can I choose another one?'

'Sorry!' Sammie replied. 'Only one pick per person and most of the others have already been allocated.'

'But it's not even romantic!' Halle protested.

'Why? What is it?' Sammie said.

'It can't be that bad.' I tried to steal a look.

'No, it's worse than bad. It's *that* scene from *When Harry Met Sally*...'

10

HALLE

'I don't see the problem?' Jake said as we returned to our sun loungers.

'Of course you don't,' I grumbled. 'Because you're not the one that has to do the main part.'

'The main part?' He frowned.

'You know *exactly* what part I mean,' I scowled.

'I think you'll need to refresh my memory,' he smirked.

'The part where Meg Ryan's character, Sally, is at the diner with Harry and she fakes having an orgasm at the table to show him how easy it is.'

'Ohhh...' he chuckled, even though I knew full well that he was familiar with that scene. 'Still don't see why that's an issue. Unless of course you're telling me that you've never had to do that.'

'Ha!' I laughed. 'I can't remember a time that I *haven't* had to fake it.'

'You're joking, right?' His brows knitted together.

'I wish I was,' I mumbled.

'That's pretty sad.'

'What?' My head shot up. 'You're blaming *me*?'

'No! I don't mean that *you're* sad. I'm saying it's sad that the guys you've been with didn't take care of business. There's no way I'd let a woman leave a bed or wherever we'd fucked without knowing that I rocked her world.'

'*Yeah, right.*' I rolled my eyes. 'You're so self-centred that just like Billy Crystal's character, Harry, you wouldn't know that she was faking it. That's why that scene is so iconic.'

'I *would* know. And I also know for a fact that no woman that's ever been with me has ever had to pretend. They've always got off. Zero exceptions.'

As I looked at Jake, I swallowed hard. I barely knew him and although he still definitely wasn't my favourite person, somehow I believed him.

Then again, given the number of women he'd slept with, he'd clearly had a lot of practice.

And when he'd said 'or wherever we fucked' I couldn't help being curious about where he'd done it before. Probably down an alleyway, in the toilets or backstage. Someone like him probably had a queue of groupies lining up to jump his community cock.

Gross.

Anyway, I had no business thinking about what Jake was like in bed or up against a toilet wall. Men like him should come with a health warning. You never knew what you could catch from them.

I swallowed the lump in my throat and pushed away the painful memories that flashed into my head.

'Whatever,' I said. 'If you want to continue your delusions, it's no skin off my nose.'

'You know what they say, Smiley: the proof of the pudding is in the eating, so if you *really* want to be sure that I'm telling the truth, there's only one way to find out. But seeing as you seem to hate me, I guess you'll never know...'

'Suits me just fine.' I wrinkled my nose.

Now that I thought about it, I'd overreacted about the scene we'd been given. Clearly I was no Meg Ryan but if I tried, I reckoned I could ace it. God knows I'd had to do it enough times. The men I'd been with couldn't find my clit if I gave them a map, compass *and* sat nav.

'We'd better rehearse,' Jake said. 'If I have to try to convince a bunch of strangers that I don't know how to make a woman come, it's gonna take a lot of work!' A mischievous grin spread across his face.

'Jesus.' I shook my head like a disappointed parent. The ego on this guy. 'I reckon you'll be a natural. And I'm sure there's thousands of dissatisfied women you've slept with all around the world who'd back me up on that.'

'Dream on, Smiley. Let's get to work.'

'No need,' I said, thinking if he wanted to play confident, that I could too. 'Thanks to my lacklustre experiences with big-headed guys like you, I don't even need to rehearse how to fake an orgasm. I've got this.'

11

JAKE

'Oh, God, right there, yes, yes, *yesssss!*' Halle cried out as she raked her fingers through her hair, before tipping her head back and groaning loudly just like Meg Ryan's character did in *When Harry Met Sally*.

As I sat opposite her and watched the Oscar-worthy performance, even I had to admit that she was scarily convincing.

Especially when she started banging her hands on the table for dramatic effect.

'I'll have what she's having!' Sammie laughed, quoting the line from the same scene. The rest of the group erupted into fits of giggles. 'That was excellent! Well done, you two!'

'I just have to add that Halle is clearly an excellent actress and her performance in no way reflects my bedroom skills, because no woman has ever had to fake it with me,' I grinned.

'Damn straight!' another guy called out from the audience.

'Yeah, yeah! Keep telling yourself that, guys, if it makes you feel better,' countered the redhead.

'Now, now,' Sammie smiled. 'I'm sure that *everyone* in this group is fully committed to delivering mutual satisfaction. And if you have the chance to get intimate with your match in the future, may you *all* enjoy a thoroughly, completely, earth-shatteringly satisfying happy ending!'

'Hear, hear!' two women chorused.

'So Halle and Jake, now you've done your performances, I need you to tell the rest of the group a bit about your match. Sorry, I should've got you to introduce yourselves first. Can you tell that I'm new here?' Sammie joked.

'You're doing great,' Halle said reassuringly. 'Well, I'm sure most of you know this guy already, but just in case you don't, this is Jake. So, three things about him: he's a successful musician and as well as being a hopeless romantic, he likes taking photos,' she said into the mic before moving it away from her mouth and muttering 'and he loves himself' at a volume that only I could hear.

I looked at her and flashed a fake smile. Halle handed me the mic.

'Thank you,' I said. Her intro was surprisingly complimentary, even if it was still inaccurate. 'Hey there, everyone. So this is Halle and as well as being a big fan of romcoms, she makes a mean green juice and she loves to smile – especially whenever she sees me.' I grinned and right on cue, Halle shot me an unimpressed look.

'Oooh! That's what we like to hear,' Sammie said, her eyes flicking to Halle as if she wasn't completely convinced that what I'd said was true. 'Wonderful performance and intros, guys, thank you. Dwayne and Miley, you're up next.'

Halle stormed back to her seat and I followed. I could tell she was pissed off.

Once the other couples performed various scenes including *Sleepless in Seattle*, *You've Got Mail* and *The Holiday*, Sammie said she needed a moment to decide on a winner so said we could take a break for half an hour.

Halle immediately pulled out her cell, which reminded me that I needed to take more photos.

This morning, I'd gone to breakfast expecting to see Halle there, but when Sammie told me she hadn't arrived yet, I thought I'd make the most of my time and take some photos before Wilma started busting my balls again.

I felt like a fucking idiot, posing on my own in front of the pool, then the beach taking selfies, then making the corny video Wilma had insisted I shoot telling the world that I'd met the woman of my dreams and to 'stay tuned' for more details and to follow our 'love story'. Just hearing myself repeat those words made me want to barf.

Seemed like Halle had no interest in chatting, so I pulled out my cell too.

Unsurprisingly, there were messages from Wilma.

> **WILMA**
>
> Great job with the video post. You've already got a couple hundred likes. But now that you've teased them, you're gonna need some content with your match.
>
> No kissing yet. Just some cute selfies of you two cosying up together will do for now.
>
> Don't leave it too long. Gotta keep the momentum going.

I dropped my cell on my lap and groaned. There was no way I was gonna convince Halle to take photos 'cosying up' with me.

And the 'no kissing yet' comment Wilma made was freaking hilarious. Forget licking a pig's butt. Halle would rather make out with a poisonous snake than lock lips with me.

Once upon a time, I could've had my pick of women. Some of

them would go to crazy lengths to just be in the same room as me. I'd lost count of the number who'd tried to sneak into my hotel room, break into my home or make up stories to get backstage.

But Halle acted like even breathing the same air as me was a chore.

I knew I shouldn't give a shit. My presence here was strictly professional. Whether she liked me or not shouldn't matter. Yet for some weird reason it did.

I guessed it was like whenever I used to do shows. When I looked out in the crowd from the stage if I saw 59,999 people loving my performance, but one person looked bored, I'd worry about why they weren't vibing with my music instead of appreciating the majority who were.

It was dumb, but I couldn't help it.

If I knew what Halle's problem with me was, maybe I could fix it. But until then, I'd just have to do what I always did: put on a brave face, crack some jokes and act like it didn't bother me.

'If I could have your attention, please, folks!' Sammie called out. 'It was a tough decision, but I'm delighted to announce that the winner of today's competition is Stuart and Mandy with their performance of *Titanic*! Give them a round of applause!'

I clapped politely. Their performance was okay, but Halle's was way better.

'We were robbed,' I whispered in Halle's ear, trying to ignore her sweet scent. I'd noticed it last night and again when I'd first sat next to her earlier. It smelt like strawberries and coconut. And as much as I hated to admit it, I fucking loved it.

'Yeah,' Halle replied.

'Thanks so much!' Mandy said as she opened the envelope. 'We've won a couple's massage!'

Everyone cheered. Except me and Halle.

'Maybe it was a good thing that we didn't win.' I turned to face her, trying to ignore her long, toned legs, which were spread out in front of her. Halle's skin looked so smooth and for a second, I wondered how it would feel to run my hands over it.

What the hell?

It was a good thing I was wearing my shades so she couldn't see where my damn eyes had roamed.

'Yeah.' She swallowed hard. 'Definitely for the best.'

12

HALLE

'Sorry I haven't called sooner,' Vanessa said as I got comfortable on my bed. It was now the start of my second full day at the hotel and I wanted to speak to her before I went to breakfast. 'It's been crazy busy with this case at work and then with the time difference...'

'No worries!' I said, propping a pillow behind my back.

'I still can't believe they matched you with Jake Myers!'

'Tell me about it!'

'I mean, the man's fit as fuck, but he's *shag* material, not *boyfriend* or *husband* material.'

'Exactly!'

'If it helps you feel better, he's smitten with you.'

'Yeah, right!' I scoffed. 'The only person Jake Myers is smitten with is Jake Myers.'

'*Nah-uh*,' Vanessa protested. 'Apparently you're the woman of his dreams.'

'Bullshit.'

'That's what he said on his Insta, and everyone knows that if it's on social media then it *has* to be true!' She laughed.

'Wait, what? He put me on his Instagram?'

'Not pictures, he just mentioned you in a reel. When I listened to your voice note and you said how obsessed he was with taking photos *for the 'gram*, naturally I had to check it out. And sure enough, although he literally had zero posts before he arrived, he's done loads since he got to the hotel. There's photos of the restaurant, food, the beach and the pool. Then yesterday he posted a video saying that he was so happy that he'd met the woman of his dreams and to stay tuned for more deets.'

That made zero sense. I'd done nothing but give him dirty looks and monosyllabic answers since we'd been introduced.

I'd made it crystal clear that I wasn't interested in him, so why the hell would he say that? Did he get off on knowing I didn't like him or think I was just playing hard to get?

Weird.

'Can I ask you something?'

'Sure, babe!'

'Do you think I'm overreacting? I've been on a bit of a downer since I got introduced to Jake and he's started winding me up by calling me things like *Smiley* as a joke because he said I always glare and never crack a smile. But you understand why I'm not thrilled with this match, right?'

'Course I do! You've shelled out a shitload of cash to find a serious match who's looking for something long-term and they've set you up with a fuckboy who probably has a longer relationship with a disposable cup of coffee than he's ever had with a woman, so it's understandable that you're disappointed.'

'Yeah,' I said, my shoulders relaxing. 'That's exactly what I thought.'

As hard as it was to believe based on my actions over the past couple of days, I generally was a happy person. I wasn't smiles and sunshine all the time. But who was? There was just something about Jake that pushed my buttons.

Well, it was more than just *something*. It was *many* things.

'And when you add in the experience you had with your dickhead ex into the mix, being set up with another popstar is the shittiest scenario. Other than being set up with your ex, of course. Now *that* would be a disaster.'

'Ugh,' I shuddered. 'Just the thought of that makes me want to throw up. I heard that'd happened with one of the couples at the Spanish Love Hotel. It worked out well for them, but there's no way it would for me. I guess it shows that things could always be worse.'

'Yep. So what are you gonna do? Stick it out or ask for a refund?'

Vanessa's question made my mind drift back to what happened after the film scene performances had ended.

We'd had a group lunch on the beach then I'd spent most of the rest of the day chilling by the pool with a book, which was bliss. Especially because it meant I had zero obligations to spend any more time with Jake.

When I was going to my room, I spoke to Sammie again and asked if they did refunds. She repeated what she'd said before and encouraged me to stick it out for a few more days because she really believed it'd be worth it.

I couldn't face having dinner with Jake, so I opted for room service instead.

I'd eaten dinner on my balcony whilst admiring the amazing sea views. Then I'd reluctantly submitted my playlist.

As well as the three songs I'd thought about earlier, I also added: 'All Eyez on Me' by 2Pac, 'Attention' by Charlie Puth and 'What's My Name?' by Rihanna and Drake, which fitted Jake's personality perfectly. After that I'd crashed out.

'The hotel only does refunds under very extreme circumstances, like if the match is abusive or threatening,' I said, bringing my thoughts back to Vanessa's question.

'Shit. Looks like you have to stick it out then. What's the plan for today?'

'Breakfast, then our first excursion.'

'Oooh! Where you off to?'

'No idea. Apparently they keep the locations a surprise.'

'How fun!'

'The excursion will be. The company not so much...'

'I feel for you. At least you'll be with other people so there won't be any awkward silences.'

'True,' I said. My stomach rumbled loudly. 'And that's my cue to go and get breakfast!' I laughed.

'Enjoy! And good luck.'

'Thanks, hon. Don't work too hard!'

'I will!' she joked, before hanging up.

Vanessa was the ultimate career woman and she was killing it, but sometimes I worried that she spent too long at the office. In her defence, she played as hard as she worked. She wasn't interested in a long-term relationship. When she wanted some fun with a guy, she went and found one.

I admired how she lived life on her terms. If Vanessa wanted something, whether it was a successful career or some fun between the sheets, she was a go-getter.

Which was more than could be said for me. I didn't have a career or any noteworthy conquests to speak of. But on the bright side, at least I was in California, a state I'd always wanted to visit. So although the circumstances weren't perfect, especially considering it was where my ex was based and I'd been matched with someone who reminded me of him, I was gonna try my best to make the most of it. Starting with a great breakfast.

Once I'd showered and got dressed, I picked up my bag and rifled through it. I probably wouldn't get time to come back to my room before we headed off on the excursion, so I needed to make sure I had everything with me now.

They'd told us to wear trousers and closed-toe shoes, so maybe we were going for a hike? I hoped it wasn't anywhere too high. But they'd also asked us to pack sunscreen and sunglasses too.

The essentials like my purse, phone and make-up bag were already in there, but I added a jumper and an umbrella just in case. Although this was the sunshine state, I was an English girl at heart and I knew it was always best to be prepared for all weather possibilities. Speaking of which, I should also pack a rain mac. And some snacks.

I threw in my battery power pack and some insect repellent spray. The last thing I wanted was to get bitten by mosquitoes. Better add some bite cream.

That should be everything.

I picked up the bag and winced. Wow. It was heavy.

After sliding it onto my shoulder, I contemplated removing some stuff, but without knowing where we were going, it was hard to know what I'd to take out. Everything was essential. I'd just have to take it all.

When I got to the restaurant, the maître d' showed me to the table where Jake was already seated.

'Hey, Smiley!' he grinned and my stomach flipped.

The action shocked me. Stomach flipping for men like Jake wasn't acceptable. I'd make sure that nonsense didn't happen again.

In my stomach's defence, Jake was looking annoyingly handsome. Again.

He was wearing black jeans and a plain white T-shirt which

on anyone else would look ordinary, but on him, for some reason it looked... good.

Maybe it was the way it clung to his muscular chest. Or the way the short sleeves hugged his biceps. I had no idea why, but knew that hating him would be much easier if he had the face and body of an ogre.

'Hi,' I said flatly, before pulling out my chair and plonking myself down.

'So I've just been looking at some very cool photos of you.'

'What?' My brows pinched together. 'From where?'

'Yesterday's activity.'

Shit. I forgot about that. Sammie had mentioned that every morning the hotel would print photos that they'd taken of us and that we'd submitted so that we could choose our favourites for the silly memory book.

I'd declined Jake's requests to take selfies (I really didn't want to be featured on his Insta), but now I remembered that Sammie had taken some during our performance, but I couldn't exactly stop mid-fake orgasm to protest.

'Aren't we supposed to go through those together?' I raised my eyebrow.

'Technically, yes. And I would've waited, but I got the impression that you weren't interested in photos, so I thought I'd save you the hassle.'

'Let me see.' I thrust my hand in front of him.

I hated looking at photos of myself and the idea that he'd already seen and studied them made my stomach churn.

To me, photos highlighted your flaws. They were like a permanent reminder of all of the things about yourself that you hated. In my case it was my thick thighs and my height. I was six feet tall, so I often towered over other people and I'd developed a bad habit of slouching and trying to make myself small, so I didn't look like a giant.

My ex was a few inches shorter than me and had a real complex about it. I didn't mind the fact I had to bend down to kiss him, but he never liked standing beside me if we were out, he'd insist we sat down. And he hated me wearing heels.

Jake put the photos in my palm and I took a deep breath, bracing myself.

As I flicked through the photos a deep frown formed on my face. They weren't as horrendous as I'd feared.

The first one was of me standing next to Jake, looking at him as he said something. And there were two things that immediately struck me. Firstly, I was looking *up* at him. Obviously I'd realised that Jake was tall, but somehow I'd been so busy snarling at him that I hadn't realised that he was a good few inches taller than me, which felt like a first.

And instead of glaring, which had become my default setting for him, I was actually smiling. Cue dramatic gasp.

That couldn't be right.

Sammie must've changed my expression in photoshop. I couldn't think of a single thing that would have caused me to grin at him.

I flicked to the next photo and there it was again. A bloody smile.

The one after that made me blush. I had my head tipped back and my mouth was open. That was clearly the point where I was faking my orgasm as part of the performance. The interesting thing was that Jake was staring at me like he was in awe.

Nah. It couldn't be *awe*. He was probably just shocked at how convincing I was and questioning whether other women he'd been with had pulled the wool over his eyes too.

'Pretty cool, right?' he said. 'My favourite one is where you're grinning and giving me heart eyes. I *told* you that you always smiled when you looked at me,' he teased.

'I do not! I was probably just laughing at something ridiculous you'd said.'

'If you say so, Smiley.'

'Stop calling me that!' I huffed. 'And what about this one?' I held up the photo where he was staring at me with the sort-of-but-clearly-it-couldn't-be awestruck expression.

'That one's cool too. I think that was when you told me that you were already falling in love with me and I was feeling flattered.' His mouth tilted into a devilish smile.

'I was *not*...' I was about to protest again, but when I saw him smiling like an idiot, I realised that he enjoyed winding me up and I was playing right into his hands by letting it get to me.

But not any more.

I hoped Jake got a good look at me smiling at him in those photos because it wasn't gonna happen again.

13

JAKE

'Nice wheels!' Stuart, the guy who'd won the performance with his match, said as he stepped onto the bus in front of me.

He was right. This was kinda fancy. Like a smaller, more modern version of the tour bus we used to ride in when I was in the band. It had a glossy black exterior, shiny wooden flooring, plus a panoramic glass roof and large tinted windows, which I guessed was designed to make it perfect for sightseeing.

I scanned the large black leather seats to see if Halle was already here, but there was no sign of her. After breakfast she'd raced off to her room to get something she'd forgotten to pack in her purse.

I was relieved when she left because I needed to collect my thoughts. When I went to pick up those photos, I was expecting to see shots of her glaring at me. But what I said was true. There were multiple photos of her actually *smiling*.

At first I was happy because it felt like a victory. I'd told her that I'd make her like me and I had, which was a win. But then when I found myself looking at those same photos multiple times, I realised that I actually liked her smile and the way it made her whole face light up.

I'd put the photos back in their envelope and thought that was the end of it. But when she sashayed into that dining hall for breakfast looking more delicious than a stack of pancakes drizzled in maple syrup, I'd started to worry.

She was wearing a yellow sundress with pink flowers printed all over it and cherry-red lipstick which captured my attention more than it should've. Her toned shoulders were exposed and the way the dress clung to her curves had me thinking all kinds of things that had no business being in my head.

I was here for *work*. Although Wilma's objective was to get me a reality TV show, the way I saw it was that I just had to get along with Halle enough to take photos that'd raise my profile and make the right people take my calls once I left here.

But I couldn't see how that was gonna happen, considering Halle's photo aversion. Sure, I had the pictures Sammie had taken, but there was no way I'd post them without Halle's permission. And while Sammie might be fooled by the smiles Halle was flashing in those photos, I knew the truth. Halle wasn't remotely interested in me.

At least the fact that she didn't like me meant I didn't have to worry about leading her on or breaking her heart.

A woman a few rows in front kept turning around and looking at me. The first two times I thought nothing of it. But now it was getting weird. She got up and came over, holding her cell phone.

'Hi!' she beamed, twirling her dark hair around her fingers. 'I wanted to come over during the activity yesterday, but anyway, I'm Sally.'

'Hey, Sally.' I gave her a weak smile. I wanted to think she was just being friendly, but the way she was clutching her cell, I suspected she wanted to ask for a photo.

Most of the guests that had recognised me had just nodded and smiled in acknowledgement and left me alone, but something told me Sally was different.

'I can't believe it's really you! Y'know, that we're here, staying in the same hotel! I crushed on you so hard in high school! You used to be so hot.'

'Uh, thanks?' Nothing like being told that you *used to be* hot.

'I don't mean *used to be* like you aren't now,' she corrected. 'If anything, you're even hotter...'

'That's nice of you,' I said, craning my neck to see where her match was.

'Can I take a photo?'

I knew it. This was awkward. I didn't want photos of me with another woman circulating on the internet. It'd get messy. The only one I should be pictured with was Halle and that wasn't gonna happen in this lifetime.

Just as I was working out how to wriggle out of this, Sammie came over.

'Everything okay?'

'Yes!' Sally said. 'I was just asking if I could have a photo with Jake!'

I flashed Sammie a *please save me* expression and she gave me a small nod.

'Sorry, Sally, but remember the NDA agreeing not to take photos of other guests, including celebrities? Ordinarily, I'm sure Jake wouldn't mind, but we need to ensure everyone's privacy is respected here.'

'Okay.' Her shoulders slumped. 'Sorry.'

'No worries,' I said. 'It was nice to meet you.'

Sally shuffled back to her seat and I mouthed a thank-you to Sammie.

Halle rushed onto the bus clutching a huge bright pink purse. It was like she'd packed for a week's vacation, not a day trip.

'Saved you a seat, darling.' I patted the space beside me.

She looked down at it like it was covered in shit, before scanning the rest of the interior, probably searching for an alternative seat. When she didn't find one, she reluctantly sat down, dropping her purse on her lap, then wincing.

'Maybe you should put that under the seat.'

She did as I suggested, then sat back down. It was a good thing this bus had a lot of legroom.

Halle's sweet scent surrounded me, just like it had at breakfast.

Damn. She looked fine and she smelt even better.

I didn't know if it was her shampoo, hair products or perfume, but I liked it way too much.

Sammie stood at the front of the bus with a mic and I was grateful for the distraction.

'Hey, everyone! Did you all have a good breakfast?'

'Yes!' the guests chorused.

'Excellent! Hope you enjoyed looking through your photos from yesterday and have picked out your favourites for the memory book.' In the end, Halle agreed on the photos of me looking at her with heart eyes. That was kinda embarrassing, but what can I say? Faking it or not, I challenged any red-blooded male not to get affected by an attractive woman telling you that you're making them come.

I, of course, chose the photos of her smiling at me. Just to remind her why I'd given her that Smiley nickname.

'And hopefully you all submitted your playlist selections too.'

Nope. Not me.

Taking photos was one thing, but playlists were something that I did for someone who was important to me. Which was why I hadn't made one for Halle. That shit was too personal.

I poured my heart and soul into making a playlist for someone I thought was special before and I sure as shit wasn't spending time doing that for a stranger who hated my guts.

Plus, the last thing I wanted to do these days was listen to music. I didn't need a reminder of what I couldn't do any more.

Fuck that.

'So the first part of today's activity will be... drumroll, please... a tour of Hollywood and Beverly Hills!'

'All right!' a woman at the front who I think was called Maisy called out.

As multiple other guests whooped and cheered, my stomach dropped like a stone.

That was up there with the activity from hell. As well as driving past all the tourist hotspots, those kinds of tours usually involved gawping at celebrities' houses.

I could understand why it might be interesting for a lot of people, but for me, it was just another reminder of my life before. The last thing I wanted to do was cruise by the homes of people who pretended to be my friends when I was riding high in the charts, but ditched me quicker than a hot potato the second things went to shit and I'd outlived my usefulness.

I dragged my hand over my face. There was no way I wanted to go on this trip, but if I refused, I'd draw more attention to myself. But if I went and the paps were around, that'd draw even more attention too.

Then again, the last place they'd expect me to be is on a fancy tourist bus. I was overreacting. It would be uncomfortable as hell, but it'd be fine.

'I know for some of you, it might seem a bit touristy,' Sammie continued, her gaze flicking to me for a second, 'but I know for most people it's one thing they'd like to do when they visit LA, so we thought we'd do this as the first excursion and then we'll be turning up the romance...'

Several guests whooped enthusiastically as the driver started the engine and set off.

'Great,' Halle muttered under her breath.

Looked like we were both dreading this trip.

'Want the window seat?' I asked Halle. 'It's your first time here, so I figured you'd want to see the sights.' Her eyes widened with surprise. 'If you don't want to, it's fine.'

'No, I... that'd be great. Thanks.' She winced like it physically hurt her to show her appreciation.

Halle stood in the aisle whilst I slid out. My arm brushed against hers and my pulse spiked. I quickly stepped back to give her more space to climb into the window seat.

Her scent hit me again and I groaned internally. I hated it how it affected me.

'So I guess you're excited about going to Hollywood,' I said, attempting to make conversation and to avoid thinking about how damn good Halle smelt.

'Yeah,' she said flatly. I was about to roll my eyes about the fact that she'd just given me another monosyllabic answer when she continued to talk. 'I always wanted to go.'

'What stopped you?'

'Just...' She paused. 'Circumstances.'

'I suppose it'd be asking too much for you to elaborate by responding with a full sentence.'

'Yep! You guessed it.'

She turned back to stare out of the window.

I was done. It was exhausting trying to make the effort when she wouldn't even meet me halfway.

What could be her reason for not coming to LA? I could understand it would be triggering if maybe she was an actress and spent years there trying to make it, but it was already clear that she had no interest in that path.

Fuck it. I had better things to think about than her reasons.

I pulled out my cell and saw that Wilma had sent multiple text messages reminding me to post. *As if I could forget.*

As the driver got closer to Hollywood, my chest tightened.

The roof of the bus slid back and the windows went down, transforming the vehicle into a luxury open-top bus and giving everyone clearer views of their surroundings, making it easier to take photos.

Sammie stepped up to the front of the coach.

'Welcome to Hollywood!' she said excitedly.

As we drove down the palm-tree-lined street, I prepared myself for the excitement that I knew was coming.

'OMG!' Mandy shouted and pointed. 'It's the Hollywood sign!'

Halle stuck her head out of the bus to get a closer look and I saw her eyes light up.

'Can we go and take photos?' Stuart, Mandy's match, asked.

'We'll be going to multiple cool places this week that will give you opportunities to take photos of the amazing views, so don't worry,' Sammie said.

As the bus continued down the boulevard, everyone started snapping away, posing for photos with the sign in view. I should do the same, but like Sammie said, there were better places to do that.

Soon afterwards the bus pulled over and Sammie announced

that we were getting off to be shown the Hollywood Walk of Fame.

Halle's face lit up again.

'I've always wanted to see this!' she said.

'It's not that special.'

'Just because you've probably seen it a million times doesn't mean you have to rain on everyone else's parade.'

'Just trying to manage your expectations.' I held my hands up in surrender.

Halle heaved her bag up off the floor.

'Sure you don't want to leave that here?'

'I can't leave it! It might get stolen. I've got a lot of important stuff in here.'

'You sure look like you have a lot of stuff... whether or not I'd classify it as important though is another question.'

Halle hoisted her luggage (that was the only appropriate word for it) over her shoulder then winced at the weight. If she wasn't so damn salty, I'd offer to carry it for her.

Sammie led us down the Hollywood Walk of Fame and guests cooed as they spotted different names engraved onto the stars.

'Like it?' I asked.

'It's...' Halle scanned her surroundings, then switched her purse to her other shoulder. 'It's not what I was expecting. I thought it would be all glitzy and glamorous, but it's just a normal kind of street with pretty paving stones.'

'Yup,' I said, resisting the temptation to say *I told you so*.

With every step Halle took, I could see her struggling under all of the weight her poor shoulders were carrying.

'Give it to me,' I sighed, then held out my hand. Watching her struggle was painful.

'Give what to you?'

'Your bank account details.' I rolled my eyes. 'Your purse, of course!'

'Why do you want my purse?' Her brows knitted together. 'Don't you have your own money?'

'Huh?' Now it was my turn to frown.

'You asked for my purse. Surely you're richer than me?' I almost laughed out loud. If only she knew I was broke. 'Wait. Sorry. I've just realised you're talking about my *handbag*.' She slapped her forehead. 'For a second I was in British English mode and I forgot that's what you call it here.'

'Yeah. But we're both wrong. That shit on your shoulder isn't a purse or a handbag. It's more like a damn suitcase!' I laughed and a reluctant smile tugged at her lips. I liked it when she smiled. 'Give it to me.' I held out my hand again. I expected her to protest, but she didn't.

'Thanks,' she muttered, dragging it down her shoulder ready to give it to me.

'Sorry, what did you say?' I cupped my ear. 'I couldn't hear you.'

'I said, *thanks*.'

She dropped it in my palm and my arm bucked under the weight.

'Damn, girl! What the hell do you have in here? Rocks?'

'Just a few essentials, you know, like sunscreen, insect repellent.'

'Why would you need insect repellent?'

'In case we went to the beach or near the water and there are mosquitoes. Maybe if I put it on it'll work on you too!' She grinned, clearly pleased with her dig.

'So I offer to carry your bag of bricks and you insult me?' I clutched my chest like I was wounded.

'I was joking! And you love to joke, right?' She flashed a

mischievous smile and I instantly dismissed the idea of winding her up.

'Okay, those things account for about 1 per cent of the weight. What else is in here?'

'A change of shoes, a jumper, umbrella, raincoat...'

'And what about the kitchen sink?'

'Ha bloody ha! Have you ever been to England? Anyone will tell you that it's good to be prepared. You never know what the weather's going to do.'

'I hear you. As you mentioned at dinner, I lived in the UK for a while, but I don't know if you've realised, we're in LA, not London right now.'

'No!' she mock gasped. 'Why didn't anyone tell me?' She deadpanned. 'Of course I know that, but still... like I said, it's always best to be prepared.'

'Yeah, if you're going camping for a week! Not an excursion for a few hours.'

'Whatever.' She tried to suppress a laugh but it came out anyway. 'By the way, it suits you,' she smiled and warmth flooded my chest. I wished she'd do it more often.

'What can I say?' I chuckled. 'Pink is definitely my colour.'

14

HALLE

It'd been a busy morning of sightseeing. As well as checking out the Hollywood Walk of Fame and seeing views of the Hollywood sign, we'd also visited the famous Dolby Theatre where they hosted the Oscars and drove to Beverly Hills where the other guests took photos of the sign before we cruised down Rodeo Drive.

Although I could tell Jake hated being here, probably because he'd visited these places a million times before, I got a real thrill from seeing everything in person.

When we drove down Rodeo Drive, I immediately pictured the scenes from *Pretty Woman* where Julia Roberts's character Vivian goes into that fancy shop and they were rude to her because they thought she didn't have any money. I could relate. All of the luxury boutiques were filled with clothes, shoes and handbags I couldn't afford.

Seeing the Beverly Hills sign made me think about the times I'd spent watching the *Beverly Hills Cop* films with my dad.

Although the Walk of Fame wasn't as glamorous as I'd imagined, it was still great to visit the place where I'd seen so many celebs famously posing with the brass stars embedded on the pavements.

Those weren't the only revelations of the morning. Jake offering to carry my bag was a surprise. I was glad that he did because I may have gone a teeny, tiny bit overboard on what I'd stuffed inside.

It was kind of him. Especially given how heavy it was. But although he'd commented on it weighing a tonne of bricks, he carried it around like it was filled with feathers. I guessed that was what happened when you had big broad muscular shoulders like his.

Not that I'd been staring at his shoulders or anything because of course I had no interest in admiring any part of his body.

After stopping for a group lunch, our driver had given us a tour of some other popular areas like Sunset Strip and Mulholland Drive and now Sammie had just stood up to let us know about our second activity for today.

I hoped that it was something relaxing like going to Santa Monica beach which was another place I'd heard about and always wanted to visit.

'Hey!' Sammie moved the mic closer to her mouth. 'Did you enjoy seeing the sights and lunch?'

'Yes!' the whole coach, well, except for Jake, chorused.

'Great! Now that our food's settled, it's time to reveal our second activity.' The coach pulled into a dusty-looking road track and started climbing some hills. 'Earlier I told you we'd have more opportunities to see the sights and take photos of the Hollywood sign, and I'm a woman who likes to keep her promises.' She smiled. 'Which is why I'm excited to tell you that this afternoon we'll be doing a horseback riding tour in the Hollywood Hills!'

As whoops and cheers erupted around me, the blood drained from my face.

The words 'horseback' and 'hills' were two of my least favourite words in the dictionary.

I had nothing against horses per se. They were pretty and I knew they brought a lot of people joy. But the idea of riding on one made me break out in a cold sweat. I'd had a bad experience when I was in my teens that was enough to put me off going on one for life.

I wasn't keen on the word 'hills' either. A gentle hill in a park, for example, was generally fine. But they were talking about high hills. With a big drop. When you put the two words – horseback and what would no doubt be very steep hills – together, the combination spelt the word: nightmare.

As a flurry of other words like *danger* and *fear* flooded my mind, I gripped the armrest, hoping that it would somehow help to steady my nerves.

'Cool,' Jake replied and from the corner of my eye I saw a wide grin spread across his face. 'I love me some horse riding!'

'Glad you're excited!' Sammie added as we pulled into a ranch.

There was a man and a woman both in cowboy hats waving at us as the driver parked up.

'The coach will be locked so you can leave your bags and heavy items on it. Just bring your phones or a small camera and a bottle of water to keep you hydrated. Let's get ready to giddy up and ride those horses!' Sammie said in a very bad American accent.

As everyone filed excitedly off the coach, I wondered if I could sit this activity out.

'You coming?' Jake said as he stood in the aisle.

'Um... I... I'm not sure.'

'Come on, Smiley.' He gestured towards the door. 'It'll be fun!'

I stood up and trudged reluctantly behind him, racking my brains for an excuse not to take part that wouldn't make me look like a scaredy cat. I came up with nothing.

The staff welcomed us to the ranch and explained the history and although they said the horses were trained and gentle, it didn't stop my heart from racing.

Once we'd been briefed, they started handing out the helmets and inviting us to be allocated to our horse. I tried to move, but I was rooted to the spot. My legs felt like concrete and I could feel sweat trickling down my forehead.

'Halle?' A deep voice sounded from beside me, but everything seemed to be spinning. 'Halle? Are you okay? You're shaking.'

Warm hands landed on my shoulders and my body temperature spiked, snapping me out of my trance.

I blinked then blinked again. That was when I realised that Jake was standing in front of me. His thick, dark brows were furrowed. Concern was etched all over his face.

His large hands had slid down to my upper arms and I noticed again how warm they felt. It was like the sensation of a hot drink heating up your body from the inside out on a cold winter's night: comforting and soothing.

'I... it's...' I was trying but it was hard to get the words out.

'Hold on,' he said, before removing his arms. I instantly missed the sensation. I saw him go over to Sammie and I could see their mouths moving but I couldn't make out what they were saying.

Sammie nodded and seconds later the group mounted their horses and set off on the trail, leaving me alone with Jake.

Huh?

'Come on.' Jake gestured for me to follow him. 'Let's sit.'

He sat down on a backless wooden bench and patted the space beside me.

I attempted again to put one foot in front of the other and thankfully this time I was able to actually move.

'Where did everyone go?' I asked as I sat down, leaving as much distance between us as possible. Sitting beside him on the coach had been challenging enough.

I'd had to make sure that his muscular legs hadn't brushed against mine, which wasn't easy. And his scent wasn't easy to avoid either. At least now we were out in the air, it wouldn't be so potent.

Well, that was what I thought until he turned to face me and a cloud of his fragrance assaulted my senses. I swallowed hard, trying to not let it affect me.

'They've gone off to start the trail.'

'But why didn't you go with them?' My head bolted up. 'You were looking forward to it!' Jake might not be my favourite person, but I hated the idea that he'd missed out because of me.

'Because, despite what you think, I'm a gentleman. You seemed like you were freaking out and I wasn't gonna just leave you by yourself. I'm guessing you're not a fan of horses?'

I shook my head.

'Wanna tell me what happened?'

I dropped my gaze to the ground. I couldn't tell him. He'd laugh at me.

'Fair enough. We can just sit and wait for the others to come back. The views are pretty great. We have water so we'll stay hydrated. And if we get hungry, we can always break into the bus and raid your purse. You said you had snacks, right? And judging by how much it weighed, we'll have enough food to survive for a year, so we're all set.'

A soft smile formed on my lips. I lifted my head and when I looked at Jake there was kindness in his eyes. He genuinely wanted to make sure I was okay.

He was excited to go horse riding but he was prepared to miss out on it just to sit here with me. That actually meant a lot.

'It was at a summer camp.' I started talking. 'One of my aunts arranged it. I thought it would be relaxed, but when I got there, turned out it was full of rich kids. I was grateful, but I stuck out like a sore thumb. They were always talking about stuff that I didn't know anything about like going skiing in the Alps and how they'd be joining their family for holidays in the South of France once the camp was over. And they all had horses. Because I wanted to fit in, I pretended to have one too. I didn't think there was any harm in telling a little white lie. But then I found out that there was a horse-riding activity scheduled.'

'Shit,' Jake winced.

'Yeah. They all got on the horses like it was the most natural thing in the world, but of course I had no idea what I was doing. When I tried to mount the horse, it was obvious and they all started laughing loudly at me. The horse got freaked out with all the noise and threw me to the ground. At one point I thought it was gonna crush me. It was terrifying. I damaged my shoulder and hurt my leg and since then I just...'

'You've been afraid to go anywhere near them.'

'Yep.' I dipped my head, not wanting to see his expression. He hadn't laughed yet but there was still time.

'I get it and your reaction is totally normal. Once bitten, twice shy, right? If they hadn't laughed, you would've been fine. Some horses can get startled if they feel scared or threatened. But the ones here will be gentle. And no one will be laughing at you. Nothing beats sitting on a beautiful horse. There's something about the sound of their hooves connecting to the ground, feeling the breeze when it moves forward and just being surrounded by nature. It's so damn calming. It's like therapy. I fucking love it. So if you wanted to try again, I'm pretty sure you'd like it too.'

'You seem to know a lot about horses,' I said, avoiding responding to his suggestion.

'I spent a lot of time on my uncle's ranch during the summers growing up. Pretty sure he had me riding a horse as soon as I could walk!' Jake laughed and the warm rumble sent a strange sensation running through me.

It felt a lot like happiness. He had a nice laugh. It was deep and infectious. I instantly felt my shoulders loosening and my heart rate slowing.

'That young? I'm not sure toddlers are allowed on horses, are they?'

'Probably not,' he grinned. 'I'm exaggerating, but the point was, because I grew up around them, I learnt not to be afraid. But if you're new to it, then I can understand how it can be scary. I'm not gonna push you to do anything you don't want to, but the hotel wouldn't bring us here unless they knew that the horses would be fine for beginners. And if you want to try, I promise I'll be right beside you, so nothing will happen to you.'

I looked into his eyes and saw that sincerity again. I actually believed him.

'But what if I fall?' I asked.

'I'll be right there to catch you.'

My heart fluttered. That was so sweet. He certainly looked strong enough to do that. With those arms, he could probably carry me and the horse without breaking a sweat.

'And it looks pretty high up, which means there'll be a steep drop and I don't see any railings or anything to stop us plummeting over the edge.'

'I'll ride on the outside, so you'll be safe. I got you, Halle.'

Jake rested his palm on top of mine and as our skin connected a bolt of electricity rocketed through me.

Whoa.

I thought him holding my shoulders before did things to me, but *this*?

A kaleidoscope of emotions fluttered in my stomach. Goosebumps erupted across my skin and my heart galloped out of my chest faster than a horse racing at the Grand National.

Maybe given the circumstances, thinking about a horse riding fast wasn't the best analogy to convince me to face my fear, but it was exactly how I felt.

The sensation of Jake's hand on my skin was reassuring and downright electrifying.

Just as I was revelling in the sensation, he yanked his hand away. And despite it being at least twenty-five degrees up here, suddenly my hand felt like it had been plunged into a bucket of ice.

'Sorry.' He shuffled away from me on the bench. 'I didn't mean to...'

'It's fine!' I squeaked. 'Thanks for... talking about it actually helped.'

Jake beamed like I'd just told him he'd scored top marks in an empathy test.

'Yeah?'

'Yeah.'

'Enough to convince you to give horse riding another try?'

I paused.

Could I really do this?

My chest tightened again. The ranch owners had said the horses were gentle and suitable for beginners. I was wearing a helmet and Jake said he'd be beside me and catch me if I fell.

I'd come to the Love Hotel to push myself out of my comfort zone.

Although romance sadly wasn't on the cards, that didn't stop me from making the most of this experience.

When else would I get the chance to come to LA and do a horse-riding hike with breathtaking views?

Probably never.

If I didn't do this, I'd regret it.

As I looked into Jake's eyes, a wave of reassurance surrounded me.

It was going to be fine.

'Okay,' I said. 'I'd like to try again.'

15

JAKE

'See! You're a natural!' I said as Halle cautiously swung her right leg over the top of a pretty chestnut-coloured horse called Champ and slid her foot into the stirrup before gently and slowly sinking into the saddle like I'd told her.

'That's it!' Aidan, the guide, said encouragingly. 'You comfortable?'

'Yeah,' Halle nodded, her eyes wide like she was surprised that she'd mounted the horse without falling.

When she told me what happened the last time she tried to ride a horse, my heart squeezed. I really felt for her. That must've been terrifying, especially because she was surrounded by people who didn't give a shit about her. I knew exactly how *that* felt. But I'd meant what I said: I'd make damn sure that she was safe.

'Ready to go?' Aidan asked. I climbed up on my horse, Fire-cracker, which had a gorgeous reddish-brown coat.

'I think so...' Halle looked at me for reassurance.

'I got you, girl.' I nodded and she smiled.

Goddammit.

Seeing Halle smile like that... like she trusted me to take care of her hit me right in the feels.

Just like it had when I'd stupidly put my hand on top of hers.

I knew better than to make physical contact with a woman without her permission, but seeing her so upset was like a punch in the gut and I just wanted to make her feel better.

But I wasn't prepared for how good it was gonna feel. Her skin was so soft and inviting. It sounded dumb but it was like when my hand connected to hers, it cast some kind of spell over me. I wasn't even the one who was scared or worried, but somehow it made me feel calm.

For those few moments I forgot about everything. The shit show that my life was right now, all the missed calls from Wilma hassling me about taking more photos, worrying about where I was gonna live after I left the hotel... all that shit sailed clean out of my head.

But then when I heard a horse neigh in the stables, I snapped out of my thoughts and realised what I was doing.

Upset or not, Halle wouldn't want me putting my hand on hers. Hell, most of the time she acted like existing on the same planet as me was too much for her, so I pulled it away.

I couldn't lie, I was kind of disappointed because I liked how it felt, but it was for the best. I wasn't here to start touching hands with Halle. She was scared about getting on the horse, I helped her out and now she was on it, job done.

For the first ten minutes or so, we pretty much rode in silence, but this time I didn't take offence. I knew Halle wasn't staying quiet because she was deliberately ignoring me. She was just focused on trying to stay calm.

'You good?' I asked.

'Mmm-hmm,' she replied, her eyes firmly fixed on the trail ahead.

'Great views, huh?' I said, taking in the mountains and canyons in front of us.

'Yeah.'

'Anytime you wanna stop to take photos, y'all just let me know,' Aidan called out. He was slightly ahead of us whilst I rode beside Halle.

'Thanks. We're good,' I said, knowing that Halle wouldn't want to take photos.

'I know you like taking pictures, so go ahead and take some of the views,' she said. 'I'm just worried about stopping the horse.'

I could easily remind her how to do it, but she was doing so well I didn't want to disrupt her progress just to take a few photos.

Maybe we could stop later or I'd just take some selfies.

'It's okay, let's carry on,' I said.

As we continued riding, Halle's shoulders loosened. I was glad to see that she was more relaxed.

'I can't believe I'm actually riding a horse!' She cautiously turned her head towards me before swiftly moving it back to look straight ahead.

'You better believe it!' I said, trying to ignore the way my chest had expanded when I saw her smile again. 'And you're doing great.'

'Thanks. For listening. And for encouraging me to try again.'

'My pleasure,' I said. Knowing that I'd helped her in some small way to conquer her fear made me feel ten feet tall.

When Halle spotted a great view of the Hollywood sign her face lit up again.

'Now you've *gotta* let me take a photo of y'all here.' Aidan turned back and headed towards us. 'This view's too good to miss. Give me your cell.' He held his hand out.

He was right. It was a great view. But I didn't want to make Halle uncomfortable.

'Aidan's right,' Halle said before I even had a chance to ask her if it was okay.

'I can just take a selfie, so you don't have to be in it,' I said and her face fell. Shit. I'd upset her. 'Unless you want to be,' I added quickly. 'It'd be cool if you were, but I know you don't like to take photos – that's the only reason I said you don't have to be in it.'

'Oh. Okay. I thought that... well, okay. But I don't remember how to stop.'

'Let me help you,' I said. Once I'd guided her through the steps to bring Champ to a gentle halt, I handed my cell to Aidan.

'Come on, you guys! You can do better than that!' Aidan shook his head. 'Jake, bring Firecracker closer to Champ. You two are a beautiful couple, no need to look like strangers.'

'We're not...' Halle and I chorused our denial, turning to face each other before laughing.

'He's right,' I whispered. 'The photo would look less awkward, but if you're not comfortable...'

'It's fine,' she said. 'You can move.'

'Off the cliff?' I smirked.

'That sounds like a very tempting offer, but if you go over the edge, then who'll save me if my horse goes feral?' The corner of her mouth twitched and I was glad that she was relaxed enough about the situation to crack a joke. Especially considering her past experience.

'I reckon Aidan will step in to help.'

'He'd do his best, but with your beefy arms, you'd probably do a better job.'

'So you think my arms are beefy?' I cocked my head. 'How beefy we talkin'? Like a regular hamburger or prime ribeye or T-bone?'

'Well, I was thinking more about the minced beef you find in cheap hamburgers or the stuff they put in dog food...' She grinned.

'Unbelievable,' I snorted, fighting the urge to laugh.

'What? I'm sure the dogs love their tinned food just fine.'

'Gee, thanks for the compliment.'

'You two lovebirds finished whispering sweet nothings yet?' Aidan raised an unimpressed eyebrow.

'Sorry, we, er, got distracted,' she said.

'Yep. Halle was just admiring my *beefy* arms.' I flashed a mischievous grin.

'I was not...!'

'Say cheese!' Aidan called out, ignoring her protest.

'Cheese!' I said loudly, turning to face her. I expected to be met with a glare but instead her mouth tilted up into a half smile.

Well, won't you look at that.

Not only was Halle taking a photo with me, willingly, she was almost cracking a smile.

Turned out miracles *were* possible.

* * *

'I did it!' Halle said, a giant grin splitting her face. I got off my horse and watched her excitedly wriggle around on the saddle. 'Not only did I do the whole ride without falling off, this time I also made the horse stop all by myself too.'

'You sure did!' I said. 'I'm proud of you.'

Her eyes widened.

'You are?'

'Yeah. That can't have been easy. You could've just sat it out and hidden inside the bus, but you didn't. You faced your fears. That took guts.'

Halle blinked a few times before swallowing hard.

Seemed like she wasn't used to compliments.

'Thanks,' she said sheepishly, before swinging her leg back over the horse to dismount. Halle paused midway. 'I forgot to say thank you to you too, Champ.' She patted her horse on its side.

My chest immediately tightened. Depending on how the horse had been trained, patting it like that could be seen as a signal for it to move or follow a specific command.

Less than a second later, just as I feared, Champ did a quick turn, causing Halle to lose her footing.

'No!' I called out as the movement sent Halle crashing towards the ground...

16

HALLE

'Shit!' I let out a desperate ear-splitting scream as I tumbled from the horse in what felt like slow motion.

That'd teach me to brag about how well I'd done riding a horse.

I'd jinxed it and now I was fucked.

I squeezed my eyes shut, bracing myself for the worst.

But just as I thought I was about to crash to the ground and meet my maker, strong arms gripped my body.

My eyes flew open and I saw Jake towering above me, fear etched into his features.

He'd caught me.

Jake told me he'd keep me safe and he'd kept his promise.

As he lifted me into his arms I melted against him.

He'd saved me. Like a real-life hero.

'I... I almost fell on the ground!' I said, still trying to get my head around what had just happened.

'*Almost...*' He gripped me tighter. 'But you're fine.'

'Thanks to *you*!' I clutched my heart. It was racing at a million miles an hour and I was worried that it would shoot from my chest. 'I could've *died*!' I said dramatically. 'You literally saved my life!'

Yeah, I was wearing a helmet, but what if I'd snapped my neck?

I knew that telling Jake that he'd saved my bacon wasn't a good idea, because it'd mean that I owed him and he'd use it against me. As far as he was concerned I didn't even like him and up until we'd arrived at this ranch, I was perfectly happy to keep it that way. But right now, I was so grateful for what he'd just done, I didn't care if he reminded me at two-second intervals how he'd literally ridden in on his white horse and saved me.

'It was nothing.' Jake looked down at me and shrugged.

He'd must've taken off his sunglasses when we'd stopped like I did, so I now had an uninterrupted view of his eyes. They were really pretty. Especially framed by those long lashes.

And his brows were great too. Thick, dark and well-shaped. I wondered if they were naturally like that or if he did the whole male grooming thing.

Then I realised I'd been staring at him for way too long. I quickly shook myself out of my daze and attempted to remember what he'd just said.

Wait. Instead of using the opportunity to gloat at my hero gushing, he'd tried to play it down. I wasn't expecting that. At all.

'It *was*!' I argued. 'You actually gave a shit,' I said, remembering how no one had cared about what happened to me all those years ago. 'You saved me from falling and for the reasons I explained before, that's a big deal, so thank you.'

Jake's eyes locked with mine. After several seconds, my eyes floated down to his mouth. Then his lips parted as if he was about to speak.

I noticed (admittedly not for the first time) that he had a very nice mouth. Jake had full, pink lips which looked extremely soft, like he followed some kind of daily plumping and moisturising regime.

My gaze moved to his chin and jawline. Normally I didn't like facial hair. I preferred men to be clean-shaven, but Jake's stubble suited him. It looked sexy. And I heard that helped to intensify the sensations when a man went down on...

What the hell?

'I should...' I said, desperately trying to push the illicit thoughts out of my mind. Maybe I'd actually hit my head and was suffering from concussion. That was the only logical explanation for why I was suddenly picturing Jake's face buried between my thighs.

'Sure.' Jake tore his gaze away. 'Okay if I put you down now?'

'Course!' My voice shot up like I'd just sucked on a helium balloon. 'Don't want to break your arms!'

'Why would you break my arms?' His brows knitted together. 'I can carry you back to the bus, or *coach* as you Brits like to call it, if you want. I know you must still be in shock.'

My traitorous body was screaming *yes, please! I would very much like you to carry me everywhere in your big, muscular arms.* But luckily, common sense was still in the building, or should I say, on the hiking trail.

'No, it's okay.' I waved my hand in the air. 'I'm fine, but thanks.'

As Jake lowered me to the ground, my knees wobbled. And to be honest, I wasn't sure whether that was because like he'd said, I was still in shock or if I was still swooning over him.

I really, really hoped it was the trauma, because I couldn't start liking Jake.

No way.

Forget the damage falling off a horse could cause.

Falling for a man like Jake would be catastrophic for my heart.

17

JAKE

As the bus pulled away from the hotel's reception, Halle and I stood in front of each other in silence.

I'd lost count of how many times she'd thanked me for catching her during the journey back to the hotel and each time she did I told her the same thing: it really wasn't a big deal. I saw that she was about to fall and I caught her. I insisted that anyone would've done the same thing if they were in my position.

That was when she reminded me that her campmates had no problem standing back and laughing when they saw her fall.

She had a point. My statement had suggested that all people were good, when I knew from first-hand experience that they weren't. So I'd corrected myself by saying that it'd take a special kind of jerk to leave a good woman to fall to the ground without trying to help her.

Halle had nodded in agreement before launching into a full-on account of how much she'd enjoyed the horse riding (up until she'd fallen off) and what a buzz she'd gotten from seeing the views of the city.

She probably spoke to me more in that one ride back here than she had in the whole time we'd been at the hotel.

But I wasn't complaining. And as tempted as I was to say that maybe we'd turned a corner (I mean, we even took a photo together), I wasn't gonna jinx it, because for all I knew, tomorrow she'd be back to hating me again.

Which meant that instead of staring into her pretty brown eyes and wondering if her lips were as soft as they looked (something I'd done way too many times already today), I was gonna go back to my room and... well, I didn't know what I was gonna do yet, but it wouldn't involve thinking about Halle.

'So I should get back...' I said.

'Yeah, me too.' Halle said. 'I'm bursting for the loo. Sorry. TMI. You didn't need to know that I need to wee.'

'Speaking of that, what's the fascination you Brits have with taking a leak?'

'Eh?' She frowned and I started to wonder why instead of going to my room like I'd planned, I was still choosing to have a conversation with her. And one about urinating. Jeez. I really needed to work on my conversational skills.

Well, I guess I'd taken a turn down this alley, so I had to see it through.

'You talk about pissing a lot. I mean, we talk about being pissed off here too, but one of my British friends, or should I say, my *mate*,' I said in a terrible English accent, 'taught me a lot more.'

'Go on then,' she grinned and suddenly I didn't regret my choice of subject after all. 'Let's see how many references you can remember.'

'Sure thing!' I mirrored her amusement before puffing out my chest like I was ready for battle. 'Okay, so there's taking *a* piss, not to be confused with the teasing phrase: taking *the* piss.'

'Well done,' she clapped.

'Then you have *a lot* of drinking-related ones, right? Like *being on the piss*, *having a piss-up* and *being* or *getting pissed*, which is when you're drunk.'

'Correct.' Halle's smile widened.

'Did I get them all?'

'Not quite. There's the weather one – so when it's raining you can say *it's pissing it down*.'

'That's kinda gross.' I winced.

'I don't make the rules,' she chuckled. 'And then there's *pissing around*, which is when you're wasting time, or *pissing away something*, so you'd use that to say you're wasting an opportunity or something. Hmmm, what else?' She paused as she racked her brains. 'Oh, yeah! There's also *piss-take*, which is like when something's ridiculous, like, "Fifty dollars for a bit of mince? That's a piss-take!"'

'Not if it's prime beef mince though, right?' I teased, remembering our conversation about my 'beefy' arms.

'Right. In that case, the beef would be worth every cent...'

Her eyes dropped to my arms and when I caught her biting her lip, I had to admit that I enjoyed knowing that she liked my arms. If ogling them is what it took to get her to smile, I'd take it.

'I should...' She broke the silence.

'Go and take a piss?' I lifted an eyebrow.

'You taking the piss?' she joked and the sound of her laugh was almost as thrilling as watching the way her face lit up when she smiled. 'No, seriously,' she started jiggling around on the spot, 'I really need to go. Bye!' Halle ran off. 'And thanks again, *Hero*!'

And with that, she was gone.

Hero, huh?

I had to admit, as nicknames went, that wasn't a bad one.

I walked back to my room with a spring in my step and a stupid grin on my face.

Today was one of the best days I'd had in ages. I actually felt... *good*. I loved being out in nature and being back on a horse, but it was about more than that. As much as I didn't like to admit it, I'd enjoyed spending time with Halle.

She wasn't the hard, cold woman I'd first thought she was. She had a softer side. But for some reason she didn't like to show it. It was like she had her walls up. There was a hundred-foot-tall fortress surrounding her and she didn't want to let anyone in. But why? Had someone hurt her?

Halle had mentioned before that she'd stayed in the US because she'd met someone. I wondered what happened.

I didn't get the chance to try and dissect Halle's past any more because my cell vibrating in my pocket snapped me out of my thoughts.

It didn't take a genius to work out who was calling. I'd avoided her all day, but it was time to face the music.

After opening my room door, then closing it again, I pulled my cell out and hit the green accept call button.

'Wilma,' I said flatly.

'Where the fuck have you been?' she snapped. 'Why haven't you been answering my calls and why haven't you posted more photos?'

I rubbed my temples then flopped down onto the bed.

'I posted this morning.'

'Yeah. Some shit picture of an empty beach.'

'It wasn't shit. It was pretty.'

'People aren't following you for pictures of the goddamn beach! They want to see you and your match. Why the hell haven't you posted any pictures of this chick yet? Is she ugly?'

'No!' I said quickly, thinking about how damn beautiful she

was. I used to think I didn't have a type. But now I was worried that Halle was *exactly* the kind of woman I'd like to be with.

What the fuck?

That was clearly my dick talking. I had no interest in *being with* any woman right now. My priority was to get my life in order.

'She's... not ugly,' I said, trying to keep my voice measured.

'Well, why the hell haven't you posted any photos of her then? If she's really pretty then we could get some endorsement deals. I'm thinking couples holiday resorts, jewellery companies... you could become the new Victoria and David Beckham. The possibilities are endless!' Excitement fizzed in her tone.

'That's...' I was about to say that was never gonna happen, but I needed to keep Wilma on side. 'The reason I haven't posted any photos of her is because she doesn't like having her photo taken.'

'What?'

'She doesn't even use social media.'

'What the actual fuck?' She gasped like I'd just told her that Halle was born in outer space and looked like a three-headed green alien. 'Who *doesn't* use social media?'

'Well, up until a few days ago, me,' I reminded her.

The handful of posts that I had before were made by my management or someone else on my team, but not by me. I hated that shit. Which was why what Wilma wanted me to do was so freaking painful.

'This is insane! You must have at least one photo with her!'

'Nope,' I lied.

Thanks to the photos Sammie had taken, I now had several. Plus, there were the ones Aidan took of us on the horses today, which I'd forgotten to check, but there was no way I was posting those.

For whatever reason, Halle didn't like having her photo taken or having a social media presence. I was hoping that wasn't because she was a criminal mastermind on the run (joking – despite her attempts to act tough, I doubted Halle would hurt a fly). But just because I didn't know why, it didn't mean I had the right to put her photo online without her permission.

'You need to do better, Jakey boy.' Wilma said and I cringed at the nickname. It was so condescending.

'Maybe if you'd arranged for me to be set up with someone who wanted to raise their profile like you'd promised, I wouldn't be in this mess,' I snapped back.

'*Everyone* wants to be famous!' Wilma spat, ignoring my comment.

I disagreed. If I could sing and make music without the fame, I'd do it in a heartbeat, but they worked hand in hand. In order to make a decent living, people needed to know who you were and if they knew who you were, they would always want more. More photos, more access, more of everything.

'I can tell you with absolute certainty that she doesn't.'

'You just need to be more convincing!' Wilma countered. 'Everyone has their price. Give me her name and I'll do some digging. Maybe she's got debts to pay off or skeletons in her closet. Once we know what she needs or what she's hiding, we can wear her down. I'm sure a big cheque will make her forget about her silly little photo and social media aversion. Get some photos of her posted by tomorrow or kiss goodbye to any chance you have of reviving your career.'

Before I even had a chance to argue, Wilma hung up.

Shit.

Wilma was asking for Halle's name. She was contemplating doing some digging on her.

And I could tell from her tone that she wasn't playing.

That was bad. Very, very bad.

It looked like I had two choices: continue to refuse to post photos of Halle which would lead to Wilma digging up some secrets that maybe Halle didn't want uncovered. Or posting photos of Halle and risking her wrath and destroying whatever small part of trust I'd built with her today.

Neither option was a good one.

Whatever way I looked at it, I was well and truly fucked.

18

HALLE

I washed my hands in my bathroom and exhaled. I wasn't joking when I told Jake that I desperately needed a wee. A few minutes later and I might've wet myself, which would've been embarrassing.

As I headed out to the bedroom and thought about our 'piss' conversation, a smile touched my lips. I'd never really thought about how many weird sayings we used with that word. And until today, I never thought that a man like Jake would make me laugh, smile and feel safe either.

What a difference a few hours could make.

It pained me to admit it, but I'd had a good day. I'd conquered a fear and actually enjoyed the horse riding.

I'd seen some great views of LA and I'd voluntarily posed for a photo for the first time in years.

That wouldn't seem like a big deal for most people, but it was for me.

In hindsight, it probably wasn't the smartest thing to do, but I was on a high.

Now though, I was questioning my judgement because no

doubt that photo and the ones Sammie took yesterday were probably already plastered all over social media.

My stomach sank as the painful memories came flooding back of how Brett's fans used to pick me apart whenever a photo of me appeared on his social media or in those trashy gossip magazines.

The criticism was relentless. They hated my hair because it was too short, my body (obviously I was too big/not sexy enough), everything about my face, my skin colour, my clothes. You name it, if it had anything to do with me, it was ugly.

Every day they commented on the fact that I wasn't good or pretty enough to be with a guy like Brett and constantly questioned why we were together.

We were introduced at a party – *before* he got his record deal. I didn't even realise he was an aspiring singer until our first proper date, but I said I'd happily come to his next show.

Within days, I was watching him perform at a dingy bar in New York, but I didn't care. I loved that he was following his dream and there was something intoxicating about watching a man with a guitar, singing a song to you, like you were the only woman that existed. Truth be told, the bar was empty, so that was pretty accurate, but it wasn't long before I was head over heels.

I went to all of Brett's gigs. Whether it was a crowd of three or thirty people, I did whatever I could to support him. When he got heckled, I cheered louder for him. When he didn't have the money to travel to shows out of town, I got extra shifts at work to pay for it.

He told me that he loved and appreciated me and that one day, when he hit the big time, he'd show me how much.

And stupidly, I believed him.

I remembered joking that when he was famous, he wouldn't

want to hang out with 'little old me' and he'd roll his eyes, saying he'd never change.

What a load of bollocks.

When he got signed, I was thrilled for him. But then he started hanging out at industry parties and moving with a different crowd. As Brett became more famous, he changed and the media started taking an interest not just in him, but who he was dating. That's when all the trolling started...

Even though I'd deleted all the social media apps from my phone so that I didn't have to see their cruel comments, the damage was already done. I felt so hideous and alone.

Brett thought I was overreacting and needed to grow thicker skin. And at no point did he ever stick up for me.

So I guessed I shouldn't have been surprised when I discovered he was seeing other women on the side, including the supermodel that he went on to marry just months after we broke up.

My chest tightened. I shouldn't have agreed to take that photo. And I didn't even ask to see how it looked afterwards. I was probably all hot and sweaty and looked awful.

I reached for my phone to look up Jake's Instagram, but then stopped.

My heart raced.

My stomach lurched.

I couldn't.

It was better that I didn't see whatever he'd posted or the comments.

If I ignored the haters, I'd be safe.

My phone rang, causing me to almost jump out of my skin.

It was Vanessa. Maybe she'd seen the photos and was calling to warn me like she used to do when things got really bad.

'So how many pictures of me are plastered across social

media right now and how bad are the comments?' I blurted out quickly. I needed to know.

'Eh?' Vanessa replied. 'What do you mean? There aren't any photos of you on Jake's Insta. Why? Did he say he was gonna post something?'

Tension immediately slid from my shoulders. That was a relief.

'No, but we had a load of photos from the first activity that Sammie, my Love Alchemist lady, took and then there were more pics taken earlier.'

'Well, there's none of you. Is that why you thought I was calling?'

'Yeah.' I lowered my voice, embarrassment washing over me.

'Oh, hon. Sorry. I was just calling to see how your first outing went. I didn't mean to trigger you.'

'It's my fault. I shouldn't have jumped to conclusions. I just got worried. I shouldn't have agreed to take one with him, but I was kind of on a high about the whole horse-riding thing.'

'Wait, what? You did *horse riding*?'

'Yep!' Pride filled my chest.

'Horse riding *and* posing for photos? Wow. Who are you and what the hell have you done with my bestie?' she laughed.

'I know, right? Next thing you know I'll be bungee jumping.'

'If you do that, I'll definitely know you've been abducted by an alien!'

'Very funny. Seriously though, are you sure there's no photos?'

'Nope.'

'He must not have got round to posting any yet.'

'I'm not so sure... He's done several posts today. He did a few of the beach this morning. Then there's some cool ones of the views of the Hollywood Hills and yeah, now that you've mentioned horse riding, I do remember that the most recent posts were of some horses, but like I said, there's none with you.'

'Oh.'

That was weird.

Good weird.

I didn't want him to post photos of me and he hadn't.

I should feel relieved, but of course my brain had to take me to dark places and make me wonder why. And the default reaction for my mind was to tell me he didn't want me on his social media because I wasn't pretty enough and because he knew that his followers would rip me to shreds.

For fuck's sake.

This was exactly why I couldn't handle dating anyone in the public eye. It brought out all of my insecurities and a load of bad memories came flooding back.

If I dated Joe Bloggs who worked in accounts for a local company, I wouldn't have these kinds of concerns. We'd just be two normal people, doing normal things that no one cared about.

I wouldn't have to worry about women questioning why he'd picked me and not one of the many gorgeous supermodels and actresses that must slide into his DMs along with zillions of fans who'd do anything to breathe the same air as him.

Yeah, I knew that even 'normal' guys got attention, but it was always going to be significantly less than a man who was as recognisable as Harry Styles.

'You sound disappointed,' Vanessa said, reading my mind. I hated when she did that.

'Course not!' I lied. 'You know how much I *hate* having my photo taken. And that's almost as much as having my photo plastered online.'

'Hmm-mmm,' she replied, clearly not convinced. 'I know, but

you shouldn't let that stop you from taking them to keep as mementos of your time there. *And* to share with your best friend! You know how gorgeous I think you are.'

'Like you said, you're my bestie, so of course you're gonna say that.'

'Nope. If you were a munter, I probably wouldn't say anything at all. Actually, I'd just pay for you to get a decent haircut and buy you some good make-up and pretty clothes. Everyone has potential. But luckily you don't need a makeover.'

'Er, thanks?' I said, thinking she meant well, even if her statement didn't come across that way. Vanessa wasn't one to mince her words.

'So tell me more about this horse riding? I thought that would've been your idea of hell.'

'It was. At first.'

I filled Vanessa in on what happened and how understanding Jake was.

'Oooh!' she said excitedly. 'So let me get this straight. He carried your bag *and* he promised to keep you safe when you were facing one of your biggest fears?'

'Yeah...' I said reluctantly, feeling relieved that I hadn't shared the part about how good it felt when he rested his hand on top of mine. Telling Vanessa that would just be asking for trouble.

'And then he basically saved you when you fell off the horse?'

'Yep.'

'Bloody hell. If an ordinary man did that, I'd be dropping to my knees to thank him, but for a hottie like Jake, forget about going horse riding. I'd be pushing him down on the ground and offering to ride *him*!' she cackled.

'Classic Vanessa,' I said, trying to resist the urge to laugh with her.

'Come on,' she scoffed. 'You can't tell me you weren't tempted.'

'Of course I wasn't! I've *told* you. I'm not interested.'

'If you say so...' Clearly she didn't believe me, but that was on her because it was true. Yes, Jake was really sweet today but it just wouldn't work.

Nope. No way. I couldn't go there again.

'Tell me at least that you showed your gratitude in other ways?'

'I must've thanked him a million times. And I was surprised, because I thought he'd get all big-headed and gloaty, but he was actually humble.'

'So does that mean you're warming to him?'

I paused, considering my response.

'Let's just say that I've seen another side of him. It's possible that he's not as arrogant as I thought, but that doesn't mean we're best buddies now or that I want to jump his bones.' A disobedient wave of tingles shot down my spine. 'Just because he was sweet for one day doesn't mean he's like that all the time.'

'True. So do you know where you're going tomorrow or is that another surprise?'

'Haven't got a clue.'

'Well, wherever you go I'm sure it'll be fun. Especially now you know you've got your very own knight in shining armour! Anyway, babe, I'd better go. Be good and if you can't be good, be careful!' A mischievous laugh echoed down the phone.

And before I had time to tell her that I wouldn't have any need to be careful because I had no intention of doing anything at all with Jake, she hung up.

19

HALLE

It was Tuesday morning and we were on the luxury coach heading to another secret excursion.

I was so tired after the excitement of the horse riding and sightseeing that I'd passed out on my bed and missed dinner.

When I woke up, I saw that Jake had messaged to ask if I was coming to the restaurant, but by then, it was too late. It was sweet of him to text though. And when I replied to tell him I'd fallen asleep, he was understanding. I'd ordered room service, then went to bed.

Breakfast with Jake this morning was surprisingly fine too. We'd talked more about the horse riding and he told me about the horses at his uncle's farm. We were chatting so much that before we knew it, we had to leave to board the coach. And it was only when it set off that we realised we hadn't collected the photos from yesterday's excursions.

I didn't tell Jake this, but I was dying to see the pictures. I was tempted to ask him if I could take a peek at the ones on his phone, but I was too embarrassed. Looking at the printed versions as part of our daily 'love' tasks was fine because that was one of the 'rules'. But I'd told Jake repeatedly how much I hated photos, so suddenly begging to see them would sound contradictory.

'Thanks for the playlist,' Jake said.

'Did you like the songs?' I asked.

I'd chosen 'Hollywood' by Madonna, 'Dark Horse' by Katy Perry and Juicy J, 'Crazy Horses' by The Osmonds, 'Lost Angeles' by The Aces and 'Holding out for a Hero' by Bonnie Tyler.

I almost added 'Thank You' by Dido, but when I remembered that the lyrics included her gratitude for giving her the best day of her life, I thought it'd be way too gushy.

Even though I'd wanted to include 'Hero' by Mariah Carey and the same title by Enrique Iglesias, three knight-in-shining armour songs seemed like overkill.

'I...' He paused. 'You were showing your age a bit with The Osmonds and Bonnie Tyler.' The corner of his mouth turned up.

'You can blame that on my dad. He loves seventies and eighties music, so it rubbed off on me.'

'Your dad has great taste. I'm a fan of those decades too.'

'Yeah?' I frowned. 'Who do you like?'

'I loved bands like Guns N' Roses, Bon Jovi, Kool and the Gang, singers like Prince, MJ, Lionel Richie, Stevie Wonder, Elton John, Luther Vandross, Phil Collins, Tina Turner... I could easily list dozens more.'

'Yes! As Dad says, they don't make them like they used to.'

'Your pops is right. That's why so many modern songs sample the classics.'

'And the remakes are never as good as the original.'

'You're...' Jake suddenly paused and several people on the coach started whooping and cheering.

I frowned, but then the volume on the song playing in the background was turned up and it started to make sense.

They were playing one of Jake's songs on the radio. I turned to him, expecting a smug look to be written over his face, but instead he looked mortified.

'Fuck,' he muttered under his breath, barely loud enough for me to hear it.

'It's your song!' Mandy called out, her eyes wide.

'Yeah,' Jake replied with a tight smile.

The coach erupted as some of the guests started clapping and singing along enthusiastically.

But the more they sang, the more Jake retreated in his seat.

'Not a fan of your own music?' I frowned.

'This song is... let's just say it's kinda personal.' He dragged his hand down his face.

I knew this one. It was called 'Somethin' Special' and was all about the joy of falling in love. It was one of his most romantic tunes. And it was definitely one of his biggest hits, so it was weird that he seemed to hate it.

Unless...

Then it dawned on me that maybe it was personal because it was about one of his past loves. And obviously they weren't together any more.

The thought of a man like Jake ever being deeply in love was a complete contradiction to his playboy image.

I'd always assumed that these songs were just written to sell records because it appealed to his female fan-base. But judging by the look of horror on Jake's face, there was more meaning to the words.

I could be wrong, but it seemed like Jake was in love.

Clearly, I didn't know what had happened and I wasn't about to ask him in front of a coach full of strangers, but if I had to guess, Jake had experienced real, deep, soul-crushing heartbreak.

A wave of sympathy and understanding instantly flooded my chest.

Maybe we had more in common than I thought...

20

JAKE

Of all of the songs they could've played on the radio, it had to be that one.

Although it was one of my biggest hits, at times like right now, I wished I'd never fucking written it.

My chest tightened as the painful memories of discovering my ex-girlfriend's betrayal whooshed into my mind like a tsunami.

As the cheers around the bus got louder, my throat constricted and my pulse rocketed. I felt like I was gonna barf.

Everything started to spin.

Was the song always this long?

It felt like it'd been playing for hours rather than minutes.

I wiped the back of my hand over my forehead as I tried to calm my racing heartbeat.

Halle must have thought I was a weirdo. Most people would be psyched to hear their song on the radio and here I was sweating like a criminal on trial for murder.

I still remembered the first time I heard my song on the radio.

I was buying some candy from a local store and suddenly it started blaring through the speakers.

I'd run up to the old guy stacking shelves and given him a hug, screaming, 'That's my song!' Then I'd ran over to his wife and hugged her before jumping up and down like a lunatic.

Yep. *That* was a great feeling. But *this*? This felt like someone had taken a machete to my heart, put it in a blender then fed it to a pack of lions.

Just when I thought I was about to embarrass myself by passing out in front of a bus full of strangers, I felt something soft and warm rest on my hand.

When I looked down, Halle's palm was on top of mine.

'Breathe,' she whispered. 'It's okay.'

My head flicked up and when I met Halle's gaze I saw kindness. Did she know?

There was no way that she could.

But even if she didn't know or understand, she still was trying to calm me down and that meant a lot.

As she held my gaze, with empathy and sincerity in her eyes, my heart rate started to slow.

Halle squeezed my hand tighter and I squeezed back, hoping that one action conveyed my gratitude.

Seconds later, the song ended and an upbeat Lizzo track blasted through the speakers.

I exhaled deeply, glad that the torture was over.

'Thank you,' I whispered, wondering how long I should leave my hand entwined with hers.

I wasn't in a hurry to remove it. This was the second time that I'd felt the softness of Halle's palms and I liked it way more than I should.

I wasn't here for romance, so I didn't want to lead her on.

Loosening my hold, I slid my hand out from under hers as gently as I could.

Shock flashed over Halle's face and an expression that looked a lot like hurt replaced it. Shit. She'd done something kind and now she thought I'd rejected her.

'I...'

'It's fine,' she said quickly, waving her hand around like it was no big deal, but I knew that when a woman told you something was *fine* there was a strong possibility that it wasn't.

'You... that really helped. That song is a bit... I just could've done without hearing it right now, so, thanks.'

I wanted to explain why I'd pulled my hand away, to tell her it was because I was trying to protect her, but then the bus slowed down. When I looked out of the window and realised where we were, excitement filled my chest.

'Welcome to The Huntington!' Sammie said enthusiastically.

'Yes!' I said, louder than I should've.

'What's The Huntington?' Halle called out.

'I was just about to explain,' Sammie replied.

'Sorry!' Halle chuckled.

'It's a really cool place, that has a massive library, art museum and loads of stunning botanical gardens. Someone will explain it more eloquently once we're off the coach, but I'm sure you're gonna love it.'

'It's one of my favourite places in LA,' I added.

'Yeah?' Halle frowned like she was surprised.

'The library and museum are cool but the gardens are my favourite. There's sixteen different ones over about 130 acres.'

'That's a lot!' she said. 'I can't wait to see it!'

I pulled my baseball cap out of my short pockets and pulled it down low. I often wore a cap when I went out in public to avoid drawing too much attention. But on a hot day like this it was also good to shield my face from the sun.

We all filed off the bus and Sammie explained that we would get to spend the whole day here. She handed everyone an envelope with cash to cover our lunch and refreshments. I felt like a kid on a school trip, but I wasn't complaining. Maybe I could even save the cash to use once I left.

Thinking about how far I'd fallen made me wince. I'd gone from having millions to having to save a fifty bucks lunch allowance because I didn't know how I'd be able to pay for the most basic things after my hotel stay was over.

Things were bad.

Which was exactly why coming here today was what I needed. Spending time exploring the gardens would help me forget about what just happened on the bus and all my other worries.

As the rest of the group filed off in different directions, Halle faced me.

'So do you come here often?'

'You hitting on me?' I asked, my mouth tipping up in the corner.

'What?' She frowned. '*Ohhh...*' Halle slapped her forehead. 'That did sound like a bad chat-up line! What I meant was...'

'Whether I came here often?' I joked.

'Yeah. But in a non-chatting-you-up kind of way.'

'I know. I'm just *taking the piss!*'

'Good one,' she grinned and my chest inflated.

Every. Single. Time.

Halle's smile was gonna be the death of me.

'To answer your question, *yes*. I come here as often as I can.' I led Halle through to the Rose Hills Foundation Conservatory for Botanical Science.

'Whoa.' Her eyes widened as she stepped inside. 'This is like a massive greenhouse.'

'Yep. There's different types of habitat here: a tropical rainforest, cloud forest and a carnivorous plant bog and a lab. People can study plants from all over the world here. Let's go to the rainforest, there's a plant there that I'd like you to see.'

'I wouldn't have put you down as a guy who loves flowers and gardens.' She raised her eyebrow.

'Gardening is one of my favourite things to do.'

'You're joking, right?'

'No. Why do you find that so hard to believe?'

'Because you're a rockstar. A bad boy. A love 'em and leave 'em kind of guy. I thought you'd prefer touching different women in bed rather than tending to flower beds!'

I stopped in my tracks.

'*That's* what you think about me?' I ground my jaw and Halle's face fell.

'Sorry. I didn't mean to offend you. It's just what I...'

'What you heard? Or saw in a trashy magazine?' I shook my head like a disappointed parent. 'You shouldn't believe everything you read.'

I could've launched into a rant about all of the lies that have been printed about me and lectured Halle on the damage that reading that trash does and how those stories can literally destroy people's lives, but what would be the point? Most people believed that bullshit. They thought that just because it'd been written in black and white that it had to be true.

But I decided not to say anything more about it because although I hadn't known her for very long, my gut told me that Halle was a decent person and she didn't mean any harm.

'Sorry. You're right. I...' she stuttered. 'I shouldn't have said that. I know better than most people that what's printed in those magazines is rubbish. I apologise. So you actually like gardening?'

Her response caught me off guard. She'd read my mind. She understood.

'Yep,' I said still processing the fact that she'd apologised and actually seemed interested in finding out more about the real me. 'I love it.'

'What do you love about it?'

'It's satisfying. You plant a seed and then every day you get to watch it grow into something beautiful. Ain't nothing more rewarding than going to the garden and picking, then eating and cooking something you grew with your own bare hands.'

'Oh, wow, so you have an allotment?'

'It was one of the first things I created when I bought my first home. I always wanted a garden big enough for me to grow things.'

'What sort of stuff do you grow?'

Halle was using the present tense because obviously she didn't know that my house, my garden and everything I loved had been ripped away from me. And I wasn't in the mood to talk about it or correct her.

'All sorts. Tomatoes, peppers, carrots, lettuce, watermelons, sweetcorn, squash...'

'That's really cool.'

'Thanks. Gardening is really calming too. Almost like meditative. When you're in the fresh air, watering or weeding or planting, it's like you zone out from everything else.'

A pain shot through my chest. Damn. I missed my garden.

'What about you? What do you like doing?' I asked, desperate to draw the attention away from me. 'What's your passion?'

'I don't really have one.'

'Come on. Everyone has a passion. If you could do anything or be anyone in the world, what would you choose?'

She paused, looked at me then diverted her glance quickly, like she was assessing whether or not to share. Maybe it was too personal.

'You'll laugh.'

'Why? Do you want to become a comedian?' I joked.

'Very funny.'

'I try. Come on. I won't laugh, I promise.'

'A nail artist,' she said softly, like she'd just confessed to being caught watching porn at work by her boss.

'That's cool!' I smiled. 'That explains why your nails always look so pretty. Why would I laugh at that?'

'I used to love going with Mum to get her nails done when I was younger. Seeing how the technicians transformed people's nails and the way it boosted their confidence was amazing. So I started practising on my friends after school. Eventually Mum didn't go to the salon any more. I did her nails for her instead. Both my parents encouraged me to pursue it professionally. Vanessa did too. But other people think it's silly.'

'Those people are jerks,' I replied. 'Don't listen to them. It's an important form of art and creativity. It requires real skill to create designs on such a small area like nails. It's impressive. If that's what you'd like to do, you should pursue it. Don't let the haters stop you. It's your life, not theirs.'

'Y-yeah.' She blinked quickly, like she was shocked. 'Thank you. Not everyone gets it.'

'No problem.'

'Wow, what's that?' Her eyes bulged at the tall plant.

'This is what I wanted to show you: it's the Corpse Flower or they call it the Stinky Plant. It only blooms once every two or three years for twenty-four hours and when it does, it smells awful. Apparently, everyone describes the smell differently. Some say it's like rotting meat, others say sweaty socks, boiled cabbage or stinky cheese.'

'Nice.' She scrunched her nose. 'I'm not sure whether I should feel fascinated or offended that you took me to see a plant that smells bad.'

'I was definitely going for fascinating. This is one of their star attractions.'

'Phew, I thought you were trying to hint or use it as a segue to encourage me to use a stronger deodorant!' A nervous smile touched her lips.

I sensed that she was only half joking and that made me feel kinda sad. I didn't know her well yet, but I sensed that someone had done a real number on her. She seemed insecure. Vulnerable. Like she was afraid to be herself. Afraid of being judged. I knew the feeling.

Whoever did that to her deserved to be knocked out. People didn't seem to understand the power their words had. I hated that Halle's confidence had been damaged.

'Are you kidding? You always smell fantastic. If they had a Halle plant, it would smell like fucking roses.'

Halle's eyes popped.

Goddammit.

I wanted to make her feel better, but I wasn't supposed to lay it on so thick.

If Halle was the rose plant, then after that comment, I was the freaking cheese plant. That sounded so corny.

And it was inaccurate. Halle didn't smell like roses. She smelt like fruit-flavoured candy.

Anyway, enough thinking about how good she smelt.

'Er, thanks...' Her brows furrowed.

'Let's go,' I said quickly. 'There's something I wanna show you.'

'In public? Won't you get arrested?' she said, her face turning serious.

'What?' I frowned, then as realisation of what she was suggesting hit me, I shook my head. 'No, I meant, some place, not a... I wasn't...'

'I was pulling your leg.' She slapped my arm playfully before laughing. '*Of course* you're not going to show me your...' Her eyes dropped between my legs then travelled slowly back again.

Whoa. That went from zero to sixty fast.

One minute we were talking about stinky plants and her smelling like roses and the next she interpreted an innocent comment about me wanting to show her *something* as meaning I wanted to show her my dick?

But it was interesting because it raised two important questions:

One: why was Halle even thinking of my dick?

And two: did that mean she liked me, romantically?

21

HALLE

This was exactly why I didn't date any more. Because I'd inevitably end up doing or saying something to embarrass myself.

I couldn't believe I had just suggested that Jake might want to show me his dick.

Honestly. Where the hell had that come from?

I'm blaming the roses comment. When he said... wait, please allow me the indulgence of quoting his *exact* words: 'You always smell fantastic. If they had a Halle plant, it would smell like fucking roses,' I swear I almost passed out.

I wasn't used to getting compliments from a man.

My ex made me feel repulsive. He never wanted to go down on me because he said women smelt 'down there' and he'd wrinkle his nose whenever I came back from a run. I didn't know anyone who wasn't sweaty after running for miles and I'd always shower afterwards, but Brett made me feel like I was a human stink bomb.

Anyway, so yeah, the roses comment must've scrambled my brain.

That and Jake telling me he liked *gardening*. I used to love doing it with Dad too when we had a house in London. I'd help him out at weekends. There was something so satisfying about seeing an overgrown garden, tackling the weeds, planting new flowers, then seeing the transformation.

Having a garden in New York wasn't an option. There was barely enough room to swing a cat in my apartment, let alone being lucky enough to have any outdoor space. But I digress... What I was trying to say was there was something about Jake liking gardening and growing his own vegetables that made him... attractive. Well, *more* attractive, because the man was clearly already blessed with all the prime pickings from the gene pool.

I was blown away by how supportive he was of my passion for nails, plus there were those glimmers of vulnerability I'd seen. Like when we were on the coach. Holding his hand wasn't the smartest thing to do, but for some reason he seemed really freaked out and I wanted to help.

I thought I'd overstepped when he pulled away and to be honest, I felt a little rejected. Which was probably why I made those comments about him being more interested in women than flowers, but as soon as I'd said it, I felt bad. I knew first-hand how much things could be twisted and he genuinely seemed to be hurt.

And then later, the roses comment floored me again.

Jake was like a lucky dip: he was full of surprises.

Just when I'd think I'd figured him out, he'd drop something else about his personality that'd blow my perceptions out of the water. He'd taken me through so many different emotions, I felt like I had whiplash.

'So, er, where are you taking me?' I said.

'To the Chinese Gardens. They're one of my favourites,' he said and his face lit up. Jake had a nice smile.

Actually, *nice* didn't do it justice. Truthfully, it was pretty spectacular. *Blinding.*

Ever since he caught me falling off the horse yesterday, I felt like something had shifted. I'd noticed that when he smiled, my stomach did weird things. It was like a swarm of overenthusiastic butterflies were having a table tennis tournament inside it.

That wasn't good. I needed them to take their energetic fluttering elsewhere.

As soon as we stepped into the gardens, I gasped. I immediately understood why Jake loved it here.

'Wow.'

'Pretty special, huh?' he said as I took in the views of the Chinese plants, pretty pavilions, paths, courtyards and traditional-looking buildings. 'They brought architects over from China to work on it.'

'It looks amazing!'

'You haven't seen anything yet. Come on.' He grabbed my hand and led me to the lake.

Electricity rocketed through me. Jake was holding my hand.

I should be shocked or repulsed, but somehow it also seemed like the most natural thing in the world.

I dipped my head, taking in the sight of our intertwined fingers.

Did he even realise that he'd taken my hand?

I was probably reading way too much into it. He was just excited to show me, that was all.

Just as Jake was explaining how the gardens were filled with plants and flowers that either represented the seasons (for example, peach blossoms for spring) or human qualities, like purity (lotus) or humility (orchid), I heard our names being called from behind us. We both spun around at the same time and saw Sammie walking towards us.

I looked down at our hands and instantly pulled away.

Just a couple of days ago, I was asking Sammie to find me another match because Jake wasn't a good fit. And now here I was holding his bloody hand.

Yes, I was getting on much better with him and surprisingly he seemed like a really cool guy. But just because we were sort of friends now, it didn't mean that I'd changed my mind about him not being serious boyfriend material.

I still needed to find someone who wanted something long-term. I hadn't paid thousands of dollars to find another friend.

'There you are!' Sammie said when she caught up with us. 'I was just going to call you.'

'What's up?' I said.

'When I gave you your lunch money, I forgot to give you this.' She held up an envelope. Jake took it from her before I got the chance.

'What is it?' he asked.

'It's your photos. From yesterday's activity. When I went to reception before we got on the coach, they said you two hadn't collected them, so I brought them with me. I thought about giving you this envelope on the coach, but then I decided it'd be better for you to go through them in private.'

My stomach tensed. I hoped that didn't mean they were bad.

'Thanks, Sammie. We forgot to get them because we were rushing.'

'No worries! I'll leave you two lovebirds to it!' She winked at me, then walked away.

She must've seen us holding hands. Shit.

'Wanna go through them now?' Jake asked.

I was torn. Part of me wanted to toss them straight in the bin so that I didn't have to bear the embarrassment when I didn't like them.

I knew Jake must've sent Sammie the photos that Aidan took and I think I spotted Sammie taking some candid shots when we'd finished the horse ride.

But the other part of me was curious to see how they'd come out.

There was only one way I'd know…

'Okay,' I said, swallowing the lump in my throat.

'Let's sit.' He pointed to a bench. Once we were seated, he handed me the envelope. 'Here. You do the honours.'

I took a deep breath. As I slid my fingers under the seal, my hand trembled. I hated that I was so nervous. I didn't use to be this way. I used to take pictures all the time, like most people did. Now just the mention of the word *photos* made me break out in a cold sweat.

My heart thundered in my chest as I removed the pile of pictures. The first photo instantly made my shoulders loosen. It was a shot of us with the Hollywood sign in view, but our backs were facing the camera. Phew.

'I like this one,' I beamed.

'Is that because you can't see my ugly face?' Jake teased.

'You and I both know that your face isn't ugly.' I rolled my eyes.

'All I'm hearing is that you think I'm hot,' Jake replied with a mischievous grin.

'If you're fishing for compliments, you need to find another ocean to throw your rod into.'

'Sounds like a euphemism to me. I'm very particular about the oceans I dip my rod into.' He smirked.

'Your reputation says otherwise. Sorry.' I winced. 'I did it again. I know what's in the media isn't always true.'

'Glad to hear that.' He nodded. 'I'm not denying that I've done a lot of *fishing* in the past but my frequent ocean-dipping days are over.'

'Ugh,' I winced. 'Hearing the word *ocean* like that makes me think of something cringy.'

'Yeah?'

'The last date I went on, well, it wasn't a date, but anyway, the guy told me that he wanted to *slip and slide in my ocean.*'

'You're kidding?' Jake laughed. 'Full disclosure: I and many other artists do use the word "ocean" when talking about sex in songs. But that's different to saying it in real life.'

'Exactly! That wasn't even the worst part. He also asked if I wanted to take a ride on his *jumbo jet*. Apparently, if I had one ride on it, I'd be *begging for more.*'

'No, he didn't!' Jake snorted and the sound made me laugh so hard, my stomach hurt. 'And did you beg for more?'

'Of course not! Do you actually think that I'd let a man who referred to his dick as a bloody jumbo jet slip and slide in *my* exquisite ocean?' I giggled.

'Preach! A pretty lady like you could have her pick of the guys, so settling for a dude like that would be a damn shame. Plus, if you'd shacked up with Mr Jumbo Jet, you wouldn't be here with me right now.'

My eyes widened and my stomach flipflopped.

Jake just called me pretty.

I was a grown woman, not a teenage girl, so I had no idea why a whole basket of butterflies had suddenly ambushed my belly again. I'd thought they'd finished playing table tennis, but now they were having a full-on rave.

My gaze locked with Jake's and just like yesterday I thought about how gorgeous his eyes were.

Right now, they were a darker shade of green, almost verging on brown. There was something burning in them. I wanted to say it was desire, but that'd be ridiculous. Up until we'd arrived at Huntington Gardens, I'd never even considered whether or not he found me attractive. It was irrelevant because I'd had no intention of continuing with him as my match. But now, something was different and I couldn't help but wonder if he did?

He'd said that I wouldn't have been here with him now like he was enjoying my company. And I had to say, the feeling was mutual.

Still, that didn't mean that I was interested in him romantically, because I definitely wasn't.

I couldn't be.

'Should we look at the next photo?' I said, breaking the silence.

'Uh... um, sure,' Jake stuttered, his eyes travelling down to the stack of pictures in my palms. I moved to the next photo and swallowed hard.

'I like this one too,' Jake said. 'It's cute.'

'Y-yeah,' I said, struggling to believe how much it actually was. We were both on the horse and this time Jake was staring at me whilst I was smiling at the camera.

His expression was a mixture of happiness, but also pride? Like he was impressed that I'd ridden the horse.

I didn't hate it.

There were several other photos and all of them were really, really nice. I didn't look as shit as I'd feared and was actually smiling a lot, which surprised me. Aidan had asked us to say cheese but I didn't realise how wide my grin was.

As I came to the last photo, I gasped.

It was a picture of Jake holding me in his arms after I fell off the horse. And I was staring at him with love-heart eyes like he'd just shown me how to walk on water *and* given me the secret to eternal youth.

If I could put my expressions into words, I'd be saying 'my hero' in a breathy, *damsel-in-distress-saved-by-her-knight-in-shining-armour* voice.

And I wasn't gonna lie. I remembered how I'd felt in that moment and Sammie had captured it perfectly.

Wow.

I didn't even know how to feel right now.

'This one is...' I searched for the right words but came out blank. 'Good.'

It was a million times better than *good* but I didn't know the best way to express how much I loved it without gushing like a fountain.

'Happy with the photos?' Jake asked.

'They're better than I thought they'd be.'

'Good. I'm glad. I've been wondering... why don't you like having your picture taken?'

The question was a reasonable, but it still caught me off guard.

I contemplated trying to get him to change the subject, but that'd probably just make him more interested in finding out the truth. Like when someone says, 'I've got something to tell you!' then instead of spilling the beans, they say, 'Actually, I'd better not...' I hated that.

I took a deep breath.

'I used to date someone famous. And whenever he posted photos of me online or I was papped, let's just say that the comments weren't always kind.'

'Shit,' Jake said quickly. 'That sucks. I'm sorry you had to go through that, Halle. Those damn keyboard warriors are just a bunch of sad, jealous little fuckers who are so unhappy with their own lives that they think it's okay to talk shit about other people.'

'Yeah. I know. Doesn't stop it from hurting though.'

'I hear you. I've been through a tonne of shit over the years, but women get it a lot worse. Especially when they're the girl-friend of someone in the public eye. It's fucking bullshit. If you don't mind me asking, who were you dating?'

'Brett Burch.'

'Oh. That asshole,' he snarled.

'You know him?' My eyes bulged.

'Unfortunately. The guy's a dick. Arrogant, shady and overrated.'

'Sounds about right. Although I'd use much stronger words than that.' I gave Jake a weak smile.

'How long did you date?'

'Four years.'

'*Sheesh*! And how many medals did you get for your service?'

'Hah. If only.'

'And I'm guessing he did you dirty?'

'Yep.'

'Wanna talk about it?'

'Not really,' I said quickly as my chest tightened.

Jake had actually been really easy to talk to, but I didn't want to dredge up those painful memories right now. I was enjoying my time here. And I'd actually appeared in some photos that looked half decent.

'No problem,' Jake said softly. 'Come on. Let me take you to the desert gardens.'

'A garden filled with cake and ice cream?' I teased, trying to lighten the mood. 'Sign me up!'

'*Desert* gardens, not *dessert* gardens,' he chuckled. 'But if you like we can stop off at one of the cafés first and I'll buy you ice cream.'

'Deal!'

22

JAKE

As I watched Halle licking her ice cream enthusiastically, a wide grin spread across my face. She looked so happy. Such a contrast to half an hour ago when she was explaining why she didn't like having her photo taken.

My heart went out to her. My skin was a lot thicker now, but I'd been in this business for over fifteen years so I'd had time to get used to it. But when you were thrust into the limelight like she must've been, it would've been a real shock.

And I bet her ex wasn't much help.

Brett fucking Burch.

What I'd said was true. The guy was an asshole.

I'd seen him backstage at some festivals we were both playing at and the women he had in his dressing room were not in there playing Monopoly. And this was before he married that supermodel. I didn't know when Halle dated him, but I'm guessing from the sadness in her eyes that he cheated.

Dick.

If I had a good woman like Halle, there was no way I'd fool around. I could tell she had a good heart and was genuine.

Something that was rare these days. Her confidence seemed low and I could definitely relate to that. But something told me that once Halle started to believe in herself, there'd be no stopping her.

'That was so good!' she beamed as she finished the last bite of the cone.

When I looked at her, I grinned. She had ice cream around her mouth and on the tip of her nose.

'I can tell you enjoyed that,' I chuckled. 'You've got it all over your face.'

'What?' Her eyes popped. 'Nooo!' She reached in her bag for a Kleenex, then started frantically dabbing her mouth and chin. 'Has it all gone?'

'Nope!'

She tried to clean herself up again, but although she'd caught the bits on her nose and chin, she missed a spot on her cheek and just below her lips.

'Let me.' I reached towards her face, then paused. 'Is it okay if I...?'

'Y-yeah. Course. Thanks.'

I gently swiped my thumb over her cheek before moving it down slowly. As it brushed across her lip, Halle's breath hitched and her eyes locked on mine.

Damn. Those eyes.

And her lips.

They were so tempting. I wondered how they felt. How they tasted.

I wanted to trace the whole of her mouth with my thumb, but I was only supposed to wipe away the ice cream. I couldn't betray her trust.

Reluctantly, I removed my thumb.

'D-do you want a tissue?' she asked.

'No. Don't need it,' I said before, licking my thumb clean. 'You're right.' I held her gaze again. 'That does taste good.'

Halle's eyes widened then she bit her lip. I loved when she did that and the sight sent a shot of lightning straight to my dick.

Shit.

I wasn't supposed to be thinking about her in that way.

This was just business. I couldn't get involved.

My pulse spiked again, just like it had when I held Halle's hand, just before Sammie found us.

As crazy as it sounded, I didn't even realise that I was doing it until I felt my body temperature rise a few seconds later. It just felt so natural. I was gutted when she'd dropped my hand, but it was the right thing to do. I couldn't start getting addicted to her touch.

But yet here I was, licking the thumb that had brushed her lips and now willing my dick not to get hard.

Fuck.

'Desert,' I said quickly, trying to bring my thoughts back to safer ground. 'Let me take you to see the gardens. They've got all kinds of different cacti, they're all green and spiky and... let's go.' I groaned inside. *Green and spiky? Seriously, dude, get it together.* I guessed that was better than calling them *tall and erect.*

By the time we got to the desert gardens the sun was strong and there wasn't much shade.

Halle wiped her forehead with the back of her hand and fanned her face. I wasn't surprised she was hot. The only thing keeping me cool right now was my baseball cap. But I couldn't let her overheat.

'Take this.' I whipped off my cap. 'It'll help you cool down.'

'But don't you need it so people won't recognise you?' Her brows furrowed.

'Doesn't matter. I don't want you to get burnt.'

'But if you give it to me then *you'll* get burnt.'

'Don't worry about me, sweetheart. According to your playlist, you need a hero, so I'm just making your dreams come true,' I laughed. I'd done a lot of that today. Although I hadn't listened to the songs on the list, I'd seen the titles.

'But you already demonstrated your hero status by rescuing me from falling off a horse yesterday.'

'Can't rest on my laurels,' I shrugged. 'A hero's only as good as his last heroic gesture.'

'Very true,' she nodded, then flashed me a warm smile. 'Play your cards right and I might accidentally fall into a pond or something just so you can pull me out and save me again.'

'Wow,' I mock gasped. 'You'd do that for me? *Gee, thanks.*' I exaggerated my accent earning me another smile.

Damn. Right now I felt like a dog, desperate for its owner to throw it a bone. Every time Halle smiled at me, I felt like I'd just won the lottery.

It was such a shame she didn't like taking photos because if you asked me, she looked pretty in every single one of them.

Obviously I'd seen the ones Aidan had taken because I'd looked through them before emailing them to the hotel. But Sammie's shots of me catching Halle took my breath away.

Wilma had asked before if I was reluctant to upload photos of Halle because I didn't think she was attractive. But the opposite was true. If Wilma knew how fucking gorgeous Halle was, she'd piss her panties.

Anyhow, it was irrelevant. No matter how good Halle looked, I wasn't going to put her on my Instagram.

There was the shot where our backs faced the camera that I considered for a millisecond. Posting that would stop Wilma hassling me, but it was still a hard no. I was reluctant about doing it before, but now I was even more certain.

From what I could tell, Halle had been through enough trauma. And I wasn't gonna be the one to cause her more pain.

There had to be another way to save my career without hurting her.

Now I just had to work out how to find it...

23

HALLE

Was it possible to become addicted to someone's scent?

It was Wednesday evening and as Jake got off the coach ready for today's group activity, I followed behind him like a sniffer dog, inhaling his gorgeous woody cologne.

Well, at least I thought it was aftershave. And if it was, I'd have to buy a bottle in New York and spray it on my pillow so that I could get my Eau de Sexy Jake fix when I got back.

Yep. It was clear. With every passing minute, I was becoming more attracted to him.

If I didn't already realise it yesterday when he said I smelt like roses, when he wiped the ice cream off my lip then licked it off his thumb, I got all the confirmation I needed.

Shamelessly, when I saw his tongue wipe off the ice cream that had been on my mouth seconds earlier, I wondered if he would be into licking other things. From what I'd learnt about Jake so far, he seemed kind and considerate. I mean, the guy risked getting hassled by fans to give me his baseball cap so I wouldn't overheat. So sweet.

Jake seemed like the kind of man that would actually care

about satisfying a woman in bed and not just be focused on his own pleasure, which was very appealing.

The sun may have been hot in those desert gardens, but that wasn't the only reason I'd started overheating. For the first time in ages, I'd felt a sensation that I thought had left me forever after my last relationship collapsed: desire.

When I looked at Jake I got goosebumps and tingles between my legs, which wasn't like me. Especially considering we hadn't known each other that long.

Then again, we'd spent a lot of time together over the past five days, so that was bound to accelerate things like feelings.

After we'd left The Huntington yesterday, we'd chatted easily all the way back to the hotel. Then we'd met up for dinner where we'd spent more time talking about our visit and discussing gardening. I know, right? Sounded weird, and probably a bit boring to other people, but somehow I found it fascinating.

After dinner, he'd asked if I wanted to get a drink at the bar, but I'd said I was tired, which was partly true. But mainly, I declined because I could feel myself being drawn to him and I needed to shut it down before my feelings escalated.

That was also why I'd spent most of the day reading on my balcony because I was too worried about bumping into Jake by the pool or on the hotel's beach. Fully clothed Jake was hot enough. I wasn't prepared to see shirtless, muscles-on-show Jake.

If it was just the fact that he was beautiful, I could've handled it. I'd met a lot of good-looking guys who were dicks. Being hot alone wouldn't have been enough to move the needle. But there seemed to be so much more to him.

Jake was a walking contradiction. A tough-looking rockstar with a bad boy reputation, who also seemed gentle and kind.

He appeared arrogant, yet he also seemed vulnerable. I

couldn't figure him out and I was intrigued. I really wanted to find out more about him.

There was something drawing me to him. And it was more than just his delicious scent.

'So,' Sammie said as she stood in front of our group, 'if you haven't already worked it out, this is The Griffith Observatory. It's the most-visited observatory in the world. It doesn't get more romantic than doing a spot of stargazing, so that's what we're here to do tonight.'

'Whoop!' someone near the front cheered.

'There's telescopes so you can gaze at the stars and see the city with your match. This place was also featured in the movie *La La Land*!'

'That's so cool,' a guest called Annie called out.

'It is! There's also some interactive exhibits for those who are interested in learning about space, time and the universe,' Sammie added.

Once Sammie had shared more interesting facts and told us what time we had to meet back at the coach, the couples went their separate ways.

'I need to go to the john,' Jake said. 'You okay to wait for me here?'

'Sure,' I replied.

The views here were magical. As I looked up and saw the City of Angels lit up underneath the twinkling sky, I thought about how much Vanessa would love to see it too. Maybe I could take a few snaps. Just to show her.

Seeing the photos yesterday reminded me how nice it was to have memories in print. And if they were on my phone, *I* could decide whether or not to share or delete them. I didn't need to be so afraid any more.

I pulled out my phone, took a few snaps, then checked them

on the screen. They didn't come out very well. My phone was too old.

Oh, well. At least I tried.

Just as I was about to move to another position, Sammie came over.

'Hey, where's Jake?' she asked.

'He went to the john. I mean, the toilet.'

'Why do Americans call the loo "the john"?'

'Maybe it's something to do with the name of the guy who invented the toilet? I'm not sure.'

'They have so many different words, it's hard to believe we speak the same language.'

'I've lived here for years and even I forget the lingo sometimes!'

'I can imagine! So...' Sammie said, 'did you enjoy the excursion yesterday?'

'It was great, thanks. So many beautiful gardens.'

'And how's it going with Jake? Those horse-riding photos were cute and you two seemed to be getting on better yesterday.' She smirked.

'Yeah...' I paused, thinking how best to phrase my response. 'We're getting on much better. He's sweet.'

'I'm glad you're hitting it off.'

'That's a bit strong, we're just... friends.'

'And friends hold hands, do they?' She cocked an eyebrow. I *knew* she'd seen us.

'That was just... that didn't mean anything.'

'Hmm-hmmm,' she nodded, clearly not believing a single word. 'Sure, sure. If you say so. I've seen the way he looks at you and the way you look at him and *nothing* about it is friendly.'

'How does he look at me?' I blurted out.

'Notice how you asked how he looked at you instead of

denying it...' Sammie grinned. I opened my mouth to protest, then closed it again. She'd got me. 'He looks at you like he thinks you're amazing. And let's be honest, like he wants to devour you. And from the way that you look at him, the feeling is mutual, right?'

I didn't even know how to answer that without incriminating myself.

I couldn't confirm how Jake looked at me, but I'd admit that there had been a few moments lately that I'd wondered whether he did fancy me.

But although something told me that Jake would give me the best sex of my life, I couldn't go there. I wasn't here for a hook-up. I could've got that in New York.

And after the other thing that had happened to me before, even the idea of having sex again scared me. Doing it with someone like Jake was particularly risky, given the amount of women he'd slept with.

No. I couldn't deny I was attracted to Jake, but that was all it could ever be: an attraction that I could never act on. The consequences would be catastrophic. I just needed to keep my desire under control. I'd gone without sex for years. Another week and a bit would be a walk in the park.

'He's...'

'You ladies talking about me?' Jake appeared and I was relieved to see him because it saved me from answering Sammie's question.

'How did you guess?' Sammie said.

'All good, I hope?' he replied.

'You'll have to ask Halle about that...' She winked at me. 'Oh! You forgot to collect your photos again.'

'Yeah.' Jake slapped his forehead.

I'd remembered at breakfast, but wanted to get back to my

room to avoid spending more time with Jake. Ditto for the rest of the day.

'Here you go.' She handed the envelope to me. 'There's some real crackers in there. I reckon you're gonna love them. Laters!' Sammie disappeared.

'So... want to look at them now or after we see stars together?' I said.

'You want us to see stars together?' Jake quirked an eyebrow. 'That can be arranged.'

My face contorted, then I realised what I'd just said.

'I meant, see *the* stars, not, seeing stars together as in... you know what I mean!'

'Oh, but I don't,' Jake teased. 'Care to elaborate?'

'No!' My cheeks heated. 'Photos first or stargazing through a telescope?'

'We gotta look at the photos! Seeing you giving me heart eyes in print is becoming my new favourite hobby.'

'I don't give you heart eyes!' I protested.

'We'll see, shall we?' He smirked and I sent a silent prayer that I hadn't.

I pulled out the pics and in the first shot, I wasn't giving Jake love-heart eyes.

It was much worse.

There was a photo of our backs to the camera again and we were holding hands.

After our conversation a few minutes ago, I knew that Sammie had seen us, but I didn't realise she had photographic evidence. So sneaky!

'Cute,' Jake said.

'Yeah.' I didn't bother denying it because it was.

And I liked the way he was looking at me. I couldn't

remember what we were talking about at that point but he seemed really engaged in whatever I was saying.

There were a few photos of us in various different places around the gardens that Sammie must've snapped and some photos of the back of me that Jake must've taken when I wasn't looking.

'I hope you didn't mind me taking those photos from the back. I took them mainly for you. In case you wanted a memory of being there. But I made sure I didn't show your face because I didn't want you to feel uncomfortable.'

'They're great, thank you. I tried to take some photos just now of the views, but my phone is old, so the camera's pretty shit.'

'Want me to take some on mine?' he asked. 'You don't have to be in them. Unless you want to. Or I can take the back of you again? It's up to you.'

'O-okay,' I said, feeling a bubble of excitement forming in my stomach.

'I know this is a big deal for you so I'll...'

'Excuse me.' A guy tapped Jake on the shoulder. 'Can I get a photo?'

'Um...' Jake paused and looked at me nervously. 'Sure.' He flashed the man a smile. But it wasn't like the smiles I'd become used to. It seemed stiffer.

'Want me to take it?' I offered.

'You sure?' Jake flashed me a look which said *thanks but you don't have to.*

'Course!' After the man gave me his phone, I took a few snaps. There was one where Jake's eyes were closed so I quickly deleted that and another where he wasn't quite ready for the photo. If he had to take a photo with a fan, I wanted to make sure that he looked his best.

'There you go.' I handed back his phone.

'Thanks,' he said. 'My wife isn't gonna believe that I met you. She had the major hots for you before we started dating. What was up with that butter commercial, though dude? That blowed!'

The blood drained from Jake's face and I instantly wanted to protect him from this man's insults. Yeah, that ad wasn't his finest moment. Even I was surprised when I saw him singing that cheesy song, but I kept my opinions to myself. Saying something hurtful like that to someone's face wasn't cool.

'Just one of those things,' Jake shrugged. He was pretending that it was no big deal, but I saw how stiff his shoulders were and his smile was so tense, his face could shatter any second. He was hating every moment of this.

'Bet you went out and bought the butter though, right?' I jumped in.

'Yeah,' the man laughed. 'My wife bought enough butter to make two hundred sandwiches!'

'Then it worked! Just shows the power of a memorable advert, right?'

'Right,' the man nodded. 'Thanks for the photo.' He walked off.

When the man was out of earshot, Jake exhaled.

'Thanks for that,' he said. 'You didn't have to take the picture.'

'It was nothing. And I sensed you were uncomfortable.'

'Yeah. We were in the middle of a conversation. You were trying to get the courage to take a photo which is a big deal and even though he wasn't to know that, I didn't like that he inter-rupted us.'

'You could've just said no.'

He laughed then shook his head.

'If I said no, I'd look like an asshole. That's the thing I always found difficult to navigate with fame. It's great that people listen to my songs. I'll always be appreciative of that. But the other side of the coin is that you're always expected to be "on" twenty-four seven. You become public property. People ask for photos, and they expect you to smile, right on cue, but they don't know that five minutes earlier you just received a shitty call about someone close to you. All they want is a photo. To them you're not a human being, you're a ticket to popularity. Half the time they're not even a real fan. Take that guy. He didn't even introduce himself. He wasn't interested in having a real conversation. He didn't care whether or not it was convenient for me. He just wanted to take a photo to show his wife who "used to" like me. Others just want to get a picture to tell their friends that they met me, or to sell for money.'

The way Jake spoke was such a contrast to my ex. He loved the limelight. Craved it. When someone came up to him to ask for a selfie or autograph it was like a shot of adrenaline. Jake, on the other hand, talked about the spotlight like he hated it.

But if that was true, why was he constantly taking photos and documenting everything on social media?

Something didn't add up. His words didn't gel with his actions. And I needed to find out why.

24

HALLE

As I curled up on the daybed by the pool with my iPad, I tried to think about what to add as the final song for yesterday's playlist.

I'd already chosen 'Stargazing' by Myles Smith (obviously – I freaking loved him), 'Sky Full of Stars' by Coldplay, 'All the Stars' by Kendrick Lamar and SZA and 'Counting Stars' by OneRepublic. But I couldn't decide between 'Waiting for a Star to Fall' by Boy Meets Girl or 'Stars' by Simply Red.

Sod it. I was adding both.

They were classics and I knew Jake would appreciate a bit of eighties and nineties music mixed in with the more recent tracks.

Last night was actually really romantic. I loved gazing at the stars with Jake beside me. So I wanted the playlist to reflect that.

Just as I was clicking the add to playlist button, a gorgeous scent hit my nostrils. My head snapped up and...

Oh. My. God.

It wasn't just Jake standing in front of me.

It was the version of him that I'd been trying to avoid for days: Shirtless Jake.

As my eyes scanned him from his broad shoulders, down his

muscular chest, continuing south to take in the sight of his six-pack, I swallowed hard.

His body was even more incredible than I'd imagined.

Apart from that BUTT-RRR ad, Jake hadn't done many endorsements that I could remember, so there were no bill-boards of him advertising underwear. Which meant this was the first time I'd been treated to this delicious view. Thank God I was wearing my sunglasses so he couldn't see me gawping.

'H-hey,' I stuttered, quickly lifting my gaze back up to his face.

'Hey!' He smiled and yep, there went that pesky stomach flut-tering again. 'Thought I'd find you here. What you doing?'

'Yesterday's playlist. Speaking of which, we've been here six days now if you include when we arrived on Saturday, and I haven't received a single playlist from you. Am I worth so little of your thoughts that you can't be bothered to make the effort?'

It wouldn't be the first time.

'No!' Jake said quickly, concern etched on his face. 'Sorry. It's not about you. It's a me thing.'

'Care to elaborate?'

Jake was silent for several beats, then rubbed the back of his neck.

'Do you have time for a walk?' His shoulders sagged.

'Yeah. Our activity isn't until this evening, so I've got loads of time.'

We headed to the beach and walked together in silence. The only sounds were the waves rippling against the shore and the birds squawking in the sky.

I considered filling it, but then realised that Jake must be trying to psyche himself up to talk, so thought I'd let him do that at his own pace.

'Music is...' He paused for so long I was half expecting him to abandon the conversation altogether. 'Music has always been important to me. It's not an exaggeration to say that it was my life. It was something I always loved growing up and then when I got into the band, I thought all of my dreams had come true. But it was hell, which is a whole different story.'

'Okay,' I nodded, encouraging him to continue.

'My solo career was better. After the dictatorship of being part of a boyband, where everything we did, including what we wore, what we said, how many hours we were allowed to sleep, what we ate and how often we got to see our family and friends was decided by other people, I knew I needed to do things on my terms, like writing my own songs, which I did. But then everything came crashing down when... something terrible happened and I also discovered that my accountant screwed me over, so financially I was fucked.'

'Shit.' My eyes widened with shock.

'With everything that was going on, the last thing I could think about was making music. Eventually my label dropped me which didn't help with the debts that were stacking up. Oh, and on top of that, my girlfriend sold stories to the tabloids. Now I can't even listen to music, let alone write it, so the thought of making playlists is pretty much my idea of hell.'

Whoa.

I wasn't expecting *that* to be his explanation. That was a lot to unpack. I didn't even know where to start. Although I wanted to know more, especially about what the 'terrible' thing was, I realised that if he'd wanted to go into detail, he would've said what it was like he had with the other stuff.

'Jake... I'm... I'm so sorry. That's horrendous. Just dealing with one of those things would be a lot, but all of them together? It's a miracle that you're still able to function.'

'Yep. Sometimes I can't even do it at all.'

'I'm not surprised. I'm sorry I hassled you about the playlists.'

'You weren't to know. I saw the songs you sent through, which I appreciated. I just didn't play them. And I couldn't make my own.'

'I'll stop sending you mine. I didn't realise it would be triggering for you. Is that why...' I paused, wondering whether or not I should ask the question that I wanted to.

'Is that why, what?' He looked at me.

'On the coach... is that why you were anxious when they played your song?'

Jake's face fell and I instantly regretted bringing it up.

'Partly. But mainly because I wrote that for someone who broke my heart. So every time I hear it, it reminds me of how fucking stupid I was.'

'Was it the same woman who you just said sold stories on you?'

'Yep. I started seeing personal stuff turning up in the press. At first it was little things that maybe multiple people in my circle might know, so it wasn't immediately obvious that it was her. But then I noticed that the paps always knew where we'd be. And even if we were going somewhere low-key, she'd always get dressed up. I mentioned that it was strange, but she'd always say they'd just followed us.'

'So how did you find out?'

'I laid a trap. I told her I was going to be somewhere. She was the only person I mentioned it to and sure enough, half an hour later, the paps miraculously showed up. And I made up a story and again and told her that I'd shared it with a few other people in my circle, but I hadn't – she was the only person I told.'

'And did it turn up in the press?'

'Yep. So that's how I knew for sure.'

'Shit. I'm so sorry.'

'Thanks. It hurt, because I really thought she was the real deal. Turned out she was just using me to launch her singing career. She figured the more we got papped together, the more it raised her profile. She was a social climber. Now she's dating one of the execs from my old record label.'

'Fuck.' Seeing the sadness in Jake's eyes was like a punch in the stomach.

Without even thinking, I threw my arms around him. Just as I was about to pull away, convinced that I'd overstepped, Jake's arms snaked around my back and he held me tighter.

Every atom in my body came to life. My pulse spiked. My heart raced. My brain scrambled.

There were so many sensations flooding my body I could barely breathe.

Feeling Jake's heartbeat and his warm muscular chest pressed against mine was incredible. I rested my head on his shoulder and decided that I could happily stay like this forever.

I wanted to tell him again how sorry I was for everything he'd been through, but I couldn't even speak.

Jake moved and I was literally about to beg him not to end it so soon, but instead of breaking the hug, he readjusted his arms around me and pulled me in closer.

We stayed like that for what must've been several minutes. However long it was, it wasn't long enough.

Eventually, Jake unclasped his arms from around me and drew back. As his eyes met mine, my breath hitched in my throat.

Tingles raced down my spine and a bolt of desire shot straight to my core.

God, I wanted him to kiss me so much right now.

Jake reached up and brushed his thumb gently over my cheek, setting my blood on fire.

This was crazy.

Never in my life has a man had such an effect on me just by simply touching my face and looking at me.

'Thank you,' he said softly.

'For what?' I said breathlessly, keeping my eyes fixed to his.

'For listening. For the hug.'

His thumb continued brushing my cheek before moving towards my mouth.

When he traced my bottom lip, a moan slipped out and I squeezed my eyes shut.

Shit. I swear Jake could make me come just with his hands.

I supposed I shouldn't be surprised considering the fact that it'd been years since I'd been properly touched by a man.

'Y-you're welcome,' I stuttered. When I flicked my eyes open, Jake's gaze was still fixed on me so firmly, he could probably see inside my soul.

Ordinarily, that'd make me feel flustered, but somehow I felt at ease.

'You're really beautiful,' Jake whispered and I blinked rapidly, trying to process his words. My toxic inner voice warned me not to fall for another smooth talker, but my gut told me he was genuine.

'Thanks,' I said, softly. 'So are you.'

Jake's face inched forward slowly.

He was now so close I could feel his sweet, warm breath tickling my lips.

There were a million reasons I shouldn't want him to kiss me, but it was like his mouth was a magnet and my lips were metal.

I told myself to pull away, but I was drawn to him with such intensity that there was no way I could stop the inevitable.

Just as our mouths were about to collide, an ear-piercing shriek filled the air.

'Help!'

We both sprang back and spun around.

'Sounded like it's coming from the sea!' Jake jumped up and sprinted towards the ocean. I ran after him.

Kayla, one of the guests, was flapping around in the water frantically.

Jake launched himself into the sea and swam towards her. I followed him in and it was only when we got closer that I paused.

The water wasn't deep as she was still close to shore, so she wasn't in any danger of drowning.

Shit. Maybe it was her match, who I think was called Greg, that was underwater?

'You okay?' Jake said as he reached her. 'What happened?'

'It's my phone!' she shrieked. 'I was trying to take a selfie and I dropped it!'

The woman started sobbing like a baby who hadn't eaten, slept or had its nappy changed for hours.

'You lost your phone?' Jake frowned, like he couldn't believe what he was hearing. '*That's* why you screamed for help?'

'Yes!' she snapped. 'What am I going to do?'

Jake looked at me and mouthed *what the fuck* whilst I fought the urge to laugh.

'Well, I can see that this is very important to you and obviously it'll be impossible for you to survive without your cell...' he said.

'Exactly!' Kayla nodded, clearly oblivious to the hint of sarcasm in Jake's tone.

'So let me see if I can find it for you. Okay?'

'Okay,' she said, her sobs immediately subsiding.

Jake dove under the water. As the seconds ticked by, I grew increasingly concerned. I couldn't believe he was actually risking his life, just so this woman could find her phone.

When his head bobbed up above water again, relief flooded my veins. I knew the water wasn't deep enough for him to drown, but that didn't mean that staying under water for too long wasn't dangerous.

'Still looking!' he said before ducking back under again.

About thirty seconds later (yes, I counted, just in case), he reemerged, but this time he was waving a phone in the air.

'Got it!' he said triumphantly.

'Oh my God!' Kayla squealed, jumping up and down. 'You're a lifesaver! Thank you so much!' She threw her arms around him and a bolt of jealousy rocketed through me.

'You're welcome.' Jake shot me a look which said *this is awkward* and gently lifted her arms away from his neck. 'I'm not sure if dropping it in some rice will save it, but if it does, maybe try protecting it in one of those waterproof phone holders next time.'

'Okay!' she beamed, bashing away at the phone screen.

Jake took my hand and led me out of the sea and just like before, the sensation of his fingers curled around mine sent a zing of excitement zipping through my bloodstream.

Once we were safely back to shore, we looked at each other and burst out laughing.

'I can't believe that she cried for help because she dropped her goddamn cell!' he sighed.

'I can. Some people are obsessed. I've heard about people posing for selfies on the edge of cliffs and crazy shit like that. Some of them even die trying to get the perfect shot.'

'It's insane. We've forgotten how to just live in the moment. There's been so many times I've performed and seen people with their cells, watching everything from a screen because they're filming, instead of just enjoying what's happening right in front of them. They miss most of the show because they're too busy uploading shit to social media.'

'I agree. But I'm surprised to hear you say that, considering how much you love posting stuff on the 'gram.'

Jake froze and his Adam's apple bobbed.

'Yeah... I guess that makes me a hypocrite.' His gaze dropped to the ground. 'I-I just remembered, there's something I need to do. I'd better go. I'll catch you later. Okay?'

'Okay,' I said.

But that wasn't entirely true.

Jake had opened up a lot to me this afternoon, but I still sensed there was something he was holding back.

I just had to hope that it wasn't anything bad...

25

JAKE

That was a close call.

I couldn't believe I'd almost kissed Halle.

Although I guess if I was being truthful, I shouldn't be surprised.

The more time I spent with Halle, the more I liked her. And not just physically. Although you'd have to be blind not to notice that she was as fine as hell. I meant, liked *her* as a person.

When the guy that asked for photos at the observatory dissed the commercial and Halle snapped back, I was shocked. Everyone, including me, knew that bullshit BUTT-RRR gig was fucking terrible. But Halle still defended me in a way that no one had for a long time.

The only person that I knew with absolute certainty had my back these days was Roger and my British friend, Liam, who lived in London. Everyone else was either gone or bailed, the minute the shit hit the fan.

Yet in walks Halle and after knowing me for less than a week, she's already shown me that she's got my back. And that meant a lot.

Then the way she listened to me spill my guts about all the shit I'd been through, without judgement or pity, just genuine empathy, blew my mind.

And don't even get me started on that hug.

Fuck.

I didn't even realise how much I needed that until I was in her arms.

Given the chance, I would've held her for hours, days, months until I passed out from dehydration or hunger. There was so much understanding, care and comfort in that moment that if Halle bottled it, it'd sell for millions.

Hugs like that could cure a lot of the world's problems. It sure as shit felt like it could help with a lot of mine.

And that was why I shouldn't be surprised that when I eventually and very reluctantly dragged myself away from her (only because I was worried she'd think I was weird for holding on to her for so long), I wanted to kiss her.

Sounded stupid, but it wasn't sexually motivated.

I'd be lying if I said that I wasn't hard by that point, because like I already mentioned, Halle was a freaking smokeshow. But my need to kiss her was deeper than just wanting to fuck her. It was like there was a connection. An understanding. Like we were two lost souls coming together.

I was starting to sound like an idiot. All I can say is that I didn't know how to put it into words, but it felt... *different.*

Good different.

So when our kiss was interrupted by that cry for help, I was pissed. But maybe that happened for a reason.

Kissing Halle wouldn't have been right. I didn't want to lead her on. I couldn't drag her into my bullshit. And I had nothing to offer her. I didn't even have a roof over my head.

That was the reason I left. Well, that and the fact that I'd been too honest about how important I believed it was to live in the moment. I knew that didn't align with my actions and I didn't want Halle to ask questions that would be hard to explain without freaking her out. So I'd come back to my room, which was the right decision.

Yeah. It was definitely for the best.

I needed to keep my distance and stop things from getting complicated.

But something told me that even if I didn't see her, it wouldn't stop me thinking about her.

26

HALLE

'Yay! Santa Monica!' I cheered as we got off the coach. 'This is one of the places I wanted to visit.'

'What d'you wanna see here?' Jake said.

'Everything! The beach, the pier and I'd love to go on the Pacific Wheel.' I pointed to the Ferris wheel in the distance and watched the cute red and yellow gondola-style cabins rotating.

Just last night after our group activity, which was a couples quiz night on the beach, playing games like This or That, Two Truths and a Lie and Never Have I Ever, I'd thought about asking Sammie if we'd be coming here.

The activity was fun and I'd learnt some interesting things about Jake, like the fact that he didn't lose his virginity until he was twenty (I'd assumed that because he was in the band and had girls throwing themselves at him, it would've been younger).

'Cool. Let's make it happen.' He pulled his cap down.

'Are you okay with that? If you think too many people will hassle you, we don't have to.'

'It's okay, don't worry about it.'

Suddenly I felt bad. After seeing how uncomfortable he was

at the observatory when that guy wanted photos and learning more about what happened to him, I didn't want to put him in a difficult situation.

Although he was kind of 'in disguise', if someone was really looking, I was sure they'd still recognise him.

'Does the whole cap and sunglasses thing actually work?'

'Mostly. Sometimes it might make me stand out more, but it's all I've got right now.'

'If you feel uncomfortable, let me know and we can hide somewhere.'

'Yeah?' His eyebrows shot up in surprise. 'Thanks, but you've been looking forward to this, so I'm not gonna ruin it. Let's go.'

When we went to the Pacific Wheel, the queue was too long, so we headed to the arcade, then went for a walk on the beach.

Thankfully, by the time we came back, the queue was shorter.

'You having a good time?' Jake asked.

'The best! You?'

'Same.' Jake moved closer, reached down then gently circled the back of my hand with his thumb.

Warmth flooded my body.

God, that felt so good.

I got the feeling that if there weren't so many people around, he'd hold my hand properly. I was gutted because I desperately wanted him to, but I understood why he couldn't do that in public. And it was better if he didn't. The last thing I wanted was to be splashed across the gossip sites.

My stomach twisted. This whole situation was messy. I knew I shouldn't like Jake, but I craved his touch. I hadn't been able to stop thinking about that almost kiss we'd had on the beach yesterday or that hug. Being so close to him was amazing and I wanted to feel that closeness again.

But we had to be sensible.

There'd be no touching or anything else in public.

It was too risky. And foolish.

'Ready?' Jake asked once we were in our seats. 'I know you're not a fan of heights – you sure you'll be okay?'

'They're not my favourite, but I'll be fine.'

As we climbed higher and everything beneath us got smaller, I tried to relax.

'Great views,' I said, attempting to focus on the pretty Californian coastline and not the fact that I overheard someone in another gondola excitedly shouting out the fact that we were over a hundred feet off the ground.

'Would it be cheesy to say that I prefer the view in this carriage?' The corner of Jake's mouth tipped up.

'Kind of,' I laughed.

'But what kind of cheese level we talkin'? Like mozzarella or full-on Stilton?'

'Maybe something mild like Parmesan.'

'Awesome. I love Parmesan.' He grinned and took off his sunglasses.

'Well, then, you're good!'

'If I'm being honest, I don't care if I sound as corny as a crate of stinky blue cheese because the truth is, I'm becoming borderline obsessed with looking at you. It's kinda worrying, but seeing you smile is my new favourite hobby.' He brushed a loose strand of hair away from my face. 'Does it make you uncomfortable? If it does, tell me.'

I swallowed hard.

He was obsessed with looking at me?

Bloody hell. I had no idea. I mean, I'd caught him looking at me a few times and obviously there was the stuff that almost happened on the beach yesterday, but I didn't think he liked me that much.

'No, it doesn't make me uncomfortable.' I removed my sunglasses too. 'I'm flattered. And I'd feel bad to stand in the way of your new hobby, so if you're obsessed with looking at me, maybe you shouldn't stop...'

Our eyes locked and suddenly the Santa Monica views I'd been so interested in a few minutes ago faded into the distance. Right now, the only thing that I could think about was Jake.

His face inched closer.

'Thanks for your understanding.' He flashed a warm smile and champagne bubbles popped in my stomach. 'But what if I tell you that I've *also* become obsessed with wondering how your lips taste and how it'd feel to kiss you? What would your advice be then?'

Tingles erupted between my legs. And if my vagina could talk, right now it'd be chanting *do it, do it, dooo it!*

I'd like to say that I ignored it and that my common sense took over, but what can I say? I must've left my logic back in my hotel room.

'The only way to cure your obsession of wondering what it'd be like to kiss me would be to actually do it. That way *all* your questions would be answered.'

'That sounds like excellent advice, Dr Halle.' We both moved in closer. 'And when would you recommend that I do that?'

'Now? We're up here and everyone else on this ride is probably focused on the scenery rather than us, so there's no time like the present, right?'

Before I had a chance to say anything else, Jake closed the gap between us and gently brushed his lips against mine.

My breath hitched. I couldn't believe we were finally kissing.

He'd barely touched me and I already felt like I'd been set on fire.

Jake kissed me softly, pulled away, then looked me in the eyes as if he was checking that I was sure I wanted him to continue.

To make sure he knew it was okay, I pressed my mouth on his. He reciprocated, and although he deepened the kiss, somehow it was still soft and curious, like he was savouring the taste of me.

I parted my lips, willing him to slide his tongue inside, which he did right on cue. As his tongue flicked against mine, electricity rocketed through my veins.

For what felt like the first time in years, I wanted to take things further.

I was so wet for Jake right now.

I wanted to touch him.

I wanted him to touch me.

And this time, I didn't mean hand-holding.

I wanted more.

Just as I was wondering if it'd be okay to slide my hand under his T-shirt, he slowly pulled away.

'Fuck. I want to kiss you,' he whispered. 'So badly.'

'But you just did?' I panted.

'Oh, baby, that wasn't a real kiss,' he chuckled. 'When I do it for real, you'll feel the difference. Trust me.'

Holy crap.

If he could scramble my brain and make me wet just from that and he didn't consider that a proper kiss, God help me when he did it *for real*.

If my logic was with me right now, it'd say that I should consider myself lucky that we'd stopped because we both knew that this was a very bad idea.

But like I'd said, common sense was locked away in my hotel room.

I was past the point of caring.

I liked Jake. *A lot.*

And even though I knew it couldn't go anywhere, the devil was dancing on my shoulder, willing me to live a little. To let down my guard and enjoy myself for a change without worrying about all of the things that could go wrong.

So instead of thinking I should slam on the brakes, the only thought racing through my mind right now was what Jake had just said.

He'd said that when he kissed me for real I'd feel the difference.

I didn't doubt him, but now all I wanted to know was how long I'd have to wait to find out...

27

HALLE

'So, I'll see you at dinner?' Jake said as we got off the coach.

I paused.

It was now or never.

When we'd got off the Pacific Wheel, Jake had put his glasses back on, but despite that I still knew he was looking at me, a lot, because I was doing the same.

The pull between us was magnetic.

After surviving for years without sleeping with a man, suddenly all I wanted to do was feel Jake between my legs.

I didn't just want him to kiss me for real. I wanted him to fuck me too.

But I was scared.

I was still scarred from what happened to me before.

And now that we were back at the hotel, my common sense was slowly creeping back and it was battling with my growing desire.

Whilst it agreed that it was time to sleep with another man, it was telling me that Jake wasn't the best choice.

It was advising me to go with someone less sexually active.

Not a guy who'd probably had sex with more women than the population of a small country.

It was warning me that I was on the verge of making a big mistake.

But the whole point of coming here was to push myself out of my comfort zone, right? And if I asked him to my room, I'd be making big progress.

'Unless...' *Come on, Halle, you can do it.* 'You want to come back to my room?' I swallowed the lump of concrete in my throat.

'Sure,' Jake's eyes widened, 'but only if *you're* sure?'

'I am,' I said, hoping that I would be by the time we got there. 'Okay.'

Jake followed me down the path and as I reached into my bag to get my keycard, my hand trembled. I couldn't believe I was about to do this.

I opened the door and we stepped inside.

'Nice room,' Jake said.

'Isn't it the same as yours?'

'The layout is different.'

'Cool,' I said, standing awkwardly in front of him. 'Shall we sit on the bed? Should I take my clothes off? Sorry, I haven't done this in a while.'

'Let's just sit and talk.' Jake took my hand and sat down at the edge of the mattress. 'I can tell you're tense. We don't have to do anything, okay?'

'Okay.' My shoulders loosened.

I was surprised. I thought that as soon as we got in my room our clothes would go flying in the air, like in a sexy film scene.

And given Jake's reputation, I assumed that by now he'd be shoving me up against the wall and whipping out his dick. But I should've realised by now that the Jake I'd read about in the media wasn't the Jake I'd gotten to know and like a lot this past week.

'If it helps, it's been a while for me too,' Jake said.

My eyes flew so far out of my sockets they could've landed on the moon.

'Really?' My brows furrowed. 'What do you classify as "a while" though. A week?'

'Very funny.' Jake rolled his eyes. 'No. I haven't been keeping count, but if I had to guess it'd be over a year.'

My jaw dropped. That did surprise me.

'Oh,' I said. 'Well, I win. It's been... let's just say a lot longer than that.'

'That surprises me,' he said, still holding my hand. 'I thought a woman like you would be inundated with offers.'

'Yeah. Sometimes I can't leave the house because the queue of men begging to get in my knickers is so long,' I deadpanned. 'And let's not even talk about Valentine's Day. I have to hire my own depot and delivery team to cope with the mountain of cards, flowers and chocolates I get sent.'

'Well, I'd happily queue up for you. I don't believe in the whole Valentine's Day BS – I think that if you love someone, you should make them feel special every day. But if you like flowers and chocolates, that could be arranged. You're special, Halle. You deserve the world. And don't let anyone tell you different.'

I stared at Jake, stunned at his words. I knew from the look in his eyes that he meant what he said. It wasn't just rubbish to get his wicked way with me.

And weirdly, knowing that he'd be happy just to get up and leave the room without fucking me if I asked him to made me want him even more.

'Kiss me,' I said, edging closer.

'Sure?'

'Yes.'

Jake leant forward and before I even had a chance to catch my breath, his lips collided with mine.

Bloody hell. He was right. This kiss really was different to the one on the Ferris wheel. It was hot, hungry, wild and urgent. Like this was the last thing he'd get to do before the world burned down and he needed to make it count.

As he slid his tongue inside my mouth, I moaned.

Fuck. This felt amazing.

I grabbed the back of his head and pushed my breasts into his chest.

Jake deepened the kiss and his hands wandered up my thighs.

As his warm hands made contact with my skin, I bucked against him.

'Shit,' he growled into my mouth.

Just when I wasn't sure the sensations pulsing through my body could get any better, Jake started trailing kisses down my neck. I fell back onto the bed, unable to stay upright a second longer, then pulled Jake on top of me.

He straddled me and feeling his hard cock pressed between my legs made me groan like a wild animal.

Jake leant forward and peppered more kisses along my collarbone, then down to my chest.

'Is it okay if I...' He touched my bra and dress straps.

'Yes,' I panted.

He moved them down slowly, then reached behind my back. I lifted up a little to give him access and seconds later he'd unclipped my bra.

Jake rolled my dress down further, took off my bra and tossed it on the floor.

'Holy shit,' he said. 'You're a fucking goddess. Can I?'

'Yes,' I said. I liked that he kept asking permission. Most guys just...

I didn't even get the chance to finish my train of thought because Jake took my nipple in his mouth and my brain short-circuited.

As he licked, sucked and lavished it with his talented tongue, I almost lost my mind.

I bucked against him, then gripped his arse, pushing him deeper into me. I needed more friction. More of everything.

I needed to do this quickly, before I changed my mind.

'I want you,' I whimpered.

Jake's head whipped up.

'Sure?'

'Yes,' I said. 'Do you mind if I take this off?' I gripped the top of his shorts.

'No, I don't mind. Go ahead.'

I tugged at them, expecting just his shorts to come down, but I did it with such haste that his boxer shorts rolled down too, causing his dick to spring free.

Jesus.

He was fucking huge.

'W-wow,' I gulped. 'You're... um. Can that actually... how do you even...? Sorry. I'm just... surprised.'

'We'll take it slow.' He stroked my face as I still tried to work out how the hell he walked around with a weapon like that in his pants. Yeah, when he was pressed against me, I knew he felt big, but there was big and then there was *B.I.G.*

'Can I take off your panties?' he asked.

'Yeah.'

Jake slid my dress and knickers down my legs before tossing them on the floor to join my bra.

I took in the sight of him. Sculpted chest and abs, plus the perfect washboard stomach that belonged on the cover of *Men's Fitness* magazine.

And his giant cock.

He was the most beautiful man I'd ever seen and I was about to have sex with him.

This was...

Terrifying.

As Jake edged forward and the reality of what was about to happen hit me, I froze.

'I can't.' I bolted up, my heart leaping into my throat. My body temperature rose and my chest tightened. 'I'm sorry.'

I jumped off the bed, raced into the bathroom and slammed the door behind me.

28

JAKE

What the hell just happened?

As I watched Halle sprint inside the bathroom and lock the door, my chest tightened.

What did I do?

Did I move too fast?

Did she feel pressured?

No. That couldn't be right. I checked in every step of the way to make sure she was happy.

She seemed a little freaked out by the size of my cock, but it couldn't be that either, right?

Maybe she just changed her mind, which was totally fine, it was her choice. I knew she'd said it'd been a long time for her, so maybe she wasn't ready. That was why I wanted to take my time, make sure she was warmed up properly so that I satisfied her, but it was her that suggested we get straight down to business, so I didn't understand.

I got dressed, jumped off the bed then started pacing across the room.

Something wasn't right.

The more I thought about it, the more I was convinced that it wasn't just about Halle changing her mind. There was a hint of something in her eyes.

I could be wrong, but she looked kind of terrified.

'Halle.' I knocked on the door. 'Are you okay?'

'Not really,' she said softly. 'I'm sorry I messed you around.'

'There's nothing to apologise for. It's okay to change your mind – at any point. I just wanna make sure that you're okay.'

'I just... I wanted to. I really did. But I couldn't.'

'Were you worried that I'd hurt you?' I sucked in a breath, waiting for her response. I really hoped that wasn't the case.

'No. It's not about you. It's about... I was scared. It's a long story.'

'Wanna come out here and talk about it? I'm a good listener. At least that's what my imaginary friend used to tell me when I was a kid!'

A soft laugh echoed from behind the door.

That was a good sign.

I heard footsteps then the sound of the door being unlocked. I stood back, to give Halle room as she stepped outside.

'Come sit,' I said, this time leading her to the sofa. I wanted to reassure her that sex was off the table, so the bed didn't seem appropriate.

She followed me then sat down in silence.

I didn't pressure her to talk, instead I just waited until she felt ready.

'I haven't slept with anyone in years because... because of the way my ex betrayed me. And what he... gave to me.' Halle's gaze dropped to the floor.

'What did he give you?' I asked, my heart hammering in my chest.

'He...' She took a deep breath. 'That's how I found out he

cheated, because he gave me... a sexually transmitted disease. Well, more than one. He gave me crabs and... chlamydia.'

'Motherfucker,' I said, grinding my jaw. 'Halle. I'm so sorry.'

'Yeah.' Her shoulders slumped. 'It was pretty traumatising. I was sitting on white sheets one morning and suddenly saw what looked like a little insect crawling in the bed. I was horrified. But then I saw another. And another...'

'Shit.'

'I hated creepy crawlies at the best of times so to realise that I literally had an infestation of them in my... sorry. You don't need to know the details. Anyway, I went straight to the sexual health clinic and got tested and something to treat it.'

'What did that asshole say when you confronted him?'

'When I mentioned it, first he said it was nothing to do with him. That I'd got them because I wasn't clean enough. I felt so ashamed. But when I double-checked the leaflets the clinic had given me, it said it had nothing to do with that. So when I told him that it couldn't have been down to me, he said he'd shared someone's towel by mistake on tour and must've caught it from there.'

'What a dick.'

'At first I gave him the benefit of the doubt. But when the clinic called to say that I also had chlamydia, then I knew for sure, because that can only be sexually transmitted. And I hadn't slept with anyone except Brett since my last check-up, so I knew it was him. I was so angry and this time when I confronted him I went mad.'

'Good for you.'

'He denied it at first but then owned up. He said it was unrealistic and selfish of me to expect him to stay faithful when there were so many women that wanted him. He said any man would do the same. That he was only human and it was best if we broke up because it couldn't work long term. "We're going in different directions," he'd said. "I'm a big star now and I need someone who understands the business. Who moves in the same circles. And that's never gonna be you."'

'You're fucking kidding?' Anger bubbled in my veins.

'Nope. He didn't even apologise.'

'The guy's a jerk. You're better off without him.'

'I know. It didn't feel like it at the time, but in a strange way I'm glad that he gave me crabs, otherwise I might not have got checked out and I wouldn't have known about the chlamydia. Most of the time the doctor said there are no visible symptoms. And if it goes undetected it can make you infertile.'

'That's fucked up.' I clenched my fist. If I saw that guy right now, I'd knock him out for what he did to Halle. I knew he was bad news, but I didn't realise he was that reckless. Everyone understood how important it was to wrap your dick up.

'Yeah. So because of that I've found it hard to trust. To date. To get intimate with someone again. I seize up. I worry if they're going to give me something. Yeah, a condom protects against most things, but not everything and even though it happened years ago, it still makes me feel dirty and ashamed. I feel like if a guy finds out, he won't want to touch me, I mean, Brett never went down on me because he thought I wasn't clean enough, and that was *before* he gave me those diseases, so what man would want me now?'

'Halle.' I took her hands in mine. 'I'm sorry that he did this to you and damaged your confidence. But the right man will know that what happened to you was in the past and it wasn't your fault. And he'll be grateful for the opportunity to be with you.'

'Thanks, but you don't have to just say that to make me feel better.'

'It's the truth. You got treated, so although I understand that the psychological wounds might still feel raw, anyone with half a brain would know they have nothing to fear from being with you. Don't let his selfish actions stop you from enjoying being intimate again. As long as you're safe, you'll be fine.'

She nodded.

'You're right. You *are* a good listener. Do you want to try again? Or has this conversation put you off? Telling someone about your past STIs is hardly sexy.' She winced.

'Wanna know the truth?'

'Please. Even if it hurts, the truth is a million times better than a bunch of lies.'

Hearing that made my stomach twist because I hadn't been honest about why I was here. I *would* tell her though. Not because of what she just said, but because it was the right thing to do. Especially after what she'd been through. But not now. One battle at a time.

'You think that telling me about your past would deter me, but it actually makes me like you more.'

'Seriously?'

'Yep. Because it takes guts to tell the truth. Especially when it's not pretty. I'm not glad that you had to go through that, but I'm glad that you felt safe enough to tell me about it. A lot of people wouldn't bother. Hell, some people know they have STIs and don't give a shit. They sleep with people anyway. That's why I always wear a condom.'

'Good.'

'I know I have a reputation and it's true that I screwed around a lot in the past, but I always wrapped up and got tested regularly. And as for whether I want to try again, *hell, yeah*. If I had the chance, I'd spread you out on that bed right now and not just to fuck you with my dick. I'd happily eat your pussy like it was my first meal in weeks.'

Halle's eyes bulged and her lips parted which made my cock twitch. Her ex might not have appreciated the amazing woman he had, but I was ready to worship Halle's body like she deserved.

'But not right now,' I added. 'You need time to really think about whether you're ready. Especially because...' I paused, knowing she wasn't gonna like what I was about to say. 'Because I can't make any promises about what will happen after we leave. Like I told you, my life's in the crapper right now, so I can't offer you a relationship.'

'Wait, what?' Halle's jaw dropped and her forehead creased.

'I said I'm not looking for a relationship.' Silence filled the air and I was desperate to fill it. 'I know it's a shitty thing to say, considering this is the whole point of being here, but it's complicated...'

Halle's mouth was still wide open and I could tell she was trying to process what I'd just said.

'I know it's probably a shock so...' I didn't know what to say. There was no way to elaborate without telling Halle everything, which would freak her out. But the least I could do was be clear about what I *could* offer and see whether that'd be enough. 'I like you. And I'd like to spend more time with you. With or without sex. Although, truthfully, I'd love to have sex with you, because you're fine as hell.'

'Th-thanks,' she stuttered.

Yep. She was still in shock. I had to say something to make it better. I should focus on the positives, right? Glass half full, not half empty.

'I know it's not what you're looking for but maybe not getting into something long term doesn't have to be a bad thing? Without sounding cocky, I know that I can show you how great it feels to sleep with a real man. So maybe you could use me. Y'know, to get back into your sexual groove again.'

I stopped talking and waited for her reaction. I probably sounded like a douche saying she could 'use me' like I wouldn't get pleasure from it too.

But what I'd said was true. I couldn't have a relationship. So that was all I could offer. I didn't want anything in return. I sure as shit wasn't gonna use her to help my situation. If it gave her more confidence, that was enough for me.

Any minute now she was gonna laugh in my face and tell me she didn't need my 'help'. Instead she said nothing. It was better I gave her some space.

'I'm gonna head to my room to shower and get ready for tonight,' I said. 'You good, or you want me to stay?'

'No.' She looked up at me briefly before dropping her gaze to the floor. 'Thanks for being honest.'

My chest tightened again. Yes, I was honest, but I hadn't told her the whole truth and I really should.

I'd do it.

Later.

Soon.

Just not right now.

29

HALLE

SOS! If you're not working or shagging, please call!

I tossed my phone on the bed and crossed my fingers that Vanessa was able to reply. It was just after 7 p.m. here so it'd be after ten in New York. And although it was a Friday night, Vanessa could still be at the office or hooking up.

Although I didn't want to interrupt her night, I really needed to talk to her.

Ever since Jake had left my room an hour ago, my head had been spinning faster than a washing machine.

My phone screen lit up and I quickly accepted the call.

'Thank God!' I answered.

'What's up, babe?'

'I almost had sex with Jake,' I blurted out.

Really, I should've started with the bombshell he'd dropped about not being at the hotel for love, but I was still trying to get my head around that part.

Baby steps.

'To quote Lizzo: It's About Damn Time!' she shouted. 'Wait. Did you say *almost*?'

'Yeah.' I filled Vanessa in on our almost kiss on the beach, the first kiss on the Pacific Wheel and what happened when we got to my room. 'And then I told him about what Brett gave me...'

'Wanker. I would've chopped his dick off. What did Jake say?'

I still couldn't believe I'd told him everything. It'd brought back all of the painful memories and shame, but Jake's reaction reminded me that I had no reason to feel embarrassed.

'He was really kind. He said it didn't change anything.'

'Too right. It'd only be relevant if you were still infected.'

'I know. I just... it's more the worry that it'll happen again. But I'm so tempted. He's an amazing kisser and his dick is fucking huge.'

'I knew it!' she shouted. 'You can just tell by looking at him.'

'What? How?' I scoffed. 'It's not like he walks around with a permanent boner or a metre stick with an arrow that says "this is how long my cock is"!'

'He just gives off that big dick energy, y'know? Whenever I've seen him in interviews or performing, everything about him screams, *I've got a whopper in my pants and I know exactly how to use it!*' Vanessa laughed.

'He *is* very confident and I get the feeling he'd know what he was doing. The things he said to me were downright filthy!'

'Spill!' she said excitedly.

'After we'd finished talking, I'd asked if he wanted to try again, and he said that if he had the chance, he'd spread me out on the bed not just to fuck me with his dick. He said he'd eat my pussy like it was his first meal in weeks!'

'No! If a guy like him said that to me, I'd spread my legs wider than a gymnast doing the splits. He wouldn't need to tell me twice! Why the hell didn't you jump on that shit?'

'He said now wasn't the time. That I should think about whether I really wanted to do it: especially because...' I paused. I still couldn't believe what he'd told me. 'Because he's not looking for a relationship.'

'Wait, *what*?' Vanessa shouted, echoing the words that had flown out of my mouth when I heard his revelation. 'Why the hell's he at a matchmaking hotel if he doesn't want one? That makes no sense.'

'Exactly,' I sighed.

'And it's not as if he would've come there for a hook-up. All he'd need to do is click his fingers and a swarm of women would come running. I don't get it.'

'That makes two of us. All he said was that his life was in the crapper right now and that it was complicated. I thought about pushing him to elaborate, but I could tell he didn't want to. And if someone tells you something, believe them, right?'

'Right.'

'So if he said he can't do a relationship, it didn't make sense to beg him, y'know?'

'I hear you.'

'It's just frustrating. I came here to find love. That was the whole point. When I saw it was Jake, I thought he wasn't right for me. I'd wished I could've been set up with anyone but him. But now, just when I discovered that I may have judged him too quickly and I *am* interested, he tells me he doesn't want something long term. It's fucked up.'

'Shit. Sorry, babe.'

'And the worst thing is, that maybe if I told Sammie he wasn't here for a relationship, that might be grounds for finding me someone else. But for some stupid reason, I don't want another match. I'm enjoying my time with Jake. And I *want* to sleep with him. I know it'd be amazing. But if I did it, it'd be purely casual. And I don't know if I can do that. I don't want to get hurt again. Aaargh! I'm so confused!'

'It's a tricky one.' There was a long silence. I could hear the wheels in Vanessa's head turning. Eventually, she spoke. 'Wanna know what I think?'

'Course I do!'

'I think you should just go for it.'

'Yeah?'

'Yeah. I know given your history, you don't buy into the whole celebrity bullshit, but you and I both know that you had posters of Jake on your bedroom wall. How often do you get the chance to fuck your teenage celebrity crush? It's literally a once-in-a-life-time opportunity.'

'Maybe.'

'And as well as being fit as fuck, from what you've told me, he actually seems like a caring guy. So if you're nervous about sleeping with someone again, he'd be a good choice. He'll be patient which is what you need. Thirdly, the guy said he wants to feast on your pussy. You already know how selfish some men can be, so if a man like him is offering to give you a tongue bath, jump on that shit.'

'A *tongue bath*?' I laughed.

'What? That's what it is!'

'Well, he did say that if I wanted to use him to get back into the swing of things, he'd be happy to help.'

'Awww, what a saint!' I could tell Vanessa was rolling her eyes. 'I'm sure it's not a hardship to get his dick wet. Anyway, doesn't matter. I think you should.'

'Part of me agrees. But the other part reminds me that I'm here for a relationship, not a hook-up.'

'I know, hon, but it is what it is, right? And seeing as a relationship's off the table and you don't want to ask for a rematch and if you did there's no guarantee that you'd even get one or a refund, you might as well make the most of your investment.'

'Paying a few grand for a shag is a hefty investment.'

Not just financially, but emotionally too. Jake seemed honest and trustworthy. But if that was true, then why was he here if it wasn't for love?

Then again, he could've just strung me along and pretended he wanted more. At least he'd been upfront, which had to count for something, right?

'Some things are worth paying for!' Vanessa cackled. 'Think of yourself as the female equivalent of Richard Gere in *Pretty Woman*. Jake's given you permission to use him as your personal prostitute, so if I was you, I'd accept his offer. And if you shag him as much as you can, the money you shelled out won't hurt as much when you divide up the cost per orgasm. It'll be money well spent.'

'We'll see,' I said, thinking what she said actually made some sense.

I *did* feel comfortable around Jake and I was attracted to him. It was just hard not to think about the consequences and all of the things that could go wrong.

'Hon, I've gotta go, but think about it, yeah? And I'm sure I don't have to remind you, but if you do anything, be careful.'

'Don't worry. If we do anything, I'll ask him to wear *three* condoms.'

'Funny! And if you're worried about the crabs thing, maybe cover your fanny with a plastic bag with a peep hole in it for his dick, so nothing gets transferred to your bush.'

'Not funny.'

'Sorry! I couldn't resist. Sometimes if you don't laugh about things you'll cry.'

'Yeah. Anyway, thanks. I'll keep you posted. Where you off to tonight?'

'Just heading to a bar downtown.'

'Okay, have fun.'

'You too! Happy shagging!' She let out a loud laugh before hanging up.

The thought of actually having sex with Jake caused ripples of desire to shoot through my body.

I'd never been into casual sex before, but maybe this was different.

I was going into this with my eyes wide open. I knew that it wouldn't last. It was just an experience that I could enjoy.

Something to talk about when I was old and reflecting on my youth. Like Vanessa said, it wasn't every day I got a chance to sleep with my teenage crush.

Plus, let's face it, I rarely did anything exciting these days, so maybe Vanessa was right again when she'd said I should grab this opportunity to live my life.

Maybe there didn't always have to be a permanent goal when dating.

Maybe sometimes just having fun and living in the moment was enough.

And maybe it was time to find out...

30

HALLE

Wow.

As I took in the surroundings, my jaw dropped.

Sammie had organised a movie night on the hotel's beach and it looked amazing.

The screen that had been set up was huge, but that was only one of several things that caught my eye. Instead of chairs, there was an arrangement of daybeds in a semi-circle, with white opaque privacy curtains, white and gold cushions and blankets.

I also spotted a popcorn machine, a chef flipping burgers on a BBQ and a pop-up beach bar, so if we needed snacks, we didn't have to head all the way back to the main hotel building.

'What d'you think?' Sammie appeared beside me.

'It looks incredible! Definitely beats the sticky floors and the seats at my local cinema which always have questionable stains.'

'Gross,' Sammie said. 'There's nothing sticky on these beds. They're thoroughly cleaned after each use because we know sometimes people can get a little *frisky*, hence the curtains.' She winked.

'Oh.' My cheeks heated as naughty thoughts flooded my mind. 'Good to know.'

'Speaking of getting frisky, how's things with Jake? You two seemed to be getting on *very* well at the pier...' She grinned.

Did she know that we kissed? I wouldn't put it past her. Sammie seemed to have a sixth sense for these things.

'Yeah. He's... I like him.'

'I *knew* it!' Sammie squealed. 'Although I'm with the man of my dreams, even I can see that Jake has got a lot going for him, so it'd be hard not to, right?'

'True.' I was about to go into the whole thing about him not wanting a relationship, but I was tired of overanalysing it. I was just going to try and go with the flow.

'Speak of the devil,' Sammie said.

When I turned around, I saw Jake walking towards us.

Bloody hell.

How did he look even more gorgeous than when I saw him two hours ago?

His tanned skin glowed, his hazel eyes sparkled and his hair was damp and wavy from his shower.

And don't even get me started on his body. He was wearing a black shirt which had the top few buttons undone, giving me a glorious glimpse of his chest. And the sleeves were rolled up to the elbows.

Jesus.

His forearms had no business looking that good.

My gaze dropped to his black shorts and then zeroed in on his crotch. I couldn't believe that I'd had him naked on my bed, his enormous cock inches away from being buried inside me, and I'd run away.

I'd done a lot of stupid things in my life, but that was definitely ranking near the top right now.

I wouldn't be making that mistake again.

'Hey.' As he leant down his gorgeous scent surrounded me and when he kissed me on my cheek, shockwaves raced through every part of me.

'Hi,' I smiled, fighting the urge to giggle like a teenage girl who'd just been kissed by her crush.

'You two are adorbs!' Sammie said. 'The film will start in an hour. In the meantime, there's burgers and hot dogs being served at the BBQ so help yourself and don't forget to grab a tray and load up on cocktails, popcorn and snacks for the film. You're on bed number three.'

'Cool, thanks,' Jake said.

'I'll leave you two to it!' Sammie grinned. Once she was out of earshot, Jake turned to me.

'You good?' he asked.

'I'm great, actually. Thanks for earlier. I'm feeling much better.'

'Glad to hear it. Wanna grab a bite to eat? I'm starving.'

* * *

An hour later we were on our daybed with a tray of snacks fit for royalty. The Love Hotel really knew how to pull out the stops.

As *Pretty Woman* appeared on the screen, everyone cheered, whilst I wondered whether the universe had been listening to my conversation with Vanessa and was trying to send me a message to go for it with Jake.

'Classic,' I said. 'Have you seen it?'

'Yep,' Jake said.

'Funnily enough, I was just talking about this film to my best friend,' I whispered, conscious that I didn't want to disturb anyone.

'Yeah? What were you saying?'

'I was just telling her about...' I paused. Maybe mentioning what Vanessa had said about me being the female version of Richard Gere, using Jake for my pleasure, wasn't a good idea. I was sure he'd be cool about it considering he offered to help me get back in the saddle, but I decided against it, 'just how we'd seen some of the places on the tour the other day,' I said, which was partly true.

Jake propped himself up on his elbow and looked into my eyes with such intensity he could probably see the cogs in my brain turning.

'So did you think about what I said earlier, about putting me to use? I could be the male equivalent of Julia Roberts. Although I can't give you a relationship, at least I could make your investment worth your while.'

That was exactly what Vanessa and I had said.

'I did think about it.'

'And?'

'And I'd like to try. But can we take it slow? I'm still nervous.'

'We can go as slow as you want.' He stroked my cheek. 'Just let me know when you're ready.'

'I'm ready,' I answered quickly.

'Halle!' he whisper-shouted, then clutched his chest in mock-shock. 'Are you telling me you want me to fuck you here on this bed with all these people around us? It's true what they say about the quiet ones!'

Jake laughed and I pushed the elbow he was leaning on, so he fell flat on the bed.

'Hey!' he said. 'You'll have to pay for that!'

He sat up, pulled the curtains round at the front, so there was just a thin slit showing the screen, then climbed on top of me, pinning my hands up by the side of my head.

I swallowed hard and goosebumps erupted across my skin.

'I didn't mean...'

'Don't worry. I'm not going to get my dick out here. No matter how much I know you want to beg me to,' he teased. 'You said you wanted to take things slowly, which is exactly what we're gonna do. There's a lot of things we can do without full intercourse. What do you say we start with a kiss?'

I nodded quickly.

Jake crushed his lips onto mine and I whimpered.

God. He was such a good kisser. Our mouths moved in perfect harmony and when he slid his tongue inside and flicked it against mine, I felt like I'd just been catapulted straight to heaven.

'Can I touch you?' he asked.

'Yes.'

'Let me get a blanket.' He reached across the bed, unfolded the blanket then covered me with it, placing it just below my neck.

My heart thudded against my chest. I was desperate to know where he was going to touch me first.

Jake slid his hand underneath the blanket, trailing it from the back of my knees, upwards, and as it dipped between my thighs and his fingertips skimmed my clit, my stomach somersaulted and my horny vagina tingled with anticipation. I bucked against his hand, craving more.

'Fuck, you're so wet. Can I feel you, properly?'

'Yes,' I panted.

Jake's fingers moved underneath my knickers and as they made contact with my bare clit, I threw my head back and bit my tongue, fighting the urge to cry out.

Hell yeah.

That was *exactly* where I wanted him to touch me.

'Jesus, that feels incredible,' I said as he started circling my clit. He lifted his fingers away and out of the blanket and I almost wept. 'What are you doing?' I protested, still being careful not to raise my voice too much.

'I needed to taste you,' he said before sliding his wet fingers in his mouth and licking them clean. 'Knew it,' he declared.

'Knew what?' I said, struggling for breath.

'I knew you'd taste fucking delicious. I can't wait to feast on you properly,' he whispered in my ear. 'But for now, unless you have any objections, I'm gonna fuck you with my fingers and give you your first orgasm of the night.'

I was already soaked for him, but hearing that made a dam burst in my knickers.

He was confident, but something told me he had the skills to back it up.

'Do it,' I said.

'Good girl,' Jake said. I'd always cringed when I read that saying in books, but right now hearing those words felt so hot. 'The film is great, but we've both seen it already and I promise you, you'll enjoy this performance a lot more.'

Jake slid his hand back under the blanket.

'Lift up.' He tugged at my dress. 'I'm about to make you even wetter, and seeing as you have to walk out of this place later, it's better if your dress doesn't get soaked too.'

I did as he said and he pushed my dress up around my waist. After he'd moved my knickers to the side, Jake started circling my clit again and as my body melted against his hand, revelling in the sensations, he slid two fingers inside me.

A loud moan flew from my mouth before I had the chance to stop it. Thankfully it came just as something louder happened on the screen so hopefully no one noticed.

'You feel so good, baby.'

As Jake continued fucking me with his fingers, hitting spots I didn't even know existed, I swear my eyes rolled into the back of my head and my body felt like it'd been set on fire.

He couldn't have been doing this for more than a few minutes and I already felt like I was on the verge of coming. How was that even possible?

Holy shit.

For some reason, whenever I thought about fingering, I had visions of my first boyfriend, fumbling around in my knickers in my bedroom after college when my parents were at work. But this was light years away from those amateur experiences.

Jake was lavishing my clit with attention whilst simultaneously moving his fingers inside me so skilfully, I wondered if he'd been tutored by a sex guru.

And he was definitely making sure he lived up to his rockstar status, because he was playing my body like a fucking master musician.

When Jake slid a third finger inside me and circled my clit harder and faster, I knew I wouldn't last.

'Oh, God, yes,' I panted. 'I'm... I'm, I can't hold on.'

'Come for me, Halle,' he whispered in my ear and the sensation of his sweet warm breath on my neck brought me even closer to the edge.

Jake curled his fingers inside me and I felt the wave building and building and...

'Oh, fuck!' I brought my hand up to my mouth just in time.

As my orgasm detonated, I bit down on my hand to stifle what I was certain would've been a feral scream.

My chest was heaving and my head was spinning. Eventually I removed my hand from my mouth. I'd bitten down on it so hard I wouldn't be surprised if I'd drawn blood.

'You good?' Jake said as he slowly slid his fingers out.

'More than good,' I replied, struggling to catch my breath.

'So, just to be clear, you came for real, right? This wasn't a *When Harry Met Sally* situation, because I'm pretty sure you told me that women were great at faking it and a man wouldn't know.'

My eyes flicked open and when I looked at Jake he had a devilish smile on his face.

'I'm pretty sure you *know* that I came for real.' I rolled my eyes.

'Yep,' he smirked. 'I felt it with my own fingers.' He waved them in the air triumphantly. They were drenched and I could see that he took that as a badge of honour. And just like he'd done before, he brought them to his mouth, poked out his tongue and licked every finger clean like he'd just finished devouring a box of southern fried chicken.

If the man could make me come like that just with his hand, imagine the things that he could do with his dick and his tongue.

And as much as I wanted to watch one of my favourite romcoms on the beach under the stars, now that my desire had been awoken after so long, I was desperate to skip the film and drag Jake to my room so that I could find out if it would be as amazing as I'd pictured it...

31

JAKE

If I didn't believe I had self-control before, I sure as shit believed I did now.

I was lying on the daybed next to Halle and I'd managed to sit through the rest of the film without coming in my pants.

My dick was harder than steel and was straining against my shorts so much I was surprised it hadn't punched a hole in them.

Halle had kindly offered to *help me out* with the situation (there was no way she wasn't gonna notice my boner considering the tent that formed when I tried to cover it with the blanket).

But as tempting as the offer was, I didn't want the first time I came with Halle to be from her jerking me off. I wanted to be inside her.

Declining her offer was risky because there was no guarantee that she'd even let me fuck her. And it was understandable after the trauma that asshole put her through. But I just needed to have faith and believe that she could tell that I was different.

I really hoped that she did, because after feeling how good it was to fuck her with my fingers, I couldn't wait to do it for real.

And her taste.

Jesus.

I wasn't sure what I wanted to do more. Bury my tongue or dick between her legs.

With any luck she'd let me do both.

Halle had asked if I wanted to go to her room and although I knew my cock would hate me for it, I asked if she was sure she didn't want to stay and watch the rest the movie.

She'd only hesitated for a second before saying she wanted to leave, but a second was too long. I had to make sure that she felt completely relaxed. And she'd said she wanted to take things slow, so I reassured her that we'd still have time to continue what we'd started later.

Judging by how quickly I demolished candy bars that were in reaching distance, I'd always thought that I had zero willpower. But turns out, I'd found some self-control after all.

I slid my arm around Halle's back and when she rested her head on my shoulder, I swear my heart doubled in size.

As the credits rolled, my heart thumped against my chest.

'Shall we go?' Halle bolted up.

'Only if you're sure?'

'You know earlier you made that joke about me asking you to fuck me here with everyone around us?'

'Sure,' I nodded.

'Well, if I don't get you in my room in the next fifteen minutes, I might end up asking you to do that.'

'Fuck, Halle,' I winced.

'What? Have you changed your mind?' she frowned.

'Hell, no! It's just that I was trying to get my boner to go down so I could leave this bed without drawing attention to my crotch, but you saying that has only made it harder. Pun totally *not* intended.' I laughed.

'Sorry, not sorry,' she grinned. 'It's dark. If we make a run for it, I'm sure no one will notice.'

'We should thank Sammie though, right?' I looked over and saw her chatting to a couple and a bunch of other guests were approaching her.

'She looks busy. And Sammie's cool. I'm sure she'd be *very* happy to know that we were sneaking off to enjoy some quality time together.'

'I was right what I said about the quiet ones. You're a bad influence!'

'Thanks for the compliment! Come on.' Halle took my hand and dragged me off the daybed. 'Let's run before you take someone's eye out with your cock!'

Halle and I sprinted down the beach holding hands and laughing like a couple of kids on the run after being caught with their hands in the cookie jar.

I loved how whenever I was with Halle I felt so free and alive.

'I think we're alone now!' She stopped and attempted to catch her breath.

'We are. Still a way to go to your room though.'

'Ugh, you're right. I wanted to save all my energy for... other things.'

'Lucky for you, I've got enough energy for the both of us.'

I scooped Halle up in my arms.

'What are you doing?' she laughed.

'Carrying you.'

'You can't!'

'Why not?'

'Because... it's at least another ten-minute walk and you'll break your arms!'

'I can run it in less than five.'

'I warn you now, if you break your back and try to sue me, all you'll win is my old DVD player and a load of *Sex and the City* and *Gossip Girl* box sets. That's the most valuable things I have to my name.'

'I'll take my chances. The quicker we get you back to your room, the quicker I can give you another orgasm.'

'Well, when you put it like that...' she chuckled.

I ran to her room in just a few minutes. It was amazing what I could achieve with the right incentive.

Halle had giggled the whole way like a kid and the sound of her laughter was like a balm to my soul.

I loved how good she felt in my arms, with her body pressed against mine.

When I lowered her down to the ground, she had a grin the size of the Pacific Ocean across her face.

'My hero,' she swooned. 'You and your beefy arms saved the day yet again. I'm supposed to be a strong, independent woman, not someone who keeps needing a man to rescue her when she falls off her horse or is too unfit to run back to her room. I should get back into running like I used to.'

'You can still be a strong, independent woman and let a man help you out once in a while though, right?'

'Yeah, I know,' she said as she reached into her handbag for her keycard, opened the door then stepped inside. 'I mean, I'm perfectly capable of giving myself orgasms, but as I discovered earlier, it's actually pretty amazing when a man who knows what he's doing gives them to you instead...'

A satisfied smile touched my lips.

'I haven't even got started yet. Wait until you see what I can *really* do.'

'That's big talk,' she said. 'You sure you can back it up?'

'Why don't you invite me in and let me show you?'

Without saying another word, Halle opened the door wider. I

stepped inside, closed the door behind me then stood in front of her.

'First, I'm gonna kiss you, then I'm gonna take you to bed. But anytime you want me to stop, just say, okay?'

'Okay,' she said.

I cupped her face with my hands then crushed my lips onto hers.

And this time I didn't hold back.

The kiss was hungry and urgent.

I wanted Halle.

No. I *needed* her so much that it felt like my survival was dependent on her mouth being pressed onto mine.

In this moment, nothing was holding us back. I didn't have to worry about photos, social media and all the other bullshit with my agent. Halle said she wanted me, so my only mission right now was to satisfy her.

I carried her to the bed, laid her down then gently eased her back.

'I'm gonna take off your panties, okay?' I growled.

'Yes,' she panted. After pushing her dress up around her waist, I leant forward, gripped the top of her panties with my teeth, then started dragging them down.

As my nose skimmed her pussy, I inhaled and squeezed my eyes shut.

Fuck me.

Her scent alone made my dick thicken. I couldn't wait to taste her.

'I love how wet you still are for me, baby,' I said. Her panties were soaked. I continued dragging the flimsy fabric down her legs, past her ankles, then tossed it on the floor. 'Jesus,' I said as I took in the sight of her laid bare in front of me. 'So fucking beautiful. Spread your legs for me. Nice and wide.'

I pulled Halle down to the edge of the bed, dropped to my knees, buried my head between her legs, then took a long, slow lick.

'Oh, God!' she cried out, her hips jerking up off the bed.

'I need you to stay still, sweetheart.' I lifted my head. 'I'm trying to eat here.' I smiled mischievously before continuing to feast on her.

As I licked and sucked her delicious clit, I felt myself getting harder. Halle tasted even better than I'd imagined. Fuck dining at Michelin-starred restaurants like I used to. This right here was the best damn meal I'd ever tasted.

Halle gripped the back of my head and pushed my face deeper into her.

'God, that feels too good. I don't think I can hang on,' she panted, writhing beneath me.

I loved the way her body responded to my tongue. I didn't want to stop eating her out, but I was desperate to put my cock inside her.

But first I had to make good on my promise. She said she was close to the edge, so I was gonna make damn sure I tipped her over it.

I picked up the pace, lapping deeper, teasing my tongue over her. Halle's breath shuddered.

'Jesus, Jake!' she cried out. 'I c-can't. It's too... you're too good, I...'

I continued licking, flicking and sucking, revelling in the knowledge that every stroke of my tongue was sending her one step closer to coming apart.

Her hips arched up and she gripped the sheets before calling out my name again.

Halle started trembling and seconds later, she exploded, screaming so loud that it pierced my eardrums. I wasn't gonna lie. Knowing that I'd made her come so hard made me feel like a fucking sex god.

Tonight I'd made her come twice: once with my hands, then with my mouth.

And now my cock was ready to go for the hattrick.

32

HALLE

Oh.

My.

God.

I slowly opened my eyes then squinted. Although I could see Jake's head was buried between my legs, I was still convinced that I was dreaming.

I thought the orgasm he gave me on the beach with his hands was incredible, but that? *That* was what fantasies were made of.

The man ate me out like a chocoholic devouring a velvety rich triple chocolate cake topped with Oreos, chocolate chip cookie dough ice cream *and* rich chocolate sprinkles.

And it was clear from the way he licked me over and over again so enthusiastically, he enjoyed every single second of it.

After years spent with a man who treated me like a leper and refused to go down on me (but of course he had no problem with me sucking his smelly dick), it was earth-shattering to have a man devour my pussy with such gusto.

I've never come so hard before in my life.

Agreeing to have some fun with Jake instead of overthinking

things like I normally did was definitely the right decision. Even if it all ended right now, I'd be happy to relive that experience over and over again in my mind for eternity.

Jake lifted his head up from between my legs, looked me in the eyes, then licked his lips.

'Good?' he asked.

'*Good*?' I panted, still struggling to catch my breath. 'We both know that was more than just *good*.'

A satisfied grin broke out on his face.

'A man should never assume, am I right?'

'I know I dazzled you with my acting skills during that role-play, but not even an Oscar-winning actress could fake the orgasm I just had. I'm pretty sure everyone heard me scream your name in New York.'

Jake chuckled.

'Only in New York? How about you let me see if I can make you scream so they can hear you in London?'

'Sounds like my kind of challenge!' I smiled. 'But first, I want to return the favour,' I said as I attempted to sit up, which wasn't easy, considering I still felt like I was floating on a cloud.

'Thanks for the offer, but tonight's all about giving *you* pleasure.' He stood up. 'But if you really want to make me happy, please let me fuck you.'

'Permission granted,' I said, reaching forward and placing my hands on the side of his shorts. 'Now I need permission to remove your clothes.'

'Be my guest,' he said.

As I took in the sight of his erection straining against the fabric, I swallowed hard. When we'd tried earlier I was overcome with fear and 'what ifs'. Now the only emotion pulsing through my veins was pure desire.

I tugged his shorts and slowly pulled them down along with his boxers.

His cock sprang free like a jack bursting from its box and I marvelled at the delicious sight before wrapping my fingers around it then sliding my hand up and down his long, thick hard length.

He was already leaking pre-cum and knowing that I'd got him so excited sent a fresh wave of tingles racing through me.

'Oh, fuck,' he groaned. 'Halle, baby. Please. I'm already hanging by a thread here. I won't last if you do that. It feels too damn good. Let me get a condom. I need to be inside you.'

'Okay.'

He reached down to his shorts, pulled out his wallet then took out a condom.

'Wanna do the honours?' he asked. 'Actually, scrap that. I'll do it. If I feel your hand on my cock again, I might embarrass myself by coming too quickly.'

He ripped the packet, rolled it on then straddled me.

'You good?' he asked.

'Yes. Please. Fuck me.'

'Want me to take it slow?' he asked as he removed my dress and bra then tossed them both on the floor.

'No. Don't hold back.'

Jake's eyes turned to charcoal.

'Yes, ma'am!'

He lined his cock up at my entrance, then slammed into me.

'Oh, God!' I cried out. For a millisecond I thought I'd made a mistake by telling him not to hold back but as he stretched me open and pounded into me, over and over again, my whole body pulsed with arousal and the need for more.

Yeah, it was painful at first because it'd been a while, but once I'd adjusted to his size, my God it felt amazing.

Every thrust, every pump sent a fresh bolt of electricity up my spine.

I wrapped my legs around his back, pushing him deeper into me.

As we rocked together in perfect harmony I was overcome with ecstasy.

This was how sex was supposed to feel.

This was the sex I heard people talking about but always thought they'd exaggerated because I'd never dreamt it was possible.

But now that I knew that it was, I regretted all of those wasted years that I'd settled for mediocre shags.

How had I gone so long without feeling this?

'Put your legs up on my shoulders baby, I wanna go deeper.'

I did as he asked and...

Ohhhh... yes.

Right there.

I looked up at Jake and as my eyes raked over him from his beautiful face, down to his broad shoulders, muscular chest, toned six pack right down to watching as his cock slid in and out of me, I couldn't believe my luck.

The man whose photo I'd had on my bedroom wall was buried inside me. Fucking me hard. Never mind a fantasy. This was beyond my wildest dreams.

As Jake started circling my clit, I knew it was game over.

'Oh, fuck,' I cried out. 'Yes, don't stop!'

He picked up the pace, pounding into me harder, faster, deeper, all whilst lavishing my clit with attention.

I felt the wave building. No. It wasn't a wave: it was a tsunami.

I wasn't ready for this to end yet. Just a few more minutes was all I was asking for...

Too late.

My orgasm ripped through me, sending shockwaves shooting up from my toes, then zipping through my bloodstream before rocketing up to my brain.

My mind went fuzzy, my body trembled and I swear my eyes rolled back into my head. If someone told me I'd died, floated to heaven before being transported back to this bed and brought back to life, I'd believe them.

I squeezed my eyes shut and just like Jake had predicted I screamed his name so loud that they *definitely* heard me in London. Maybe in outer space too.

I should feel bad for whoever was in the room next door and had to listen to me shrieking like a wild animal, but this felt so fucking good I didn't give a shit who I'd disturbed.

Sorry, definitely not sorry.

'Jaaaakkkkeee!' I cried out again, before my body stilled.

Jake thrust into me several times before a feral groan flew from his lips and he exploded inside me.

He collapsed on top of me, our chests slick with sweat, our bodies heaving.

'Fuck,' he said. 'That was incredible.' He tilted his head up and kissed me. As I tasted myself on my lips, I pictured him going down on me again. I'd never get tired of replaying that moment. Or the vision of him slamming in and out of me.

'It really was.'

'So I'm vindicated now, right?'

'Vindicated? Why?'

'Come on.' He rolled his eyes. 'On our first full day here, you said that you'd had a lot of practice with faking it. And I told you that if you slept with me you wouldn't need to. Remember?'

'Yes, I remember.'

'So was I right, or was I right?'

'You were right,' I sighed. 'Ever heard of this thing called humbleness?'

'Of course I've heard of it. I'm a genius!' he joked.

'Yeah, a very arrogant one! But credit where credit's due. You have a very talented dick and I thought that mouth was only good for singing like an angel. Turns out that it's good for other things too.'

'Baby, I might sing like an angel, but I fuck like a devil. Don't get it twisted. There's nothing innocent about the things I want to do to you.'

'Tell me,' I said, as molten desire pulsed between my legs.

'I think you'll like it much better if I show you...'

33

JAKE

As I watched Halle sleeping beside me, I smiled. I couldn't remember the last time I'd felt so good.

Yeah, I usually got a kick out of having sex. The adrenaline rush and the high I got from coming was one of the simplest but most satisfying pleasures in life.

But sex with Halle hit different.

When we first fucked, I thought it just felt good because it'd been such a long time since I'd done it.

But when we did it a second time and it was even better, I knew it couldn't be that. Then I'd convinced myself that it was because knowing that I was the one she'd chosen to be the first guy to help her experience pleasure again since her break-up made me feel like some kind of sex hero.

Except when we went to shower and ended up banging against the wall in front of the bathroom mirror, I realised that it was just because it was *her*.

There was something different about Halle. Something that drew me to her.

Full disclosure: watching her tits bounce in the mirror, seeing my cock slide in and out of her and the expression on her face when she screamed my name again definitely played a part in how fucking amazing I felt. But without sounding big-headed, Halle wasn't the first woman to call out my name. But she was the first that made me feel... like *this*.

I didn't know what *this* sensation was, but it didn't matter. Whatever it was I'd take it.

I leant down and kissed the top of Halle's head. She smelt of strawberries and coconut. And I'm not even ashamed to admit that I used an extra dollop of her shower gel, shampoo and conditioner, so that if I didn't get to spend time with her later today, I could still smell her sweet scent on me.

Damn. I sounded obsessed.

'Morning.' Her eyes opened slowly.

'Morning, beautiful. How'd you sleep?'

'Like a log,' she said. 'I'm exhausted.'

'Great sex will do that to you.'

'So I'm discovering!' A wide smile spread across her face.

'You ain't felt nothing yet, baby,' I grinned.

'Oh, really?'

'Yep.'

My cell buzzed on the bedside table. I picked it up, quickly glanced at the screen then groaned before dropping it on the bed.

'What's wrong?' Halle said.

'Nothing.'

'Come on, tell me. I can see you're worried about something. What happened?'

'It's my agent.' I blew out a frustrated breath.

'Why are you upset to hear from her? Maybe she's got some good news.'

'Pff,' I scoffed. 'Doubt it. I know why she's messaging.'

'Why?' Halle pressed.

She seemed genuinely concerned and I didn't like that she was worrying about me. I guessed I could tell her without going into specifics.

'She's been hassling me about posting photos... of you.'

Halle's eyes popped.

I thought she looked worried about my wellbeing before, but the expression on her face right now was pure panic.

My chest tightened. I hated that I'd made her anxious. Maybe I shouldn't have mentioned anything at all.

'Don't worry.' I took her hand in mine and gave it a gentle squeeze. 'I'm not gonna do it.'

'Why does she want you to post photos of *me*?'

'She thinks it'll help to...'

I paused. I didn't wanna lie to Halle, but if I told her that my agent wanted me to post photos so that I could get an offer to do a reality show with Halle to help revive my career, she'd run for the hills.

Halle was already borderline freaking out when I just mentioned posting a picture and I really, really liked her. I didn't wanna upset or scare her off.

'She thinks I need to show a different side to my life. The public's perception of me is trash. When they hear the name Jake Myers, they either think about that fucking BUTT-RRR commercial or me hooking up with different women. I'm trying to show that I'm moving on. *Growing*.'

'Is that why you came to the hotel?' she asked.

Sweat pooled on my forehead. This was a difficult conversation. Halle had been lied to before and I knew it took a lot to get her to a place where she not only felt comfortable talking and interacting with another guy, especially one in the public eye, but also trusting me enough for us to sleep together. If I told her the whole truth, she wouldn't trust me or maybe anyone else again.

I'd already been upfront and told her that this couldn't be anything serious and obviously, I had no intention of plastering her all over social media, which meant the reality TV show and all of that other bullshit wasn't even a consideration. So now that I thought about it, it didn't make sense to blow everything up between us unnecessarily by talking about something that was irrelevant.

The important thing was that I'd been honest about not wanting a relationship. I hadn't led her on. And I'd respected her privacy by not posting photos with her without permission.

No. It was better that she didn't know the full story. For her own protection. Once we left the hotel she would've had a good time and could go back to New York with more confidence and the knowledge that not all men, including has-been musicians like me, were total dicks.

'Kinda,' I replied. 'If I'm honest, I *did* tell my agent that I didn't think it was a good idea for me to come here, given that I wasn't looking for something serious.' That was definitely true. 'But she told me that...'

Shit. Maybe if I told Halle that Wilma said I'd be matched with someone else in the public eye it might make Halle think that I was disappointed about being paired up with her.

Obviously for work purposes and the whole objective of me being here that was true. But now I was glad that we'd been set up. That was selfish though, because Halle had come here expecting to find her perfect guy.

Fuck.

This was so damn messy. If I ever got back on my feet, I'd refund Halle for every cent she'd paid to come here. That wouldn't compensate her for the time she'd wasted or for crushing her romantic dreams though, so the only way I could make up for that would be to show her the best damn time here.

Right then and there I vowed to fulfil every sexual desire Halle ever had, to worship her body and to give her the best holiday of her life. It probably wouldn't ease my guilt, but hopefully it'd make her happy.

'My agent said that it'd be good for me.'

'Maybe she thought that once you got here and met an amazing woman, you'd change your mind about not wanting to be in a relationship,' Halle said. 'Y'know, sometimes people say they don't want something serious but then they fall in love. Happens all the time in romcoms. Maybe she's hoping that by the end of your stay, you'll be so loved up, you'll end up getting engaged!' she laughed.

My stomach dropped like a stone.

Halle had no idea how accurate her joke was.

No, Wilma wasn't expecting me to fall in love. But she *was* expecting me to go through with some fake engagement bullshit.

'Maybe.' I forced a smile.

'Oh...' Halle's face fell. 'Sorry! I was joking. I hope you don't think that I was trying to say that I want you to change your mind about what this is. I know it's just sex. You were honest about that from the start and I appreciate that. I'd be lying if I said that I wasn't... y'know, a bit disappointed. I mean, I came here for love. A relationship. I was hoping for the whole fairytale experience.'

'I'm sorry.' My chest tightened. 'I feel really shitty about that.'

'I've accepted it. I'm trying to just go with the flow for a change. And after being with so many guys that lie about their intentions, it's kind of refreshing to find someone who's upfront. You told me where you stand so I'm not gonna stalk you or start demanding that you call when we leave. I'm fine with our arrangement. More than fine. How can I not be with all the orgasms you've given me!'

'Glad I could be of service.' I flashed a small smile.

'In fact, to prove how fine I am with it, I'm gonna return the favour.' She sat up in the bed and propped a pillow behind her. 'You can post a photo with me.'

'Wait, what?' A puzzled expression spread across my face as I tried to process her offer. 'Hell, no.' I shook my head so vigorously I was surprised it didn't fall off. 'It'd make you uncomfortable. I couldn't ask you to do that. I know what you've been through. I'm not gonna expose you. No fucking way.'

'I appreciate you looking out for me, but you wouldn't be *exposing* me. I'm nervous, but it's time. Plus, this wouldn't be like before. *I'd* choose which photo you'd post. Knowing I had that control would make a big difference to me because I didn't have that before. And I already know which picture it'd be.'

'Which one?' I asked, curious but still shocked she'd even suggested it.

'The one of us horse riding where our backs are to the camera. No one could see my face and I'm wearing a helmet so my hair is covered. If you post that picture, it'd get your agent off your back and my identity would be protected. It's a win-win.'

I paused for a second. It *wasn't* a bad idea, but I still felt shitty about putting Halle in the spotlight. Then again, she was right. If no one knew it was her then maybe it'd be fine?

'I'm not sure...' I rubbed my jaw. 'Maybe it'd help temporarily, but what'd happen if she asks for more photos?'

'Then we'll take more. But none that show my face or too much of my body. I could even wear a wig. No one would know. Then we could enjoy our time here and when I leave, no one would be hunting me down because they wouldn't know what I looked like.'

'That might work,' I said, still surprised that she'd really do all that for me.

'I'd choose the photos though and if I didn't like them, you'd have to agree not to post them. Okay?'

'Okay...' I frowned. 'But what if there are comments that are shitty?'

'I'm not on social media so I won't see them. And anyway, if they don't see my face, body or any identifying features, what are they going to criticise? My hat? I can live with that.'

Good point.

'Maybe we should take some time to think about it. So I know that you're really sure. You could still be in some sort of post-orgasm haze. I need to know that you're making a decision with a clear head,' I insisted.

'Honestly, I'm *fine*! I'm tired of overthinking stuff. If I'd had too long to think about us hooking up, I never would've done it and I would've missed out on five mind-blowing orgasms. *Imagine!* That would've been a travesty. My poor pussy would never have forgiven me!'

She laughed and the sweet sound made my chest inflate.

'Look, I came here to find my Mr Right and although we're not gonna sail off into the sunset together and live happily ever after, I'm realising that doesn't have to mean that the holiday is a disaster. Life can't always be perfect. Sometimes it doesn't have to be all about finding Mr Right. Sometimes having a fun experience with Mr Right *Now* is enough.'

'I like your thinking,' I nodded.

'I know, right? Look at me sounding all mature and wise and shit! All joking aside, it's true though. I also came here to push myself out of my comfort zone and I feel like I've been doing that. I've ridden a horse, for God's sake! I've started taking photos again and allowing myself to be in them, which is a big deal for me. *And* I've had a reckless one-night stand – something I never thought I'd do. So why not continue my crazy streak by going totally wild and allowing you to post a photo of me on Instagram!' She laughed again.

'Okay. Thank you. I really appreciate you helping me out. We'll do it later,' I said, not wanting to interrupt our morning by posting. I'd rather spend that time with her.

'You're welcome.'

The fact that Halle offered to do this for me meant a lot. There weren't many people who'd try to help me out – especially if it was something that involved a personal sacrifice.

I could thank her a thousand times, but it'd be better if I showed her.

'To demonstrate my appreciation, I'd like to go down on you. Unless you have any objections?'

My cell buzzed again, making us both jump.

Halle picked it up before I got the chance to get to it.

'Yikes!' Her eyes bulged and my stomach tensed. My messages were previewed on the home screen so Halle would be able to read at least the first few lines of whatever had been sent. And if it was who I thought it was, it'd be bad news. 'I'm guessing Wilma's your agent, right?'

'Yeah...' I said, even more worried about what she'd seen.

'Well, Wilma needs to work on her bedside manner and be more polite.'

'What did she say?'

'She said, and I quote: "What the fuck are you playing at? Post the fucking photo of your match unless you want me to come down to the hotel and cut your fucking dick off!" I guess she really wants you to post a photo!' Halle laughed before handing me the phone.

I exhaled, relieved that Wilma hadn't said anything more incriminating.

'Yeah.'

'Well, after experiencing the pleasure your dick brings, I cannot in good conscience allow her to destroy it. So if I hadn't already decided to let you post a photo before, that definitely would've changed my mind. Jake Myers's dick must be protected at all costs!' she chuckled.

'Thank you. My dick appreciates your concern for its wellbeing!' I laughed and my shoulders loosened.

'So go on then, do it. Let's get Wilma the evil dick slayer off your back.'

'Sure?'

'Yes!'

I could tell she was tired of me asking and double-checking but I didn't care. I had to be sure, because something told me that once I posted this photo, even without her showing her face, there was a chance that there was no going back.

'And you know that if I post this, it might not be as easy and straightforward as you think? If someone really wants to find you, they can.'

'Maybe. But it's unlikely. All the guests signed NDAs so they're not allowed to reveal our identities and once we leave this place, we'll never see each other again, so there'll be no story for anyone to pursue and no more photos, so people will lose interest pretty quickly. It'll be fine. Find the photo of us on the horses, add it to your Instagram account images selection, then give me your phone.'

I did as she asked.

Halle selected the image, then wrote something quick in the caption.

'What d'you write?'

'I thought it was best to keep it simple so I went with "admiring the views" and a love-heart emoji. Okay with that?'

'I am if you are.'

'Great!' she said as she pressed the 'post' button. 'Done! Now Wilma will be happy and you can be more relaxed too.'

'Thanks, Halle, that really means a lot. If Wilma's happy and I'm happy, it's only right that *you* get to enjoy some happiness too, am I right?'

'You are.'

'So, how about me showing my gratitude by eating your sweet pussy for breakfast?'

'If you insist, I suppose I could let you,' she mock sighed, then laughed.

As I slipped under the bedsheet, dipped my head between her legs and tasted her, I let out a contented sigh.

Halle had said earlier that she'd pushed herself out of her comfort zone by having a reckless one-night stand with me.

But as I licked her slowly from her entrance to her clit, I knew that one night with her would never be enough.

I wanted to devour her every single day as often as possible whilst we were here.

Now I just had to hope that Halle agreed to let me...

34

HALLE

The doorbell rang just as I was seconds away from having my sixth orgasm in the last twenty-four hours.

Wait. Maybe it was the seventh? Might've even been the eighth. I'd lost count. I wondered if there was an entry in the Guinness World Records book for most orgasms delivered by one man in a day? If so, Jake should seriously consider entering.

He was so dedicated to showing me a good time with his tongue that when the doorbell rang a second time, Jake still didn't flinch. He continued licking me with gusto. And I was totally here for it.

I squeezed my eyes shut again and pushed his head deeper.

'Halle?' a voice boomed from the door. 'Are you okay?'

My eyes flicked open. That sounded like Sammie.

I wanted to cry out that I was *more* than okay and ask if she wouldn't mind returning once I'd finished coming, but when she knocked and called out again, I noticed the concern in her voice and didn't want her to worry.

And I definitely didn't want her to call housekeeping and risk them opening the door to see Jake's head between my thighs.

'Y-yeah!' I called out, trying to catch my breath.

'Oh, thank God!' she replied. 'I've been calling you because you missed the briefing and you were due to check out of your rooms two hours ago so I wanted to make sure you were okay.'

Check out? Two hours ago?

Jake's head bolted up. Clearly he was as surprised as I was about Sammie's announcement.

I reached for my phone.

'Shit! It's almost two o'clock!' I whispered.

I was about to say that I didn't know how that had happened, but we'd been up half of the night shagging. Then when we woke up after ten, Jake told me about his agent hassling him.

Once I'd posted the photo, he'd gone down on me before going another round. We'd showered, come back to bed then we must've fallen asleep. And when we woke up about fifteen minutes ago, Jake had very kindly offered to eat me out again and I was raised to have manners, so it would've been rude to refuse.

I had no idea it was so late though.

'Hold on,' I called out. 'I should speak to her,' I whispered to Jake. He nodded, gave me one last long, slow lick, then sat up.

I jumped off the bed, dragging on a dressing gown and tying it tightly before heading to the front door.

'Hi,' I said. 'Sorry. I didn't know it was so late. What do you mean we have to check out? We're here for another week?'

She smirked and I saw her eyes trail upwards to my hair. It was probably a mess and I got the feeling from the look she gave me that she knew exactly why we'd missed the briefing.

'Don't worry! We're not kicking you out. Once you've been here a week, we transfer couples to a luxury villa to help you get to know each other better. Although something tells me you've already checked that box...' She flashed a knowing smile. 'I couldn't reach Jake either. Have you heard from him?' Sammie raised her eyebrow.

Yep. She definitely knew.

Jake had also put his phone on silent once we'd done the Instagram post.

I turned back to the bed and saw him sitting there in his boxers. Fuck, he was hot. I gave him a look that I hoped said: *shall we fess up?* When he nodded, I turned back to Sammie.

'Jake's here.' I opened the door wider so Sammie could see and when she caught sight of him, her eyes bulged.

'Ohhhh... I had a feeling...' She grinned. 'But I had to make sure, y'know. Just in case you hadn't attacked each other or something!'

'We're all good,' Jake said as he walked to the door.

'So I see!' Sammie smirked. 'When you're ready, come to reception and I'll take you to your villa.'

Sammie rubbed her chin a few times as she looked at Jake, then grinned.

Strange.

'Thanks. We'll be quick,' Jake said.

'I'm sure Halle would prefer if you weren't!' Sammie cackled and walked off. 'I'll stall housekeeping for you, don't worry!' she called out.

Jake and I laughed then closed the door.

When I turned to face him, my eyes popped.

'Shit!'

'What?' Jake frowned.

'Whilst Sammie was talking to us, she kept rubbing her chin. I thought it was strange, but now I understand why.' I shook my head.

'Why?'

'Because you've got my juices all over your chin!'

'You're kidding?'

'Nope.'

'I thought I licked everything off! Oh, well,' he shrugged. 'It's a badge of honour. If you haven't already figured it out, I'm not ashamed to say that I'm addicted to eating your pussy, so sue me.'

'Sounds like something you should wear on a T-shirt!' I joked.

'*Proud Pussy Eater*,' he grinned. 'Has a nice ring to it!'

We both burst out laughing.

'Come on. We better get packing. Looks like we're moving in together!'

* * *

As Sammie waved goodbye and we closed the door to our brand-new luxury villa, I let out a squeal.

'This place is incredible!' I jumped up and down like an excited child. I thought the room I was staying in before was fancy, but this was on a whole different level.

The villa had a huge open-plan living room with a plush white sofa and massive TV screen. The neutral décor looked like it was straight out of a minimalist interiors magazine.

There were two bedrooms, but the master bedroom was insane. It had a four-poster bed, complete with translucent white curtains and gorgeous white and gold cushions.

There was a bathroom with a ginormous walk-in shower and we had a plush kitchen too.

But the outdoor area was even more mind-blowing. As well as having our own small pool, there was a hot tub outside the bedroom patio and a large daybed.

Wow.

'I guess this is all pretty standard for you,' I said, remembering that Jake was famous and probably stayed at places like this all the time.

'Not really,' Jake said as he sat down on the sofa. I sat next to him and OMG, it felt like I was sitting on a cloud. 'At the height of my fame I stayed in a lot of nice places and yeah, my house was pretty special too, but it's been a while since I stayed anywhere like this.'

'Why's that?'

'Because...' He looked at me, then his gaze dropped to the floor. 'I'm broke, Halle. Not just broke like down to my last thousand bucks. I mean, barely have a cent to my name kind of broke.'

Shock rolled through me. I mean, I knew he wasn't as famous as he used to be, and he'd mentioned his accountant screwed him over, but I kind of assumed he meant he 'only' had a few hundred thousand in the bank rather than millions. Y'know, like first-world, rich people problems.

'I'm so sorry.' I took his hands in mine. 'I had no idea. If you don't mind me asking, what happened? You've had loads of hit songs, so I thought you'd be okay?'

'My biggest hits were with the band and when we signed those contracts we were young and naïve so I never made much from that. As for the money I made from my solo stuff, my accountant screwed me over. I trusted him so didn't keep a close enough eye on him and not only did he steal from me for years, he didn't file my taxes properly so a few years ago I got stung with a huge tax bill that almost wiped me out and then... then some other stuff happened that I had to pay for which finished me off.'

'Can't you remortgage your house or something to free up some cash?'

'Had to sell my home to pay my debts.'

'Shit. So are you renting now?'

'Nope.' He blew out a defeated breath. 'Before I came here, I was crashing on my best friend's couch. His wife wants me to move out though, so I've no idea where I'll go after I leave this place.'

Wow.

I blinked repeatedly as I tried to take everything in.

'Jake.' I squeezed his hand. 'That's awful. I'm really sorry. It seems so unfair. You've worked your arse off since you were a teenager and now...' I paused, worried about making him feel worse about the situation.

'And now I have nothing to show for it,' he said.

'I wasn't going to say that. I... all I meant was, for everything you've done and achieved, it's not right that you're in this situation. But don't you get royalties or something every time your song is played?'

'Yeah, but no one really plays my songs any more. Or so my agent tells me. And anything I do earn goes straight to paying my debts.' He exhaled again. 'Fuck. Why the hell am I telling you this? We were having a good time and now I've made everything heavy. Why don't we test out that bed? Looks pretty nice, huh?'

'No,' I said firmly, looking him deep in his eyes. 'Just because we agreed that this isn't a relationship, doesn't meant that we can't talk about serious stuff. I know we haven't known each other long, but I like you. I care about you. I want to know that you'll be okay when you leave here. I don't know anyone in LA that you could stay with, but I can ask my best friend Vanessa if she does and...'

'It's okay.' Jake squeezed my hand. 'I really appreciate you looking out for me, but I'll be fine. I shouldn't have brought it up. It's kinda depressing. I'm gonna go for a walk on the beach. Clear my head.' He got up, then kissed me softly on the forehead. 'Do me a favour though, please.'

'Course.'

'When I get back, can we pretend we didn't have this conversation? My life has been pretty shitty lately and, well, this past week with you has been awesome and I know it's not the responsible thing to do, but I just wanna stay in this happy bubble a little longer and have fun before I have to face up to reality again, okay?'

'Okay.'

'Thanks.' He kissed me again, this time on the lips, sending a zing shooting up my spine. 'I'll catch up with you later.'

As I watched him leave, my stomach sank. I felt for him, so much. I wished there was something I could do to help.

Just as I was racking my brain, my phone buzzed. It was a notification that I'd had a missed call from Vanessa. I dialled her straight back.

'Hey!' I said.

'Thought you should know that Jake posted a photo of you on his Insta. Sorry, Hal,' she sighed. 'If it helps, no one will know it's you because your back's to the camera and everyone's talking about the great view and how intrigued they are to know who the mystery lady is, but anyway, I thought you should know.'

'It's okay!' I said, thinking how sweet it was for Vanessa to call to tell me. She always had my back. '*I* was actually the one who posted it on his Instagram.'

'What?' she shouted. 'But why?'

'His agent's been hassling him to share more content and to post about me. Thinks it'll help his image if he's seen to be more serious or some shit like that. And after what he did for me, I wanted to do something to help him out.'

'What, you mean, after he saved you falling off the horse?'

'No...' I paused, getting up to close the small gap in the patio doors, just in case, because I knew there'd be a lot of screaming and excitement once I spilled the beans. 'Because he gave me more than six orgasms!'

'Say whaaaaatttt?' As predicted, Vanessa screamed down the phone. The loud, screeching sound was more ear-piercing than the cries of a hundred newborn babies, so I quickly held it away from my ears. 'Oh my God! You fucked him? When? How? Where? Tell me *everything* immediately!'

I filled her in on the epic fingering on the daybed, then told her all about the sex and how he'd gone down on me multiple times. And I threw in the fact that Sammie caught him with my juices on his chin which of course she thought was hilarious.

'I am *so* fucking happy for you! You deserve this! A man with a big dick who not only knows how to use it but is also obsessed with eating you out is the dream hook-up!'

'Right? I can't even believe this is happening!'

'You better believe it, sweetie! And lap it up, pardon the pun! I know you wanted to find your happily-ever-after, but sometimes it's not that deep. Sometimes getting multiple happy endings is all a girl needs to put a smile on her face!'

'Yeah. That's what I told myself. I'm happy to have a Mr *Right Now*. I still have time to find my Mr Right. And I really feel like this will be good for me. Jake has shown me that not all guys are arseholes. He's been really open and honest about a lot of personal stuff with me. That's refreshing.'

Although Vanessa was my bestie, I didn't feel right sharing the things that Jake had told me about his personal situation. He'd confided in me and I didn't want to betray his trust.

'It really is. Too many men are too afraid or closed up to talk about anything related to their feelings.'

'Exactly. And the whole going down on me thing was pretty

great too. It's like he did it not just because he enjoyed it and was determined to make me happy, but also because he wanted me to understand that I *am* desirable and worthy and that I shouldn't feel ashamed about what happened before with he-who-won't-be-named.'

'That's good, because he's right. That arsehole refusing to eat you out wasn't a *you* problem. That was a selfish prick problem.'

'Right. And Jake definitely isn't selfish in the bedroom. I asked him multiple times to let me return the favour, but he kept saying that he wanted to give *me* pleasure and watching me come and having the opportunity to fuck me was enough.'

'*Damn.* That is *gold*. This man's a walking, talking, *fucking* green flag. Shame he doesn't want anything serious.'

'Yeah...' My voice trailed off.

Never mind keeping count of the orgasms. If I had a dollar for every time my mind had drifted, thinking about how great it would be if Jake and I were together for real, I'd have enough money to cover at least his first month's rent on an apartment.

But there was no way I could confess to that.

As much as Vanessa loved me, she'd think I was being an idiot. It hadn't even been twenty-four hours since I'd slept with Jake, so my mind was racing forward way too fast.

And most importantly, we'd agreed that this was casual. Jake was very clear on what he could offer, and I'd said I was fine with it. I couldn't start asking to move the goalposts just because we'd had an amazing time together.

Honestly, a few orgasms and my brain turned to mush.

To be fair, it was probably because I hadn't had sex for a long time.

Either way, it didn't mean I could get carried away. I had to get a grip.

'So where is Mr Downtown now?'

'Mr Downton? As in *Downton Abbey*?' I frowned.

'No! "Downtown" as in that nineties song by a group called SWV. You're probably too young to know it. My older sister used to play it a lot and I thought it was about downtown, like the American for going into the city. Little did I know it was all about oral sex!'

'I'll have to check it out!' I said, making a mental note of it. Although I hadn't been uploading my daily playlist songs since Jake told me how triggering they were for him, I had been keeping a note of them, so that if that changed, I could share them with him. It was also interesting to see how my feelings for him had changed over the past week. I didn't see it at first, but now I realised the playlist idea was genius. 'He's gone for a walk on the beach.'

'Cool. So what's the plan for today?'

'Not sure. I'm happy to just chill at our new villa.' I told Vanessa all about how fancy it was.

'If I was staying in a place like that, they'd have to carry me out of there! It sounds like you're living your best life right now, hon!'

'I really am! Anyway, enough about me, what's new with you?'

'Nada. Just been working non-stop on a big case. Hopefully I'll get to blow off some steam later.'

'Sounds like you deserve it.'

'Yeah. Anyway, I better get back to it.'

'You're working on a Saturday?'

'Yeah. I'm on my laptop in bed, so it's fine. Don't worry.'

'Okay. Well, thanks again for calling and don't work too hard.'

'Probably will. Happy shagging, honey!'

'Thanks,' I laughed. 'Speak soon.'

I hung up then jumped off the sofa. It was time to unpack.

Then I'd do my nails. I needed something to stop me fixating on Jake and get my head on straight.

By the time he came back from his walk I'd be cool as a cucumber.

And all hopes of this holiday romance developing into anything more would be wiped from my mind.

I might be new to the whole fling thing, but I was going to learn how to stay chill and not embarrass myself.

My heart depended on it.

35

JAKE

As I watched the waves lapping against the shore and my feet sank into the golden sand I exhaled.

The proximity to the beach had always been one of my favourite parts about living in LA. I could take or leave the rest of it. There were a lot of bad memories for me in this city. The exploitation when we were in the band, people screwing me over, what happened with my sister and losing my home and everything I'd worked my butt off for...

It was better that I didn't think about that right now. I was trying to leave my past in the past. Which is why I couldn't believe I'd spilled my guts to Halle earlier.

After being burned so many times, I was usually wary of sharing details about my private life with anyone. I knew from experience that usually led to it being splashed across the internet or in some trashy magazine.

But with Halle it was different. Even though we'd only known each other a week, for some reason, I felt like I could tell her anything. That I could trust her.

I couldn't get attached though. This was only temporary. Some fun to distract me from reality.

My cell buzzed and I regretted switching it back on earlier. I'd already seen that I'd had dozens of missed calls from Wilma. She was probably pissed that the photo Halle posted hadn't shown her face.

I glanced at the screen and saw Wilma's name flashing on it.

There was also a missed call from Roger, which made me smile. It was good to hear from him.

We'd texted a couple of times since I'd arrived, but seeing as I'd overstayed my welcome at his place, he was probably glad to see the back of me so I thought I'd give him some space. I'd call him back, but first I had to deal with Wilma.

I took another deep breath, then answered the call.

'Well, well, well,' Wilma said, her voice surprisingly calm. 'I didn't know you had it in you.'

'Huh?' I frowned.

'The photo you posted earlier is blowing up! Bravo! At first I was pissed that you'd put up a picture that didn't show that chick's face, that's why I called so many times. But then, when I started to see the comments, I realised that it was part of a bigger marketing strategy.' My frown deepened. I didn't know what the fuck she was talking about, but I was gonna run with it and hear her out. 'You deliberately avoided showing her face in the first photo because you're *teasing* your followers. Building up to the big reveal, so that when you finally show her face, it has more impact. Smart! Keep up the great work, Jakey boy!'

And with that, she hung up.

Oh.

I wasn't expecting that, but I wasn't complaining. I'd finally got Wilma off my back. And it was all thanks to Halle agreeing to post that photo.

She had no idea how grateful I was for her agreeing to do that.

With a spring in my step, I dialled Roger's number.

'Hey, stranger!' he said. 'How's it going? How's the hotel? How's your match?'

'So many questions! What is this, an interview?' I joked.

'I miss you, bro,' he said and warmth flooded my chest.

'Yeah? I thought you and Cathy would be glad to see the back of me!'

'C'mon, man.' He groaned. 'You know it's not like that. I told you. I'll always have your back.'

That was true. I'd known Roger since high school. Before anyone knew my name. He was a day-one friend. When I first was in the spotlight and the other kids were crawling out of the woodwork asking me to hook them up with concert tickets or helping them meet other celebrities, Roger was one of the only ones that messaged purely to see how I was.

Even when I was riding high on success and offered him money when he was struggling to pay his rent, he refused. I found out who his landlord was and paid his rent for a year anyway. He was mad, but I knew he was grateful.

We'd always been there for each other.

'I just thought I'd give you guys some space, y'know?'

'I know, but it's not necessary. I told you, I want to make sure you're okay.'

'I appreciate that, man.'

I filled him on the hotel, Halle and everything that had happened.

'Damn, J! Sounds like you really like this girl.'

'She's cool. Different, y'know. Halle doesn't give a fuck about the whole celebrity BS, which is great. She's fine as hell, but smart too. Easy to talk to...' *Jeez.* I needed to calm down with the compliments before Roger got the wrong idea. 'Anyway, we agreed to keep it casual. I've got too much on my plate right now. And if she sticks around Wilma will wanna follow through on her stupid plan.'

'What plan?'

Then I remembered that I hadn't told Roger about it. Mainly because I knew he'd think it was batshit crazy, just like I did and didn't want him to talk me out of it because it was the only way I could leave his place.

'I guess it's okay to tell you now.' I scrubbed the back of my neck before explaining.

'Jesus, man. That's got disaster written all over it!' Roger sighed. 'Why the hell did you agree to that shit?'

'What choice did I have? And even though I still don't agree with it, and won't be following through, I've had a really cool week. It's been good to take my mind off things.'

'You mean to meet a woman who's helped you to take your mind off things?' Even though I couldn't see him, I could tell that he was smiling.

'That too,' I confessed. Now I was the one who was smiling. Memories of how amazing it felt to be inside Halle flashed into my mind. Then I thought about how kind she was when I told her about my situation. She didn't judge. She just listened.

'I'm happy for you, J. You deserve to find someone to make you happy.'

'Hold your horses, buddy. I told you, it's nothing serious.'

'Uh-huh,' he said, clearly not believing a word. 'Never say never.'

'It won't work. It can't.' For some weird reason my chest tightened.

'Like I said, keep an open mind.'

'How's stuff with you?' I asked. Not just because I wanted to change the subject, but also because I was genuinely interested.

'All good. Work's keeping me busy.'

Roger worked in IT. He was always the smartest one in class and he'd built a great career. I was proud of him.

'Glad to hear it.'

'I'd better go. Promised to go shopping with Cathy.'

'I know how much you *love* shopping!' I joked. Roger had a wardrobe filled with multiple pairs of the same jeans and T-shirts. He had his style and he stuck to it. I doubted if he went shopping more than once every few years.

'That's what you do when you love someone. You do shit that you hate, just because you know it'll make *them* happy.'

'I'll take your word for it.' I thought I was in love with my ex, but when it ended, I wasn't so sure. At least Roger and Cathy's love was real.

'When it happens, you'll know. Trust me.'

'Enjoy your shopping trip,' I said, deliberately not responding.

'And enjoy your time with Halle.' He chuckled softly, then hung up.

Even though I knew he was getting carried away with stupid ideas of me and Halle having some kind of relationship after this, he was right about two things.

One: I did like her. And two: I should enjoy my time with her.

Like I'd said, it'd never be anything serious, but if I only had one week left with her, I was gonna make damn sure that I made it count.

Starting right now.

36

HALLE

The past two days had been unreal. In the best possible way.

On Saturday evening, once Jake returned from the beach, we had dinner at the restaurant, then came back to our villa and christened the four-poster bed.

On Sunday, we almost didn't leave the villa at all. The hotel had helpfully stocked the fridge with essentials, so we'd had breakfast in our garden by the pool, chilled, had more sex, followed by lunch, then more shagging.

I hadn't realised I was so insatiable, but when you're with a guy that was as talented as Jake, it was easy to understand why I couldn't get enough of him.

By late afternoon, we were both exhausted and I could've easily just fallen back into bed (to sleep this time), but Jake said he wanted to take me to a place called Echo Park Lake. I'd never heard of it before, but they had these cool swan pedal boats.

He timed it perfectly because we were able to do a sunset ride and the boats were illuminated which made everything extra pretty. And seeing the city lights shimmering across the dark water made it extra special.

Now it was Monday and we were in a chauffeur-driven car the hotel had arranged which was taking us to Venice Beach – a place that I'd heard a lot about, but never visited. I couldn't wait.

'Nice nails!' Jake took my hand, held it up and admired my bright pink shade. 'When did you do them? They weren't that colour this morning.'

'How can you be so sure?' I said, secretly impressed at how perceptive he was.

'Because,' he whispered in my ear, and the sensation of his sweet, warm breath tickled my skin, sending shockwaves through me, 'I would've noticed them when you had your hand and lips wrapped around my cock.'

'Very observant,' I grinned.

Jake finally let me go down on him and I was surprised at how much I'd enjoyed it. That definitely hadn't been the case in the past, but as I slid him in and out of my mouth and saw how much pleasure it gave him, it made me feel so good.

I liked the fact that I was driving him wild. That he called my name when he lost control. That I was satisfying him just like he'd done for me so many times.

'I am. I already have the blueprint of every inch of your body stored here.' He tapped the side of his head.

'Oh, really?' I smiled.

'Yep.'

My stomach fluttered. I totally believed him. I had become very familiar with his body too. He had a scar on his right shoulder that he said he got when he fell off the bed when he was seven. And there was a small Minnie Mouse tattoo on his back with a series of numbers.

It seemed a bit odd for a muscular rockstar to be inked with a Disney cartoon character and I was curious to know the story behind it. But when I'd asked, he'd stiffened and changed the subject, so I decided it was best not to pry.

'You're obsessed!' I joked, expecting him to roll his eyes.

'Accurate.' He grinned, then leant forward and kissed me softly on the lips. 'I can't even pretend that I'm not. You're pretty awesome.'

'Thanks.' My cheeks heated. I wasn't used to getting compliments, but Jake had given me so many these past few days I was glad my head still fitted through the door.

The most important thing was that he genuinely seemed to mean them. I saw it in his eyes. Sometimes I caught him looking at me like I'd just casually started walking on water and he wondered how I'd done it.

'So tell me? When did you create this magic?' He ran his thumb over my nails.

'When you were in the shower.'

'Huh? But how'd you do them so quick and put that pretty little love-heart design on your thumbs?'

'Practice, I suppose.' I shrugged my shoulders. 'I always bring my nail kit with me, y'know, with my polishes, tools, UV lamp, rhinestones and other stuff.'

'I don't know much about nails, but they look damn good, Halle. Remind me again why you don't do nails for a living?'

'It's...' I stuttered. 'It just didn't work out.'

Jake stayed silent, like he was waiting for me to elaborate.

'I tried doing it for a while, but when people found out who I was dating, they were more interested in asking questions about him and then when we broke up...'

'It became awkward and uncomfortable?' he finished my sentence.

'Exactly.' It was great that he understood. A lot of people would've thought I was overreacting or just tell me to suck it up.

'And I know that the nail bar must've passed my details to the press. I used to get journalists calling and emailing all the time. They hounded me so much that I stopped answering my phone, listening to voicemails or reading messages from numbers I didn't know.'

Which was why I'd missed the original messages from the Love Hotel.

'That sucks. And sometimes even when you change your number, they find another way to reach you.'

'Yeah. It's still triggering. I never answer a call if I don't know who it's from.'

'I get that. But things would be different now though, right? Have you ever thought about trying again? You could do it free-lance. Pick and choose your customers instead of working in a shop with people all up in your business.'

'That would be a dream, but I'm not sure,' I shrugged. 'It's been ages since I've done a stranger's nails.'

'There's a lot of potential for people with your skills. Even when I was on the scene they used to have nail techni-cians or manicurists, sorry, I don't know the right terminol-ogy, but they'd have them on video shoots. And it's not just for people in the industry. Cathy, my best friend's wife, has a lady that comes to her office to do her nails when she can't get to the salon. Maybe you could do something like that?'

'Maybe. I'd need to get more experience first. No one at the juice bar is interested in getting their nails done and if I tried to promote it to customers I'd get fired. So unless I went to work at a nail bar, it'd be hard to get the word out. Plus, it's even more competitive than it was before.'

'Like I said, I'm no expert, but your nails are fire, baby. It may be a competitive market, but I bet there's not many people who could do the designs like yours. You have a gift. It'd be a shame to waste it.'

My chest expanded like a hot air balloon. He really believed in me.

Other than Dad and Vanessa I couldn't remember the last person who'd had such encouraging words. And definitely not someone I was sleeping with.

'Thanks.' I kissed him on the lips. 'That really means a lot.'

'If you want to thank me, you'll send me a photo with your first paid customer when you get back to New York. Deal?'

Hearing him mention me returning to New York made my chest deflate.

I didn't want to go home. Time was going too fast. If I didn't include today, I only had four full days left here. By Saturday lunchtime I'd be heading to the airport to get the plane home.

I gave myself a mental slap. I shouldn't be thinking of that, I should enjoy the time we had left.

'Deal,' I said, managing a half smile.

* * *

As we strolled along the Venice Beach promenade, my eyes kept popping.

It wasn't just the beautiful golden sand and sea views that captured my attention, it was all of the different sights around me. As well as the people playing volleyball on the beach and the surfers in the distance, I'd also spotted people roller skating in bikinis, belly dancers, different street performers and lots of bodybuilders. Jake had also taken me to see the canals and skatepark. How they managed to navigate all those jumps and stay on their boards was beyond me.

'This place is really vibrant. There's so much going on!' I said.

'Yeah. It was one of my sister's favourite places.' He lowered his voice.

'Nice! I forgot you have a sister!' I said, thinking it'd been a while since I'd seen photos of them in the press. Then again, I'd stopped reading those magazines a long time ago.

Jake's face fell, his shoulders slumped and he shook his head.

'*Had*,' he mumbled. 'She passed almost two years ago.'

37

JAKE

A sharp pain shot through my chest.

What the hell was wrong with me?

First, I'd told Halle about my dumpster fire of a career and that I was basically homeless.

And now I'd told her about my sister.

I should know that wasn't how flings worked.

Hook-ups didn't usually involve conversation. The point was just to fuck. And if you did need to talk out of politeness, the topics were supposed to be superficial. Y'know, like the weather, what was on TV or...

Now that I thought about it, I had no idea because most of the time I preferred the *one and done* situations.

It'd been a while since I last fooled around, but as far as I remembered, I'd ask their names, whether they'd had fun, if they needed me to call them a cab and that was it. So I couldn't understand why I suddenly kept sharing shit with Halle that I'd promised myself I'd keep locked up and not talk about with anyone again.

We were having a good time and now everything would get

awkward. She'd feel bad and worry what to say and I'd feel bad about the fact that she felt bad.

I needed to find a way to stop spilling my guts to this woman.

'Fuck.' Halle froze. 'I'm so, so sorry. I'd love to hear about her if it's not too painful to talk about.'

Wait, what?

That was the last thing I expected her to ask.

Sure, I knew that Halle would be sympathetic. She was kind and considerate. She cared about people. And I knew she cared about me.

But normally if I mentioned anything about my sister passing, people would clam up or change the subject. I understood why. It was hard to know the right thing to say and instead of saying the wrong thing, people assumed it was better to say nothing at all.

There was no one right way. We all deal with grief differently, so trying to change the subject would probably work best for most people. Hell, when it first happened it felt way too raw to talk about at all. Every day that I woke up I just hoped it was a bad dream.

Now though, even though it still felt like someone had taken a knife to my heart when I thought about what happened to her, I wanted to talk about her. I wanted her memory to live on.

I wanted people to know how amazing she was.

When I glanced at Halle, she had such sincerity in her eyes. She genuinely wanted me to talk about my sister.

Wow.

Halle didn't realise it, but somehow she'd said exactly the right thing. It was like she already knew me so well that she understood what I needed before I did.

'She was incredible,' I said, my face lighting up as I pictured her smile. 'Her name was Minerva, but we called her Minnie because she was petite and cute like Minnie Mouse.'

'Ahhhh...' Halle said, like she'd just solved a puzzle. 'Is that why you have that tattoo on your back?'

'Yeah,' I nodded. 'I... the numbers, that's her date of birth and I put it on my back, not just because I wanted to have the tattoo somewhere private where it wasn't easily visible, but because Minnie always had my back. Even though she was my baby sister, she always looked out for me.'

'That's really lovely.'

'Thanks. I always looked out for her too, when we were kids. Everyone at school knew not to mess with her or they'd have me to deal with.'

'I can totally see you as the overprotective older brother.' The corner of her mouth turned up into a reassuring smile.

'Yep. I played the role well back then. Just a shame that I failed her when we got older.' My voice trailed off and my chest tightened as all the painful memories flooded back. Maybe I wasn't ready to talk about it after all.

'I'm sure that's not true.' Halle rested her hand on my shoulder.

'If I wasn't so hell-bent on being successful, she'd still be here.'

'I don't understand. Why would you be responsible?'

I blew out an exasperated breath. I needed to tell Halle the whole story.

'Minnie was my biggest supporter. When I was a kid singing at school or in our local park, she'd come to every performance. She was always the one cheering the loudest. We were really close. So when things really took off, she wanted to come to LA to be with me. At the time, I told her no. So did my parents. We said she needed to focus on her education. She wasn't happy about it, but eventually agreed. I occasionally used to let her come to some of my gigs with my folks. But by the time my solo career really took off, she'd graduated and as she liked to remind me, there was nothing holding her back. I missed her, so I thought I was doing the right thing by agreeing to let her come here. In hindsight, it was the worst thing I could've ever done.'

'Why?'

'She was mesmerised by the industry. She thought it was glamorous. It was so different to the small town we grew up in. By then, I'd been in the business for over a decade. I'd seen what went on behind closed doors. The stars with squeaky-clean images who were really alcoholics or drug addicts. I'd had a couple of close calls where I could've gone down the wrong path, but luckily, I was able to keep my head straight. Probably because I saw how close one of my bandmates came to dying after he OD'd, and it scared the shit out of me.'

'Jesus,' Halle winced.

'Anyway, I was proud of the fact that I'd been in the business for so long, but never let myself get seduced by that stuff. But my sister was more easily led. One night she went to a party, I was too tired to go, so she insisted on going alone. Anyway, she met this guy, fell head over heels and got sucked into the wrong crowd. He and his friends were into coke. Persuaded her to try it and it all went downhill from there. She became an addict. I tried everything to get her away from him, but he'd turned her against me. When I finally got her out, she was too far gone. She was a different person. I put her in rehab over and over. She'd stay clean for a while, then relapse. The pattern continued for years. A shady journalist got wind of it and blackmailed me.'

'No!' Halle's jaw dropped.

'Said if I didn't pay up, he'd publish the story. I didn't want her to go through any more pain so I did. Cost me a lot of money.

But even though paying for that and all the rehab drained me dry, it was worth it to protect my sister. I would've given my life for her. The last time she fell off the wagon, I put her in rehab again, but when she got out, she bumped into her ex, the guy that fucked her up, and went back with him. And this time, when she shot up, she overdosed and that was it. She was gone.'

'Fuck,' Halle said. 'That's awful. But you've got to know that it wasn't your fault. You did everything you could.'

'But it wasn't enough. That's one of the reasons I don't speak to my folks any more. Because they blame me. And because I'd run out of money to give them.'

'That's really sad. But if they only care about your money and blame you, you're probably better off without them.'

'True.' It still hurt though.

Things were already on a downward spiral with my financial troubles after I got screwed over, but Minnie's passing was really what marked the beginning of the end for me. That was when I started losing it all: my family, my career, then my home and everything I'd worked for.

'None of this is on you. By the sounds of it, Minnie was determined to come to LA, with or without your blessing. You can only guide someone. Ultimately, they make their own decisions. You can't be held responsible for that. She wouldn't want you to blame yourself either. She'd want you to live your life to the full, have all of the adventures that she couldn't and give your life and career your all to show her that everything wasn't in vain. Her memory can still live on, through you.'

I stared at Halle in silence.

Her words hit me right in the gut. But in a good way.

She had a point. If Minnie could see me now, she'd be sad that I wasn't writing any more. She'd be upset with me for blaming myself.

Whenever anything bad happened to me she'd say, 'Sucks for you but sweet inspo for one of your songs.'

'You're right. She'd tell me to write a song about her.'

'That's a great idea. The Irish band The Script has a song called "If You Could See Me Now" about some of the band members' parents who'd passed away...'

'I love that song,' I nodded.

'It's brilliant. And one of my favourite parts is when they say: "Take that rage, put it on a page—"'

'"Take the page to the stage, blow the roof off the place."' I finished Halle's sentence. I knew that song off by heart.

'Exactly!' she smiled. 'That's what *you* could do. I know you normally write about love and heartbreak in romantic relationships, but there's nothing to stop you from writing about the love you had for your sister too.'

'I thought about it, many times, but it was too hard. It felt too personal. I didn't want people to think less of her. I'm always asked about the inspiration for my songs and I knew that if I said it was about her, she'd go from being Minnie, my amazing, vibrant sister, to Minnie, the drug addict sister of bad boy Jake Myers. They'd tarnish her name and assume I turned her into an addict. I couldn't protect her in life, so I at least wanted to protect her memory now that she's gone.'

'I totally get that. But maybe that song could do some good. It could let people, families who are going through the same pain know that they're not alone. Or encourage other addicts to seek help. Your words, your songs are powerful. They could change lives. It could help something positive come from this pain.'

Fuck. I'd never thought about it like that.

'Thank you,' I said. 'For listening. For not judging.'

'Thank you for trusting me enough to share something that's so painful. I'm sure Minnie was amazing. And despite what you think about yourself right now, I'm sure she'd still believe in you. You're so talented, Jake. Millions of people around the world would give their right arm to have a voice like yours and to be able to write songs like yours. You have a gift. Don't let it go to waste. I believe in you. Now it's time that you believed in yourself again.'

Once again, Halle's words hit me like a truck.

As she squeezed my hand, I knew she was genuine.

Minnie was gone, but I was still here.

I was still alive.

I could still try to write again.

I could still play my guitar.

And I could still sing.

Halle was right. I couldn't give up.

I had Roger and now I'd found another amazing person who believed in me.

I was gonna try again.

And this time, I'd make it happen.

38

JAKE

I kissed Halle on the cheek, then crept out of the bedroom door. It was only early evening, but after getting back from Venice Beach about an hour ago, Halle said she wanted to take a nap before dinner and she was sleeping so soundly that I didn't want to disturb her.

Although I offered to lie beside her, I couldn't sleep. Ever since our conversation about Minnie, my mind had been racing. So instead of tossing and turning beside Halle, I decided to get up and go for a walk on the beach.

After finding a piece of paper and a pen, I scribbled a note to let Halle know where I'd be so that if she wanted to join me later, she could.

Before I went for a walk, I needed to find Sammie. She wasn't in her office and when I checked with reception, they said she wasn't at the hotel, but suggested I message her so she could pick it up later.

There was something I needed her help with that was related to Halle, so I quickly fired off a text before heading down to the beach.

I took off my sliders and as my feet sank into the soft sand, my shoulders loosened. The beach was pretty empty, which was perfect.

I looked out to sea and listened to the sound of the gentle waves lapping at the shore. I didn't want to leave this place.

My thoughts turned back to the last few days, which had been awesome. Wilma was finally off my back (Halle posted another photo of us today that Sammie had taken of us on the beach with our backs to the camera which definitely helped). And opening up to Halle about my situation (well, most of it) was a weight off my mind.

I was starting to realise that there was a strange kind of freedom that came with hitting rock bottom, because there was nowhere else to go. I was basically homeless and jobless. My sister was gone. I didn't speak to my parents any more. I'd already lost everything, so how much worse could things get?

Despite all that'd happened to me, I could still sing. I could still play guitar. That would never change. And I had to believe that my ability to write songs would come back soon too.

Minnie would hate that I'd stopped writing. And she would've been just as excited as Roger was to hear that I was enjoying spending time with a good woman. She would've loved Halle.

Who could blame her?

Halle was a breath of fresh air. She was like a bright light in a dark room. Like sunshine on a cloudy day. A rainbow after the rain.

I paused, reached in my pocket for my cell phone and quickly opened my Notes app.

A flash of something raced through me and I smiled.

It felt like... *hope.*

I sat down on the sand with my cell resting on my knees and started typing.

With Halle firmly fixed in my thoughts, I started writing down how she made me feel. How somehow, things with her hit different.

I flicked to my voice memos app, pressed record and sang a melody.

I had no idea how much time had passed, but when I stopped I had dozens of different voice memos and pages of notes.

But they weren't just notes.

They were lyrics.

Fuck.

I'd written a song.

I'd written a goddamn song!

The first one in... shit. I didn't even know how long it'd been, but it felt fucking incredible.

I jumped up. I needed to see Halle. To thank her for inspiring me. But just as I was about to head back to the villa, I saw her walking towards me.

I raced towards Halle, picked her up and spun her around.

'Wow!' she squealed. 'What a welcome! Are you okay? Clearly you're happy, which is great, but what led to this excitement?'

'I wrote a song!' I shouted.

'No way!' she screamed, mirroring my enthusiasm. 'That's amazing, Jake!' She dipped her head and kissed me. 'I knew you could do it. I'm so proud of you!'

Hearing those words made my chest bloom. It'd been a long time since anyone had said that to me.

And I didn't care if it sounded like I was tooting my own horn, I was proud of myself too.

There was still a long way to go – I'd have to fine-tune the lyrics and find a way to record them, but I'd done the hardest part: getting started again.

I'd shown myself that it was possible.

That I hadn't lost my ability to write.

It was still buried deep inside of me. I just needed the right situation and inspiration to draw it out.

And now Halle had helped me do that, there was no stopping me.

39

HALLE

'This is so beautiful,' I said as I sat on a towel resting on top of the soft golden sand next to Jake and took in the gorgeous sea views.

Shades of orange, yellow and pink glowed in the sky. The sun would be setting soon and I couldn't wait to watch it with Jake.

'Sure is.'

'What time do you want to have dinner tonight?'

'Maybe later?' Jake shrugged. 'I'm too buzzed to go right now though. Let's walk. I need to burn off some of this excited energy.'

After picking up my towel, we strolled further up the beach, holding hands. We were just about to turn back, when Jake stopped and a mischievous smile spread across his face.

'Why are you grinning?' I said.

'Because I've just found a way to work off some energy.'

'How?'

'See that?' He pointed. I followed his finger and saw that there was a hammock nestled between two palm trees.

'Yeah, but how will lying on that burn calories?'

'Because we won't just be *lying* on the hammock. Come on.' He took my hands and led me over to it. 'How would you feel about letting me fuck you on it?' He looked at me, his eyes as dark as onyx.

'I'd definitely be up for trying,' I said as heat flooded my cheeks. 'But won't we fall out? And what if someone sees us?'

'If we do it right, we'll be fine. A hammock is basically just a big sex swing.'

'You said that so casually, like it's something that everyone uses!'

'I used to have one in every room, don't you?' he laughed.

'Yeah. *Obvs*,' I deadpanned.

'We haven't seen anyone on the beach for ages. And why else would the hotel put a hammock here at a height that's perfect for banging if they didn't want us to enjoy it?' He raised his eyebrow.

Jake had a point. I was sure hammocks were usually higher. Not that I'd seen many before. Anyway, enough of the thinking.

'Okay!' I said, not recognising myself. Two weeks ago, I would never have considered doing something like this, but Jake brought something out in me that made me want to try new things. And *hello*, who wouldn't want to dabble in some outdoor beach hammock sex with a man like Jake?

'Give me your towel,' he commanded before laying it inside the hammock. 'Now take off your panties and sit with your legs hanging over the edge.'

I quickly did as instructed. He hadn't even touched me yet and I was already wet for him.

'I wanna thank you.' Jake dropped to his knees. 'You've really helped me. I was able to write today for the first time in a very long time. So now I'm going to show you how grateful I am.'

He leant forward, pushed up my dress around my waist, spread my legs then dipped his head between them before licking me *oh-so-slowly*.

My hips jerked up and I cried out.

When Jake said he was going to show his gratitude, he wasn't joking. I came hard and fast and although I knew that should be enough, I wanted more.

He reached into his back pocket, pulled out his wallet then a condom.

'Still okay with this?'

'One hundred per cent,' I panted.

He quickly pulled down his shorts and boxers, rolled the condom on then stepped closer to the hammock.

'Try and sit upright,' he instructed. 'I'm gonna stand out here which will be good for keeping our balance and the momentum from the hammock should help. Just follow the rhythm of it, okay?'

'Okay.'

Jake lined himself up at my entrance then thrust inside me. The swing jolted back and I cried out at the sensation of him filling me up.

'Fuck.' He squeezed his eyes shut. 'That feels so goddamn perfect. The height and everything is just right.'

As the swing moved back and forth, we rocked together in perfect harmony. I couldn't believe I was out here on the beach, being fucked in a hammock by this gorgeous man.

The sun had slipped further below the horizon, so the sky was now a blend of pretty purple hues, the sound of the waves echoed around me and my nostrils were flooded with a delicious combination of the fresh sea air and Jake's manly scent. I couldn't see how anything could top this.

But then Jake started circling my clit and I knew I was a goner.

'Jake...' I forced the words out as I felt my orgasm building. 'I can't... I can't hold on.'

'Not yet,' he growled. 'I'm gonna pull out, then I need you to get up, lie down on your chest in the hammock with your butt in the air. We're gonna try doing it kind of doggy style.'

My eyes popped, not sure how that was going to work, but I couldn't wait to try.

Jake pulled out and I followed his instructions.

After taking off his shorts and boxers and straddling the hammock, he lifted my bum higher, then lined himself up with the entrance of my pussy, gripped my hips then slammed inside me.

'Oh, fuck!' I screamed.

'You good?' he checked.

'Yes! More than good. Please. More.'

He plunged deeper, fucking me like he was a jockey riding towards the finish line.

My hands latched on to the top edges of the hammock, holding on tight whilst Jake pounded into me in the most delicious way.

He removed one of his hands from my hip, slid it under me before dipping it between my legs.

Jesus.

Now it wasn't just the sound of the sea vibrating around me. It was the sound of his fingers sliding through the wetness between my legs and our skin slapping together.

This was heaven.

'Holy shit,' he moaned. 'You're soaked. I fucking love it.'

As he played my clit like a fiddle, I hurtled closer and closer to the edge.

I held off my orgasm before, but I wasn't strong enough to stop it again. The way Jake was pumping in and out of me and lavishing my sensitive bud with attention felt way too good.

'You feel fucking incredible,' Jake growled before drawing out, then slamming back in, over and over again, going harder, deeper and faster with every thrust.

My breath grew ragged and my body started to shake. Seconds later a volcano erupted within me and a strangled cry shot from my lips.

'Ohhhh, God, Jake, Jake...' I panted.

Jake gripped my hips with both hands again, pumped faster then growled like a wild animal as he exploded inside me.

He rested his chest on my back and I felt his heart racing just like mine.

'Wow,' I whimpered. 'That was...'

'Yeah,' he said, gasping for air.

I couldn't keep this position any more. My brain was fuzzy, my limbs and my whole body felt weak.

I collapsed on the hammock, trying to catch my breath. Jake removed his hands, sat back, then plonked himself down on the hammock. But he did it with such force that it tipped over.

He lost his balance and I was so weak from that mind-blowing orgasm that I didn't steady myself in time, so we both crashed to the ground. Me with my legs akimbo and Jake on his side with his sheathed dick exposed.

We both burst into a fit of raucous giggles.

'Oh my God!' I chuckled, my stomach hurting from all the belly laughs. 'I can't believe we managed to stay in the hammock for two different sex positions, but then ended up falling out of it afterwards!'

'I know, right?' Jake clutched his stomach as tears rolled

down his cheeks. 'Fucking hilarious. I guess we should be glad there's no one here to see it.'

'Or to take photos!'

'That'd be a good one for the memory book though. Admit it!'

'Ha! Your agent would love that and you'd get a shitload of followers! Imagine: I'd go from not wanting to take any photos to appearing in pornographic ones. Don't think I'm quite ready for that yet!' I laughed, but Jake froze.

'I hear voices!' He jumped up, grabbed the towel from the hammock then threw it over me.

Jake just about managed to pull on his shorts and boxers and I yanked down my dress before the couple got closer. I couldn't find my knickers, but at least my body was covered.

The sun had almost set, but it was still light enough for them to see us.

'Oh! Hi!' One of them waved, before walking towards us.

'Hey!' Jake said casually. 'You good?'

'Yeah,' the woman replied. 'Just thought we'd come for a... walk.'

'Cool,' I said, trying to act natural. 'We were just, er, watching the sunset.'

'Nice,' the guy replied, then smirked, his eyes darting to the ground near where Jake was standing. 'Well, we'll let you get back to your *sunset watching*,' he winked.

His match's gaze seemed to follow the same direction, but I didn't dare look.

'Thanks! Enjoy your walk.'

Once they'd left, I looked down to the spot they seemed to be staring at and gasped.

'Something tells me they knew we weren't here to watch the sunset,' Jake smiled.

'Yep,' I said. 'And if they had any doubts, I reckon seeing *those* would've confirmed their suspicions.'

I pointed to the ripped condom packet innocently resting on the sand, right beside my knickers.

Busted.

40

HALLE

It was Tuesday morning and I was on my way to the hotel restaurant to grab breakfast.

We'd exhausted all the supplies in our villa's kitchen and to be honest, neither of us could be arsed to cook, so it made sense to get a bunch of stuff to take back to eat.

When I'd left, Jake was still in bed. I think that all of the excitement of writing his first song for ages, not to mention our hammock activities, had tired him out.

I was so happy he'd gotten his writing mojo back. He credited me for helping him which was sweet, but I didn't really do anything. All I did was listen and encourage him. I meant everything I'd said: I believed in him. He was so talented and I knew for a fact that he had a lot more hit singles ahead of him.

'Hey, Halle,' Sammie said as I walked into the restaurant. 'I was hoping to see you.'

'Really?'

'Yeah. I wondered if you could do me a favour?'

'Course! What do you need?'

'You do nails, right?'

'Yeah...?' I frowned.

'Great! The nail technician in the spa is fully booked today, but I have an important meeting and I haven't had time to do my nails and I want them to look nice, so I wondered if you could help me out? I know you're on holiday so if it's a hassle then I understand. I don't want to put you out, it's just that—'

'I'd love to!' I jumped in, excitement fizzing in my stomach. 'I'd just need to check with Jake to see what our plans are for today first, so I can text you to let you know a time. Would that work?'

'Sounds perfect. And... actually, do you think you'd have time to do Jasmine's nails too? She's a Love Empress here. She probably would only want something simple like a French manicure. We'd both pay you for your time.'

'No, it's okay.' I waved my hand dismissively. 'I'd be happy to do it for you!'

'You're a lifesaver! I'll wait to hear from you then, thanks!'

Once I'd loaded up a tray with some pastries and fresh fruit, plus placed an order for fresh pancakes, waffles and an omelette to be delivered, I literally skipped back to our villa. I couldn't wait to tell Jake the exciting news.

When I burst through the door, I saw that Jake was already sitting outside.

I rushed over to him.

'Guess what?' I placed the tray on the table in front of him.

'What, baby?'

'I just saw Sammie and she's asked me to do her nails! And the Love Empress woman who I think is her boss or something!' I let out an excited squeal.

Jake smirked, then got up and wrapped his arms around me.

'That's so cool! Proud of you.'

'I told her I'd check with you because I didn't know if you had something in mind for us to do today and get back to her.'

'Nope. Nothing that can't wait.'

'Okay, great! I'll message to see if she's free after breakfast. Then we'll have the rest of the day to spend together.'

'Perfect! And whilst you're doing their nails, I'm gonna do some more writing. I'm feeling inspired.' He dipped his head and planted a soft kiss on my lips.

'That's what I like to hear. You going to tell me what the song you wrote yesterday is about?'

'It's a secret. And it's not ready. I wish I had my guitar.'

'You didn't want to bring it with you?'

'Roger suggested it, but I thought there was no point and didn't want to put too much pressure on myself.'

'I can understand that. Maybe we could get it delivered?'

'Yeah, maybe.'

The doorbell rang.

'That'll be the rest of the food.'

'There's *more*?'

'Yep! If you're going to be writing some hit records and I'm going to be doing my first proper nails booking in years, we'll need to keep our strength up.'

A couple of hours later, I was on my way to Sammie's office to do her nails. My heart thundered against my chest.

I couldn't fuck this up. This was a great opportunity to dip my toe back into the water and build my confidence. Apart from doing Vanessa's nails, I hadn't done anyone else's for ages. If I messed up on myself or Vanessa, it was fine, I could shrug it off and start again, but I couldn't do that today. Sammie was trusting me to do a good job and I didn't want to let her down.

I knocked on the door.

'Come in,' she called out.

When I entered, her boyfriend, Romeo, was sitting on the edge of her desk.

'Sorry, I didn't mean to interrupt,' I said.

'No worries! Romeo's on a break, so he was just keeping me company.'

'Nice to see you again, Halle,' Romeo said. 'Are you enjoying your time at the hotel?'

'Loving it, thanks. Jake and I didn't get off to the best start, but now we're getting on like a house on fire.'

'Reminds me of another couple.' Romeo turned to Sammie and gave her a knowing look. I could literally feel the electricity crackling between them. I cleared my throat, worried that if I didn't they might start banging on the table.

'It's so cool that you both work together.'

'It is,' Sammie smiled.

There was a knock on the door and a tall, elegantly dressed black woman walked in with an attractive man with dark hair and olive skin.

'Halle, this is Jasmine and her partner Alejandro, who also works at the hotel.'

'Good to meet you,' Alejandro said.

'Yes!' Jasmine added. 'It's a real pleasure.'

'Likewise,' I said. 'Wait, so you work as a Love Empress and Alejandro, what do you do here?' I asked, hoping that it didn't sound like an interview, but I was genuinely interested to find out. I had no idea there were so many couples here.

'I am a Cuisine King, which is basically the head chef,' he said in a deep accent which sounded Spanish.

'We're normally based at the Love Hotel in Spain, but we're here for a few months to help the team here.'

'Amazing! I'd love to hear how you all met!'

'That's enough to fill two books!' Sammie chuckled. 'We're not supposed to talk about it, but in a nutshell, we met and fell in love at the Italian Love Hotel. At the time it was forbidden because Romeo was my Love Alchemist.'

'No way!' I gasped. 'But what happened with your actual match?'

'Let's just say he was an arsehole.' Sammie wrinkled her nose.

'That is putting it politely,' Romeo added in his thick Italian accent.

'How come you got set up with him then? I thought the hotel were good at finding the perfect match?'

'It wasn't their fault,' Sammie added quickly. 'On paper my match seemed ideal, but let's just say he lied about a few things... Anyway, doesn't matter. I'm glad it didn't work out with him. Otherwise I wouldn't have found my *real* Mr Right.' She looked at Romeo with love-heart eyes and he leant over and kissed her gently on the lips.

'Ooops, sorry for the PDA!' Sammie said. 'We're supposed to keep things professional at work, but it's difficult. I mean, look how gorgeous he is! And with all the love floating around in the air at this place, sometimes it's just too hard to resist sneaking a little kiss here and there.' Sammie winked. 'I know we're not the only ones. Jasmine and Ale may look innocent but I'm telling you, they're feral!'

'Excuse me?' Jasmine raised a perfectly arched eyebrow. 'I'll have you know that Ale and I are always perfectly professional in front of guests.'

'In front of guests, maybe, but don't think I haven't heard you two in your office,' Sammie said.

'Wh-what?' Jasmine stuttered. 'We're always careful and I don't... we always make sure that we don't...'

'Gotcha!' Sammie cackled.

'Wait. So you *didn't* hear us?'

'I was just pulling your leg. But your reaction told me everything I needed to know. See, Halle! I told you: *feral!*'

We all burst out laughing.

'I think that is our cue to leave these ladies to it,' Alejandro said to Romeo.

'*Sí.*' Romeo squeezed Sammie's hand and Alejandro gave Jasmine a swoony look before both men left.

'Shall we get started?' I said. 'Who'd like to go first?'

* * *

Jasmine's nails were done and Sammie's were almost finished.

Although Jasmine requested a French manicure like Sammie predicted, she was up for giving it a twist, so instead of a plain white tip, I'd created a seashell design and added a baby pearl in the centre of each nail.

Sammie said she was up for trying something more adventurous, so I gave her summery nails with a mixture of designs including palm trees and an orange starfish on her nude nails.

I was nervous at first, but they made me feel so at ease that it wasn't long before I relaxed.

Happiness filled my chest. This was exactly how I'd envisaged things years ago: having my own clients and doing their nails whilst we had a chat and a giggle. I wished that I could do this all the time.

'I can't stop looking at my nails!' Jasmine beamed. 'They're stunning. And you did them so quickly! Do you have your own salon back in New York?'

'I wish!' I said. 'Then again, I'm not sure if I'd want my own salon. The dream would be to be freelance and work with different customers rather than in a fixed place. That'd keep my overheads low too.'

'Great idea. Do you have an Instagram page with all of your creations?'

'I don't do social media,' I winced. 'I had a bad experience and it put me off.'

'How so?' Jasmine said.

'I used to date someone famous and the comments got quite bitchy.'

'That's awful,' Sammie said.

'So sorry to hear that.' Jasmine softened her voice. 'Obviously it's up to you, but maybe think about trying again. You can control how it's used and I think the community would be supportive. Putting lots of photos will help you get your name out there and get more bookings. It'd be a shame for people not to see how talented you are.'

'Thanks,' I said. 'I'll think about it.'

'Why don't you take some pictures of Jasmine's nails now?' said Sammie. 'We can take some of mine too when they're dry. Then if you create a page, you'll have some content ready.'

'That's really kind.' I nodded, reaching for my phone, then tapping the camera button, before snapping away.

'I'd better head to my meeting,' Jasmine said. 'Halle, could you get my purse out of my bag? My nails should be dry by now, but just in case.'

'Oh, no, this is on the house!' I said.

'Sorry, but I can't allow you to do that,' Jasmine insisted and I reluctantly took her purse then opened it. 'Take out fifty dollars, please.'

'That's too much!' I shook my head.

'My purse is on my desk, so you can take out the same amount from me too,' Sammie said, ignoring my comment.

'I can't...'

Jasmine checked her nails were dry before taking both purses and carefully pulling out the bills.

'Oops! Looks like neither of us have anything smaller, so you'll just have to accept it.' She handed the cash to me.

'Thank you,' I sighed. The money would come in handy.

'No, thank *you*!'

My heart bloomed.

Vanessa was right before when she said I was living my best life.

I was staying in a dreamy five-star hotel, with the sweetest, kindest, hottest guy that ever walked the earth, enjoying amazing sex and now I was a step closer to pursuing my passion.

If I looked up the definition of being on cloud nine, there'd be a photo of me with a big cheesy smile.

The only snag was that things with Jake were temporary. But I wasn't going to dwell on that. I wanted to focus on the here and now.

Maybe we could talk about the future later in a few days. I didn't want this to end and I was pretty sure that Jake had feelings for me too, so there was still hope. It wouldn't be easy, but I'd like to at least try.

The same went for my career.

I could do this.

I owed it to myself to give it my best shot.

'I'm sure I'll see you before you leave,' Jasmine added. 'But if I don't, good luck with your nail business. I'm sure it'll be a huge success!'

Warmth flooded my stomach.

Just like Jake, Jasmine and Sammie really believed that I had talent.

Jasmine had no idea how much her words meant to me.

I didn't even have a nail business, yet, but seeing how happy and impressed Jasmine and Sammie were made me more determined than ever to turn my dream into a reality.

41

JAKE

I rested my guitar down on the daybed in our villa's garden and exhaled.

Another song written.

That made six this week, which was a new record.

It was always impossible to predict how long composing a song would take. Some of my biggest hits were penned in minutes. Others I'd mulled over for weeks, months and even had a couple that I'd started, but only been able to go back and finish years later.

But over the past few days, the words had flowed right out of me and straight onto the page.

I wrote that first song about Halle on Monday once we'd got back from Venice Beach.

On Tuesday, she was gone for a couple of hours doing Sammie and Jasmine's nails and during that time I wrote another.

But on Wednesday night after Halle and I got back from checking out some farmers' markets in Malibu and watching surfers at the popular Surfrider beach, magic happened. I'd told her I was gonna take her advice, call Roger and ask to meet so I could collect my guitar because I was on a roll with the songwriting.

But when I'd opened the door and stepped inside the villa, my eyes popped because right there, propped up on the sofa, was my guitar.

Halle had looked up the company Roger worked for and called him to ask if he could drop it off at the hotel because she knew it would help me write.

Damn.

I stood there in shock for minutes before I could speak. That was one of the sweetest, kindest, most thoughtful things anyone had ever done for me.

Once I'd made sure I showed Halle my gratitude, I'd put her to bed, then taken my guitar, phone, notepad and a lamp to the beach.

I'd walked to the same hammock we'd used on Monday, sat in it and with just the sound of the waves crashing against the shore and the light from the lamp, I'd written two more songs. Another one about Halle and one about Minnie.

Although I didn't get to bed until five in the morning yesterday, I made sure I woke up to have breakfast with Halle. I'd ordered some waffles and pancakes from the Love Hotel's restaurant to be delivered to our villa.

After devouring breakfast, we'd gone for a walk on the beach, before relaxing by the pool at our villa. Then whilst she did the nails for a guest who'd seen Sammie's nails and asked if Halle could do the same design on hers, I'd liaised with Sammie to set up my final date with Halle tonight.

Yep. Today was Friday: our last full day at the hotel.

My stomach sank. I wasn't ready to say goodbye to Halle. She meant too much to me.

But we'd agreed that it was only temporary, so I couldn't go back on my word. I really wanted to, but it wouldn't be fair to Halle.

Yeah, I'd written these songs, but I still had to find a way to record, distribute and market them and that would be intense and time-consuming. Halle deserved someone who could give her all the attention in the world and who lived in the same state as her. And that wasn't me.

That was why I had to make sure tonight's date was something she'd remember forever, for all the right reasons. What I was planning was ambitious, but thankfully Sammie said her partner Romeo and a French Love Alchemist guy I hadn't met, called Claude, had the skills I needed to pull everything off. I hoped she was right.

My cell buzzed and my jaw tensed. This morning was the first time I'd turned it on it two days.

On Wednesday, Wilma had called again, demanding that I reveal Halle's identity immediately. I refused. She called back and I told her no again. But when she called a third time, I switched it off.

The only reason I'd switched it on again was because Halle had another request to do a guest's nails and she didn't know when she'd be back so said she'd call to update me and the phone in the villa wasn't working properly.

I was so damn proud of Halle. She was killing it with all the nails she'd done. Just like I knew she would.

When the first guest request came in, she was gonna turn it down because she said we were on holiday and she wanted to spend the time with me, but I reminded her that this was her future and I wanted her to succeed.

Plus, I might've offered to congratulate her with my tongue if she accepted the job... That incentive seemed to work. And whilst she was gone, I wrote another song, so it worked out well for both of us.

We worked well together. Everything felt so... effortless. There was no drama, we just connected on every level.

My cell stopped ringing, then started again. I'd gotten so distracted thinking about Halle that I'd forgotten to even look at it.

It was Wilma.

Fuck it. I'd be leaving the hotel tomorrow, so I'd call her back once I'd left. I wasn't gonna let her ruin my mood or my last day here with Halle.

I switched off the phone. Halle would try and call but hopefully when she couldn't get through, she'd just come back to the villa.

About an hour later, the villa door opened.

'Hey!' Halle waved, then walked out to the garden. 'You're here! I was trying to call you.'

'Yeah, sorry.' I got up to kiss her. 'My cell was on but Wilma called again, so I switched it off.'

'She still hassling you about posting a proper photo of me?'

'Yep.'

'Maybe I could...'

'No,' I said firmly. 'You've already done enough. It's fine. We'll be leaving tomorrow, so...'

My words lingered in the air and our eyes locked. I wondered if she was dreading saying goodbye forever as much as I was.

'How'd it go with your customer?' I changed the subject.

'Amazing!' Halle beamed. 'She was so happy and asked if I'd have time to do her girlfriend's nails too for their final date tonight too. They're the cutest couple. Apparently, they hit it off straightaway and put a label on their relationship by day two. I wouldn't be surprised if they got engaged tonight!'

'Wow.'

'She said, *when you know, you know...*' Halle held my gaze. 'Anyway, I said I couldn't because I had my own match to spend time with.'

'You should do it!' I said. 'Just think of the extra photos you'll get to add to your portfolio. And, if I'm honest, I need to spend a couple of hours preparing for our date tonight.'

'Oooh, I'm dying to know what you've got planned. Can't you give me a little hint?'

'Nope. It's a surprise. But I think you'll like it. At least I hope so.'

'Aaargh! Such a tease! You won't tell me anything about all the songs you've been writing this week and now you won't tell me about our date! How will I know what to wear if I don't know where we're going?'

'Doesn't matter what you wear. You'll look beautiful.'

'Such a smooth talker!' Halle wrapped her arms around my waist, then kissed me softly. I was just about to lift her onto the daybed and ask her if she wanted a little afternoon delight, when the doorbell rang.

'Dammit,' I groaned. 'Talk about bad timing. I'll be right back.'

I strode to the door and when I opened it, my jaw crashed to the ground.

'Good afternoon, sir, Ms Beaker is here to see you. I tried to call but your phone was off and the villa phone wasn't working and she said it was an emergency so I decided to escort her—'

'I'll take it from here.' Wilma jumped in before pushing past the staff member, stepping inside the villa and slamming the door behind her.

'What the fuck are you doing here?' I spat, my heart thundering against my ribcage.

'You've been avoiding my calls,' she poked at my chest with her finger, 'so I had to come and find you. Is that her?' Wilma strained her neck to look out onto the patio where Halle was relaxing on the daybed. 'Jake, she's a fucking babe! Why aren't you putting photos of her online?' She reached in her purse, pulled out her cell, then headed towards Halle.

'Don't you fucking dare, Wilma!' I shouted, racing in front of her. 'Baby!' I called out, in desperation, deliberately not using Halle's name. I didn't want Wilma to know anything about her. 'Go to the bedroom.'

'Jake?' Halle came rushing in. 'What's wrong? Who's this?'

'This is Wilma. Go! She's gonna try and take photos of you!' I held out my arms and stood in front of Halle, trying to shield her.

'She'd better get used to the photos. When you guys appear on your reality show together, there'll be a lot more of them. The press are gonna love her!'

'Reality show?' Halle moved from behind me, concern etched all over her face. 'What reality show? What's she talking about, Jake?'

'You didn't tell her?' Wilma laughed.

'No, I... it was irrelevant,' I stuttered, the blood draining from my veins.

'I think it's pretty relevant to explain that she's about to be thrust into the limelight. We've got two production companies keen to have talks about giving you your own show, but they needed to see how she looked first. And now I've seen your mystery lady for myself, there won't be a problem. She's pretty and she's exotic, which will help the show appeal to a wider audience.'

'*Exotic*?' I ground my jaw. 'She's a person, not a piece of fucking fruit! Don't be disrespectful.'

'Reality show?' Halle repeated.

'It's not how it sounds, baby,' I protested.

'I don't want to be in a reality show!'

'Awww,' Wilma said in a condescending tone. 'Don't tell me you thought all of this was for real, honey? Jake didn't come here to fall in love. He came to relaunch his career. We planned it all together: he pretends to fall in love to get a TV show, you guys get engaged, sell the story to the media, meanwhile he just happens to mention that he's working on some new music and *boom*! He gets a record deal. Then once everything's set up, the endorsements roll in and you've made enough cash, then you two put out a statement on social media to say that after a lot of soul searching, you've decided to break up. Then you'll both go your separate ways, significantly richer, of course!'

Halle blinked rapidly, her mouth opening and closing repeatedly like a hungry goldfish as she struggled to speak.

'Tell me it's not true, Jake!' She looked at me and when I saw tears streaming down her cheeks, I felt like I'd been punched in the gut. 'Tell me that's not why you came here!'

'It's not... I mean, *yeah*, that was the plan in the beginning. But only because I was supposed to be matched with someone high profile who needed to revive their career too.'

'So you were disappointed to be matched with me?'

'No! Yes, but only because I didn't want to lead you on—'

'So instead, you lied!'

'I didn't lie, I... I said—'

'You said you were just trying to improve your image!'

'I was!'

'But you didn't say that you were trying to trick me into appearing on a reality show! Or *anything* about us getting engaged! So this was all fake? It was all a set-up?'

'No!' I went to rest my hand on her shoulder and she brushed it off. 'Everything I feel for you is real. I swear.'

'I told you how important the truth was to me, Jake. You knew how hard it was for me to trust again, but you lied to me and... Wait, are you *filming* this?' Halle glared at Wilma who was holding her cell up in her direction. 'This is fucked up!'

Halle sprinted to the front door, opened it then raced outside.

I went to run after her, then stopped. If Wilma was filming, I needed to deal with that footage first before she uploaded it or sent it to God knows who. I had to protect Halle.

'What the fuck, Wilma!' I snatched her cell from her hand and stopped the recording.

'That's mine!' Wilma shrieked. 'Give it back!'

I raced into the bathroom, locked the door, then deleted the video. Then I went in the trash and made sure I deleted it from there too.

When I went back in her photo library, I spotted dozens of photos she'd taken of the hotel and most importantly of Halle, so I canned those as well.

Once I was sure every trace of Halle was off Wilma's phone, I unlocked the door. When I came out, Wilma was in the bedroom, trying to open Halle's suitcase.

'What the hell are you doing?'

'Finding info on your mystery woman.'

'Get the fuck out of here. *Now*!' I grabbed her arm.

'Get off me!' Wilma said as I pulled her out of the door.

When I left, I saw one of the groundsmen I'd become friendly with.

'Brian. Can you call security, please? We've got a trespasser.'

'On it, sir.' He nodded.

I continued escorting Wilma down the path.

'You can't do this!' she protested. 'And give me back my goddamn cell!'

'Fuck your cell, and fuck you.'

'You better speak to me with respect, boy. I'm the key to your future. The production companies will only speak to *me* about this deal. You need me.'

'The hell I do! You crossed too many lines, Wilma. I might not have my career or a home any more, but do you know what I do have?'

'You don't have shit, Jakey boy. Especially without me.'

'Stop fucking calling me Jakey boy! And you're wrong. I'm cash poor, yeah. But I'm the richest I've ever been because I have love.'

As those words flew from my mouth, I swallowed hard.

Shit.

I didn't mean to say that.

Not because it wasn't true, though, because it totally was.

I was in love with Halle. Totally, completely head over heels.

I hadn't used the L word in the songs I'd written, but the sentiment and the meaning was there.

Halle was the first person I thought of when I woke up and the last person I thought about at night.

When I wasn't with her, I wanted to be with her.

It was a damn shame that in life you couldn't always get what you wanted.

'Are you kidding me?' She rolled her eyes. 'You think you're in *love* with this chick? *Jesus.* You've known her for five minutes! Just because a woman knows how to suck your cock and spreads her legs for you, doesn't mean it's love! You need me more than I thought!'

'That's where you're wrong. I don't need you. The only reason I thought I did was because you took me on when I was at my lowest point and you've manipulated me ever since. But the difference is that thanks to meeting an amazing woman, now I believe in myself. I've got talent and I know I'll make it on my own. *Without* doing a fucking reality TV show. Wilma, you're fired!'

Right on cue, two burly security guards rocked up.

'Is there a problem here?' one of them asked.

'Sure is,' I said. 'This woman isn't authorised to be on the hotel grounds. She's harassing me and my match. Please can you remove her?'

'Right away, Mr Myers. Ma'am. Please come with us.'

'You can't do this!' Wilma shouted as they guided her towards the gates.

'I just did.' I went to walk off, then stopped. 'Hey, Wilma. You forgot this.'

I threw her phone towards her. She went to catch it but it slipped out of her hands and crashed to the ground.

'No!' she cried out. 'It's smashed!'

'Too bad. Guess you need to practise your catching skills. Maybe there's some kind of baseball reality show you can apply for.' I smirked, then walked away.

As her screams and wails faded into the distance, pride filled my chest.

I was free.

Deep down I'd always known that Wilma was wrong for me, but I was so desperate that I thought without her, I wouldn't survive.

But now I realised that she was holding me back.

Worse than that, she was encouraging me to do things that went against everything I believed in. I'd been someone's puppet before and I sure as shit wasn't doing that again.

The songs I'd written these past few days were *good*. No. They were *great*. I felt it in my bones. And I could do this.

I'd release my music myself, on my own terms. This was my calling and I wasn't gonna waste it.

When I left the band, I thought I'd never sing again. But I did.

I rose from the ashes once and I knew that I could do it again.

But first, I had something that was even more important to focus on: Explaining everything to Halle.

And finding a way to win her back.

42

HALLE

How could I be so stupid?

As I marched along the beach, tears streamed down my cheeks. Not even the blazing sunshine, the feel of the soft sand between my toes or watching the waves rippling towards the shore could lift my mood right now.

I didn't know what was worse: agreeing to have a holiday fling with another musician or believing that I could actually trust him.

Didn't matter. Either way, I'd gone against my better judgement and now my heart was paying the price.

Jake had lied to me. He knew how important it was for him to be truthful and open. And despite that, he'd failed to mention that he wanted me to appear in a fucking reality TV show with him!

That was my idea of hell and he knew that.

Maybe that was why he was being so nice to me. He was just trying to get in my good books. He must've thought that if he gave me enough orgasms, I'd be so dickmatised that I'd agree to do anything he'd ask.

Well, he was wrong.

But it didn't make sense. He'd insisted multiple times that he didn't want to expose me by putting me on his social media, so why the hell would he think that I'd want to be on TV?

And he said he had feelings for me, yet he admitted the TV show was part of his plan.

Okay, technically this was supposed to be casual, so he didn't owe me anything. Plus, we'd be leaving the hotel tomorrow and might never see each other again. But I still felt hurt, betrayed and misled.

Maybe I shouldn't have run off. I should've listened to see if there was an explanation, but if there was and he really cared, he would've come to find me. Instead, he'd stayed with Wilma. Probably to cook up their next scheme of how to get me to take part in their stupid plan.

My mind was spinning.

I plonked myself down on the sand and dropped my head in my hands.

I really liked Jake.

So much.

I was embarrassed to even think it, but it felt like more than *like.*

Even though I'd told my heart not to want him because this was always going to be temporary, I knew I'd fallen for him.

Big time.

I was in bloody love with him.

Shit.

What a fool.

'There you are!' a woman's voice called out. My neck snapped up and I saw that it was Sammie. 'I've been looking for you. So has Jake.'

'He has?'

'Yep. Poor guy's distraught.'

Although I hated to know that Jake was down, hearing that he was upset at least showed he cared. Hope bloomed in my chest, but then common sense kicked it to the kerb.

'He's just worried he won't be able to get his stupid reality show.'

'Reality show?' Sammie frowned. I filled her in on what'd happened. She waited until I was finished before speaking. 'Obviously you know Jake better than me, but ask yourself, does that really sound like something he'd do to you? Honestly?'

'A few hours ago I would've said no. He always seemed genuine when he said he didn't want to make me feel uncomfortable.'

'And how did he react when he saw his agent taking photos?'

'He told me to go the bedroom and he told her to... stop.'

I paused and replayed everything that happened when Wilma turned up in slow motion. This time I put my emotions to one side.

Yes, he'd shielded me from her.

He'd said the reality show thing was 'irrelevant' now.

And he'd insisted that was the plan 'in the beginning' but that he had real feelings for me.

Jake wasn't trying to trap me. He wanted to protect me.

'I shouldn't have run,' I sighed. 'I should've listened to his explanation.'

'Is that what your gut tells you?'

'Yeah. My gut tells me he's a good man. He wouldn't hurt me. Not on purpose.'

'Everything I've seen of him backs that up. For example, what he did to encourage you to start doing nails again was so sweet.'

'Huh?' My brows creased. 'What did he do?'

'Full disclosure: it wasn't a coincidence that I asked you to do my nails. Obvs you know I loved your creations – it's one of the first things I noticed when we met, so that was totally genuine. But it was *Jake* that messaged me to ask if I ever needed to get my nails done and if I did, if I'd consider asking you.'

I blinked several times, trying to digest this revelation.

'He said that you were super talented and he knew you'd go far, but you just needed a break and he'd be grateful if I could give you a chance.'

My heart swelled. That was so thoughtful.

'I didn't realise.'

For a few seconds I felt awkward because I hated the thought of Sammie feeling obligated to say yes. But like she'd said, she *had* complimented my nails before and when I'd done hers, she was genuinely happy with them.

'And he's been working so hard on your date tonight. What he has planned is some next-level stuff. So if you ask me, your gut is spot on. A man doesn't go to those kind of lengths if he's not into you.'

I reflected on Sammie's words for a few beats.

Of course it was possible that he was doing this to butter me up to take part in whatever he'd planned with his agent. But if I took into account everything I'd learnt about him, that didn't ring true.

When I'd first met him, I thought he was an arrogant, self-absorbed wanker who was obsessed with posting on social media. But I sensed that he hated posting as much as I did.

So would someone that didn't like showing his life online really want to allow a bunch of cameras to follow him around?

No.

Now that I was thinking more clearly, I knew I had two options:

I could either let my fear and past experiences continue to

affect my future, not hear Jake out, waste the time I had left at the hotel moping, then go back to New York never really understanding what really happened.

Or I could be brave, put my heart on the line one more time, hear Jake out and try and make the most of the time I had left at this gorgeous resort with him, then go home with no regrets and my head held high, knowing that I'd done everything I could to make this work.

It was a no-brainer.

'I need to speak to him.'

'That's the spirit!' Sammie cheered. 'But... you can't right now.'

'Why not?'

'Because he's not here.'

'Where's he gone?'

'I could tell you, but then I'd have to kill you!' Sammie laughed. I didn't. 'Sorry! That was supposed to be a joke. I've just always wanted to say that! Anyway, Jake had to leave to sort out stuff for tonight. But he asked me to find you in the meantime and said if you can meet him at eight tonight, he promises to explain everything. So what do you say? Can I tell him that you're gonna give him a chance? Will you still go ahead with the date?'

'Yeah,' I said quickly. 'I will.'

43

HALLE

As Sammie led me to a secret location, my heart hammered against my ribcage.

She'd blindfolded me with a silk scarf, at Jake's request because he wanted everything to be a surprise. I knew we were on the beach, as I could feel the sand and smell the fresh salty sea air. I was intrigued to find out what he had planned.

'Almost there,' Sammie said. After a few more minutes, she stopped. 'I'm going to untie the blindfold now.'

I felt her stand behind me then the blindfold loosened.

'Ta-da!' Sammie whipped it off dramatically.

I blinked a few times as my eyes adjusted to the light.

There was a large projector screen, just like the one that was used for the movie night on the beach last week.

In front of it was one of the hotel's large, comfy white double sofas with cream and gold pillows and blankets.

I guessed we must be watching a film. Probably a romcom. But from the way Sammie had hyped up the date and spoken about how much work Jake had put into preparing it, that didn't seem right.

Jake stepped out from behind the screen and my heart skipped a beat.

'Hey,' he said softly.

It'd only been hours since I'd seen him, but it felt like weeks. As crazy as it sounded, I'd missed him.

And God, he looked gorgeous.

He was wearing a fitted white T-shirt and black jean shorts. So understated, but *so* sexy.

'I'll leave you guys to it – for now...' Sammie turned then left.

'Hi,' I said as Jake approached the sofa.

'Thanks for coming.' He flashed a cautious smile. 'I know you'll have some questions, but first, there's something I'd like to show you. Is that okay?'

'Okay,' I said.

We both sat down. I desperately wanted to snuggle up beside him, but instead, I sat at the furthest end. I was going to give him a chance to explain everything, but until then I had to keep my guard up. Just in case.

Jake pressed play on the remote control.

The title 'You Light Up the Room' flashed up on the screen and the sound of a guitar playing filled the air. I immediately started tapping my feet, it was catchy.

Next, a flurry of photos filled the screen.

Photos of *me*.

My jaw dropped and I looked at Jake, confusion written all over my face.

And then the lyrics started: 'Whenever I'm feeling blue, when I see you, you light up the room...'

'Wait...' I paused, my brain scrambling. 'This is your voice. Is this one of your new songs?'

Jake nodded, still staying silent.

More photos flooded the screen. This time it was photos of us together. The one from the horse riding, the pic Sammie took of us at The Huntington, a selfie Jake snapped on the Pacific Wheel at Santa Monica beach and so many others.

A million thoughts flooded my mind: how bloody brilliant this song was, what an amazing singer Jake was, how much I loved the lyrics, how cute we looked together in the photos, plus how glad I was that I'd got over my fear of having them taken so that I had all these memories to look back on. And how an earth he'd managed to put all of this together.

Now I understood why Sammie thought I'd be impressed.

She was right to, because this was epic.

It was just Jake singing and playing the guitar, so it was an acoustic performance that had the kind of pop/rock feel of bands like The Script, OneRepublic and Imagine Dragons, mixed with the soulful vibe of artists like Usher, Khalid and Myles Smith, Arlo Parks and Masego. I freaking loved it.

The song ended and I instantly wished I could press rewind and hear it all over again for the first time.

But just when I thought it'd finished, Jake appeared on screen. He was at Santa Monica Pier. I recognised the Pacific Wheel in the background.

A man with short dark hair appeared with a microphone. He seemed like he was about to interview him. I frowned, not understanding what was going on.

'So today, I am here at Pacific Park in Santa Monica with Jake Myers, who has just unveiled a brand-new single called, "You Light Up the Room". Jake, what inspired you to write this song?'

'I wrote it about a very special woman. It's been a while since I've written or released any new music. I just hadn't found the right inspiration. But then I met this amazing woman and the words just poured onto the page. I wrote the whole song in thirty minutes.'

I looked at Jake, then the screen, my face contorting in a million different directions. My brain was more scrambled than a dozen fried eggs.

My first thought was that it was a song about Minnie because we'd spoken about him writing something about her. But I quickly realised that didn't track, because Jake just said he'd *met* an amazing woman, which sounded more recent.

Then I remembered something in the lyrics talking about kissing.

Which meant that...

No way.

Could it be about... *me*?

I wanted to ask, but if I was wrong, I'd feel like an egotistical twat, so I kept quiet and continued watching the interview.

'Wow, must be a very special lady,' the man, who I noticed had a French accent, added.

'She is. She's smart, kind, caring, talented and so damn beautiful.'

'And you have brought us to Santa Monica Pier. Please can you explain the significance of this location?'

'Sure. I wanted to come here because it's where we had our first kiss.' Jake looked into the camera this time. 'Right up there on the Pacific Wheel.'

OMG. OMG. OMG!

I gasped. It really *was* about me.

'That's so romantic,' the French guy said. 'Well, "You Light Up the Room" sounds like it will be a big hit and I hope that your special lady agrees. Good luck.'

'Thanks,' Jake said before turning to the camera again then saying, 'In case you haven't already guessed, Smiley, I wrote this song for you.'

My eyebrows hit the ceiling.

My heart somersaulted in my chest.

And a zillion butterflies fluttered in my stomach.

Jake wrote me a song.

Wow.

I fanned my hand in front of my face. If I wasn't careful, I'd start crying.

The screen went blank then I felt Jake's gaze on me.

'So...' he said, as I turned to face him. 'Did you like it?'

'I...' My mouth opened and closed as I searched for the right words to convey the emotions racing through me.

Even if I swallowed a thesaurus, it wouldn't even convey 1 per cent of the joy I felt right now.

'I can't believe you wrote me a song! It's bloody amazing! Incredible! Honestly, I can't even begin to tell you how much I love it, thank you!'

'You're not just saying that to protect my ego, right?'

'No!' I protested, wondering how he could think that for a second when the song was so brilliant. 'I genuinely, one thousand million trillion per cent love it! And not just because it's about me. It's so catchy and the lyrics are beautiful, Jake. Honestly. It's a banger! It's got hit record written all over it!'

'Thank fuck.' He blew out a breath. 'I thought it sounded pretty cool, but I really wanted *you* to like it.'

'How did you prepare all of this though? Recording the song, making the video and putting it all together?'

'Sammie's boyfriend, Romeo, put me in touch with one of the guys who's here from the French Love Hotel, Claude.'

'There's a Love Hotel in Paris?'

'Shoot! It's supposed to be a secret for now. They're opening *two* new Love Hotels in France soon: one in Paris and the other in the South of France and he's one of the Love Alchemists they've hired, so he's kind of here to shadow the Love Alchemists in LA and learn from them. Anyway, he's a whizz at making videos and stuff so he helped put everything together. That was him interviewing me. We filmed that this afternoon, not long after the whole incident with Wilma...'

'Oh...' I said.

'So, about that.' His expression turned serious. 'I'm sorry if I hurt you. I wanted to tell you the full story, but I didn't want you to freak out. I thought I was protecting you, but now I can see that I fucked up. Yeah, it's true that in the beginning I agreed to Wilma's dumb reality show idea. Reluctantly.'

'To help your career?'

'Yeah. Wilma said it was my only chance of saving it. I told her I thought it was crazy and that I wasn't comfortable leading someone on. But she assured me that I'd be matched with someone in the public eye who also wanted to revive their career. She said it'd be mutually beneficial. That's why when we first met, I asked if you were an actress or influencer.'

'Ohhh.' I nodded, as I remembered thinking that was strange. 'But when you found out that I wasn't and that I was here to find love, why didn't you tell her?'

'I did! But as far as Wilma was concerned, everyone is for sale and everyone wants to be famous.'

'Not me!'

'I know and I told her that. But she insisted I continue. So I went along with it whilst I tried to figure out what to do for the best. I kinda convinced myself that because you seemed to think I was a jerk, there was no danger of you getting hurt and it wouldn't be long until we went our separate ways anyway, so I might as well enjoy my time at the hotel for however long it lasted. But then I started getting to know you and I began to like you and... when I realised the attraction was mutual, I tried to minimise the risk of leading you on by making it clear that I couldn't do anything serious. I figured that I shouldn't make the decision for you. If you were interested, you'd agree but if not, you'd say no and I'd have to walk away.'

'I respect that,' I acknowledged. 'Like I said at the time, I was glad that you were upfront, but I wish I knew the whole story.'

'I hear you. But honestly, at that point, I had no intention of ever asking you to do a reality show, so I thought it didn't make sense to worry you. Especially because it was just supposed to be casual. But I meant what I said earlier. I *do* have feelings for you. I've loved spending time with you, and I've never felt so inspired to write. I wanted to show you how much you mean to me. That's why I made that clip. I haven't done any playlists or been properly keeping up with the memory book, so I thought I'd make a mini movie with photos and write you some songs instead. This is Hollywood, after all!' His lips curved into a smile.

'Well, I really appreciate it. The song, the movie and the explanation.'

'It's the least I could do. Oh, and I fired Wilma.'

'No way!'

'Yep! I grabbed her cell, deleted all the videos and photos she took of you, told her she was toast and that I didn't want to work with her any more, then had her escorted off the property.'

'Whoa!' My eyes popped. That explained why he didn't come after me. 'Thanks for looking out for me and deleting everything. What did she say when you fired her?'

'That I needed her. But I know that's bullshit. It's gonna be hard, but I believe in myself. I can do it without her.'

'Too right! Fuck you, Wilma!' I shouted in solidarity and a wide grin spread across Jake's face. 'You've got this! There's no way that song won't be a hit.'

'Let's hope you're right. Wanna hear some more songs?'

'Yeah! I knew you'd been writing a lot, but I didn't know they were all finished.'

'I haven't been able to record them, but I've finished writing them. I told you, baby, I've been on fire, thanks to you. Not to sound obsessed, but I've written three more songs about you and one about Minnie.'

'I'd *love* to hear them.'

'Cool. I'll play them all to you. Including one I wrote in the car to Santa Monica Pier today, called "I Fucked Up".'

'You did *not* write a song called that!' I laughed.

'Sure did!' Jake got up and walked around the back of the screen, then reappeared clutching his guitar.

He stood in front of me, started playing an upbeat melody on his guitar then burst into song.

> Hey, hey, what can I say?
> It wasn't okay.
> Baby, I know I fucked up.
> Please say it's not too late.
> I'm begging you to stay.
> Baby, I know I fucked up.

As Jake continued singing, laughter bubbled in my chest. The more he sang, the more hilarious the lyrics became and when he finished, he took a bow.

'That's actually genius!' I giggled. 'I can hear men playing that song to their wives, girlfriends, boyfriends, lovers around the world. That'll become an anthem!'

'Why, thank you!' He bowed again, before resting his guitar on the sofa. 'But the real question is, did it work? Do you forgive me?'

'Hmmm.' I dramatically rested my finger on my chin and

paused like I was a judge on a talent show, drawing out the announcement of the winner.

'You're killing me.' He squeezed his eyes shut like he was in pain.

'*Of course* I do!' I jumped off the sofa and wrapped my arms around him, squeezing him tightly. 'Just please don't lie to me again.'

'Never.' He brushed a strand of hair away from my eyes. 'Can I kiss you?'

'Yes,' I said, my breath catching in my throat. 'I'd really like that.'

As soon as Jake's lips connected with mine, everything felt right in the world.

Every doubt, concern and worry washed away and the whole world fell silent.

Nothing else existed. Just us.

We kissed like these were our last moments together.

Like we wouldn't see each other for a dozen lifetimes.

Like our survival depended on our mouths being moulded together.

Jake's hands roamed hungrily down my back before clutching my arse and my greedy palms did the same to him. As his hardness pressed against me, tingles shot up my spine and my knees buckled.

'Fuck, Halle,' he gasped into my mouth, before pulling away slowly. 'You don't know how much I want to continue kissing you, but if we do, we'll end up fucking and we've only had part one of our date.'

'Part one? How many parts are there?'

'Three... maybe four.'

'And I suppose you're not going to tell me what they are?'

'Where's the fun in that?' he smirked, before picking up his guitar. 'Please take a seat.' He gestured to the sofa and I sat down. 'First, I want to play you another song. It's called "When You Smile".'

As Jake serenaded me with his soothing, soulful voice, I pinched myself. This felt like a dream. Having an amazing man standing here, singing a beautiful song that he wrote for *me*.

Jake looked at me like I'd invented sound.

Like I was the human equivalent of his favourite song.

And that made me feel like a goddess.

Once Jake finished that song, he launched into three more. The one about Minnie was so beautiful, I cried.

'That concludes tonight's performance,' Jake said.

'One more song! One more song!' I chanted.

'I've played you everything!' he laughed, a proud grin the size of the Pacific Ocean breaking out across his face.

'They're all too good! I'm not ready for this concert to end yet. *Please*. Play me something else. I love your voice so much. I don't care if you sing "Chitty Chitty Bang Bang" or "Twinkle, Twinkle, Little Star". Even if you sang the instructions to constipation tablets, you'd make it sound amazing!'

'Thank you!' he laughed. 'Well, I've done a jingle for butter, maybe it's time to branch out. Today, constipation tablets, tomorrow laxatives. I could become the face of drugstores worldwide!'

'Yes!' I chuckled, then my stomach rumbled.

'Sounds like someone's hungry,' he said, before clutching his guitar with one hand, then reaching in his pocket to pull out his phone with the other. He tapped away on his screen, then returned it to his pocket.

'Yep! Hungry for more songs! Do you want me to beg? Because I will!'

'You'll get your songs, but first, say hi to Alejandro, who'll be cooking us dinner tonight.'

I turned around and saw Alejandro walking towards us carrying a food box.

'Hi!' I said.

'Nice to see you both,' Alejandro replied. 'I will let you know when everything is ready.'

'*Gracias*,' Jake said.

'Where's he going?' I asked.

'Behind that screen is the set-up for the next part of tonight's date. He's gonna grill some ribs and dirty burgers. Sound good?'

'Sounds perfect!'

'In the meantime, I'll sing you a few songs. I can do a cool version of "Wannabe" by the Spice Girls or because I know you like eighties music too, we could have "Never Gonna Give You Up" by Rick Astley. What's it gonna be?'

'Both!' I squealed.

* * *

Three hours later, we were curled up on the daybed.

Apparently, whilst we'd been enjoying the delicious food that Alejandro had whipped up for dinner, on the other side of the screen a team had replaced the sofa with the daybed, which had been draped with pretty fairylights to illuminate our surroundings and set up a romantic film for us to watch together to round off the evening.

I was going to press play to find out what it was, but Jake said Sammie was on her way to give us something.

'Sorry!' She rushed over to us. 'I got held up with one of the other couples. Did you enjoy your evening?' Sammie faced me.

'It's been amazing!'

'Awww, so glad to hear that. So I wanted to give you this.' She handed me a big red book. 'It's your memory book. I know you've already seen the photos on Jake's film earlier, but I thought you'd like a hard copy now, to look at it together. I've got another one in my office for you too, Jake.'

'Thanks so much!' I said.

'So, we're all clocking off for the night now. This part of the beach has been sectioned off, so you'll be all alone...' She gave me a wink. 'Enjoy your time together!' Sammie raced off.

'This is cool,' Jake said as he sat up straighter. 'Shall we look at the memory book now?'

'Definitely,' I said.

As we turned the pages and saw the images of our time together, a mixture of joy and sadness filled my chest.

'These are beautiful.' Jake ran his finger over the photos, before turning to face me and stroke my cheek. 'I really wish things were different. I wish that we could be together,' he said, looking into my eyes.

'I know,' I said, a lump forming in my throat. 'Me too.'

As Jake kissed, then made love to me on the daybed, under the stars, I savoured every moment, praying that this wouldn't be the last time that I'd feel his heartbeat against mine. I hoped that it wouldn't be the final time that I'd feel him inside me or experience the intense connection we had.

Our bodies moved together perfectly and I knew this was intense, profound, and real.

This was more than just a crush, a fling or a holiday romance. This wasn't just sex. This was making love.

This felt like forever.

I didn't want this to end.

It couldn't.

As my orgasm ripped through me, an idea lit up like a light bulb in my brain.

That was it.

Yes.

That would solve everything.

I'd message Sammie first thing in the morning to see if she could help me set everything up in time.

Jake had been so kind to me. Not only had he made this whole trip unforgettable for all the right reasons, he'd made this evening magical too.

Now I wanted to show him how much he meant to me.

Jake said he wished there was a way we could be together and I was sure that I'd just found it...

44

JAKE

I put the last of my clothes in my suitcase then let out a long, defeated sigh.

I couldn't believe that in just half an hour, I'd be leaving this villa and Halle.

Forever.

Last night was off the charts.

Even when Sammie had messaged whilst I was at Santa Monica filming, to say that Halle had agreed to come on the date, I still couldn't believe it.

My heart was in my throat for the rest of the day because I was worrying whether she really would turn up and, if she did, whether she'd forgive me.

When Halle told me she loved my songs and accepted my apology, I was so happy I was convinced that if I took my feet off the ground, I'd float away. I was on cloud nine.

The evening couldn't have gone better. The conversation, the food, the sex...

Except this time, when I was inside her, it was more than that.

I felt the connection in my soul. It was like I'd come home. That being with Halle was where I belonged.

After we'd finished making love, we'd watched *Pretty Woman* again (we didn't get to watch it properly last time), then headed back to the villa where we fell asleep as soon as our heads hit our pillows.

We ordered in breakfast, then once she'd packed, Halle said she had to see Sammie about something. Now I was here, waiting for her to come back, so I could kiss her properly. For the last time.

A sharp pain shot through my chest.

I already knew that this was gonna be one of the most painful experiences of my life. I didn't want to say goodbye, but I had no choice.

'Hi!' Halle called out as I heard the door slam behind her. 'I'm back! Can you come out here, please?'

'Sure,' I shouted back, before wheeling my suitcase out, my heart feeling heavier than a bag of stones. 'Hey, beautiful.' I kissed her on the lips, wondering how I was gonna survive without being able to do that every day like I'd gotten so used to doing.

Getting over her was gonna feel impossible, but somehow, I'd have to find a way to do it. I had no other choice.

'Hey, you!' she replied, her hands behind her back. She sounded surprisingly upbeat considering we only had minutes left together.

'What you hiding there?' I asked.

'Gifts. For you.'

She thrust her hands in front of me. Halle was holding a small red rectangular box.

'You got me jewellery?' I frowned.

'Hmmm, no. Open it.'

I took the box from her and when I popped the lid, I saw that it was a key.

'So, I was thinking...' She looked at me, a mixture of nerves and excitement in her eyes. 'You said last night that you're not ready to say goodbye to me, right?'

'Right,' I said quickly.

'So, let's not. This doesn't have to be the end! Come to New York and move in with me!' she blurted out and my eyes popped. 'That's the key to my apartment. Sammie arranged for it to be cut this morning. I know it's fast, but when you know, you know, right? I remember reading something that said, "When a guy likes you, you'll know and when he doesn't, you'll be confused." And I *know* that you like me. I can feel it. *Here*.' She touched her heart and I blinked rapidly, still trying to take in the magnitude of what she was asking.

'I...' I stuttered, trying to think of what to say.

'And I believe in you!' she continued. 'Those new songs you wrote are incredible. I'm certain that you'll get your career back on track. You're gonna thrive. The world's about to become your oyster. And I want to be right beside you, cheering you on, every step of the way. So live with me and get back on your feet. My place isn't fancy, but you'll have a roof to sleep under and a slightly lumpy, but semi-comfortable bed to sleep in! I know it's early and it's a risk, but if it doesn't work, we'll find out pretty quickly, but something tells me that it will.'

I stood there, mouth open, stunned into silence.

'Halle... wow. Thanks for the offer, that's... That's so kind of you. I don't know what to say.'

'Say yes!' she beamed.

'I want to. I really do. I meant what I said last night. I don't want to lose you.' I paused for several beats. 'But I can't. My life is here – in LA. And I... I can't give you what you need. I'm not boyfriend material.'

'Oh.' Her shoulders slumped and my stomach dropped. 'I thought you had feelings for me. Our date yesterday... the songs you wrote, our connection...'

'I *do* have feelings for you. I *do* want to be with you, but I... I just can't right now. I need to get my shit together first. And it wouldn't be fair for me to ask you to wait. I know you're mainly asking because you know I don't have a home any more which is kind but I don't want you to pity me. And I don't want to hold you back.'

'Right.' The silence stretched and her gaze dropped to the floor. 'Where will you go?'

'An old friend of mine, Liam Stone, has a house in LA that he rents out that's just become vacant. The new tenants don't move in until next month, so he's said I can crash there for a few weeks.'

'That's good.' Her face brightened for a second, then fell again. 'I'm glad you'll have somewhere to stay. Wait. Liam Stone the actor?'

'Yeah. He's one of the few good ones who still checks on me every so often and didn't ignore my calls when my life went to shit.'

'And what about your music?'

'I'll keep working on it. I've put the feelers out to see if I'm able to call in some favours to get studio time. If not, I'll get a job somewhere to pay for it.'

She nodded, then got up.

At first, I thought she was so pissed off with me that she'd left. But then Halle came back holding a white envelope.

'Here.' She handed it to me.

'What's this?' I said, turning it over and ripping it open. When I saw what was inside my eyes bulged.

It was filled with cash.

'It's all the money I earned from doing nails this week. I want you to have it. Use it to put towards your studio time, food or rent.'

I opened my mouth to speak then closed it again.

My mind raced and my heart swelled.

From what Halle had told me, she didn't make much from working in the juice bar. And because she didn't get much vacation time, she wasn't getting paid whilst she was here either, so I knew it'd be a struggle for her to make ends meet this month.

The money that she'd earned from doing nails would be important to her.

That's why I couldn't believe that she'd give it all to me.

That she'd make that sacrifice *for me.*

That she'd make her own life harder to make mine easier.

'I can't take this.' I closed the envelope and handed it back to her but she refused to take it. 'You worked hard for this. You earned it fair and square and you need it too.'

'No. I want you to have it. Use it to make your career a success. I know it's only a few hundred dollars and I wish I could give you more, but it's all I have. *Please.* If you won't come to New York, and even if we never see each other again...' She swallowed hard and my stomach twisted at the thought. 'Even if we're not together, I still want you to succeed. I want you to be safe and happy.'

I had no words.

This woman was fucking incredible.

My heart squeezed and I wasn't ashamed to admit that when a tear rolled down my cheek, I didn't even wipe it away.

She'd got me good.

I stepped forward, opened my arms then wrapped them around her.

We both cried, the sound of our emotional sobs echoing around the room.

'I love you, Halle,' I whispered. 'I will *always* love you. You are the most amazing woman I've ever met. I really wish things were different. Know that if they were, I'd be with you in a heartbeat.'

We held each other for a few more minutes, before she slowly pulled away.

When I looked at Halle, her eyes were red rimmed and her cheeks were stained with tears.

Seeing her cry and not being able to do anything to make it stop was like having a machete thrust straight into my heart.

I wiped her cheeks with my thumb, still trying to stop my own tears from falling.

I wasn't embarrassed to show my emotions. There was nothing wrong with a man crying. We hurt, we felt, we broke, just like women did. But I knew that I had to leave, because if I didn't, I'd make things harder. For both of us.

I leant forward and gently pressed my lips on hers.

My cell buzzed. I ignored it.

'You should get that,' she said softly.

'I... it's not important.'

'No, it's fine.'

I sighed and reached in my pocket.

'It's... it's the driver. He's at reception.'

'So, I suppose this is goodbye?' she said, her voice cracking.

'I... I guess so.' We stared at each other in silence, seconds then minutes elapsing, both of us finding it impossible to break each other's gaze.

When my cell buzzed a second, then a third time, I knew I had to be the one to rip off the band-aid.

'Bye, Smiley.' I kissed her forehead softly. 'Don't give up on doing those amazing nails and take good care of yourself. I love you,' I said, picking up my suitcase before walking away and feeling my heart shatter into a million pieces.

45

HALLE

As I glanced at my reflection in the mirror, I wondered whether I should plaster on another layer of concealer to hide the dark circles under my eyes.

I'd already put on two layers and although it was marginally better, I still looked like shit.

The past six days had been tough.

My last long-term relationship lasted for four years and the break-up was brutal. But although I'd only known Jake for two weeks and we were never officially dating, this felt harder.

When he'd left last Saturday, I'd stumbled out of the villa in a daze. Somehow I'd managed to muster up a half smile and mutter my thanks to Sammie when she came to say goodbye. But that was all. She'd asked how it went with Jake and all I could do was shake my head before I got into the car.

I was in shock.

I really thought I'd found the perfect solution. We'd stay together and he'd have a roof over his head to help him get back on his feet. Clearly I was wrong.

I'd fought back my tears during the flight, but once I was in the safety of my apartment, they came and didn't stop. I cried so much I was surprised I didn't flood my whole building.

Vanessa had called on the Sunday to suggest that she came round for a catch-up, but I couldn't. I just needed to mope and feel sorry for myself without judgement.

I knew it was stupid to be upset, given I'd agreed to a fling and nothing more from the outset, but what could I say? *The heart wants what the heart wants.* And sometimes it's completely illogical.

So I gave myself the rest of the weekend to get all of my tears out of my system. Then promised that come Monday morning, I'd throw myself into work.

It helped a little. When we were busy, there was no time to think about crying. But as soon as I had even a pocket of stillness, my thoughts turned to Jake. I'd wonder what he was doing. If he was okay. Whether he'd found a way to record his songs.

And of course I wondered if he'd thought about me.

Probably not.

He'd had much more experience with flings than I had, so although I believed that he was sad for it to end, the bottom line was he didn't want it to work as much as I did, so I just had to accept that and move on. Just like he had.

Which was why I'd pushed myself to keep as busy as possible. During the day I'd worked at the juice bar and at night, I'd been working on a plan to try and pursue my dream of becoming a full-time nail technician.

I'd popped into a few nail bars to ask if they had any vacancies, but so far I'd had no luck, which was why I was going to give the whole freelance route a go.

I had the photos of Sammie, Jasmine and the other guests' nails, so I was building a nice little portfolio.

Now I was waiting for Vanessa to come round so that I could do her nails and take more pics.

Although we'd messaged almost every day, this would be the first time I'd seen her since I got back.

Right on cue, the bell rang. I shoved my concealer back in my make-up bag, before going to open the door. Vanessa wouldn't care how I looked. She'd seen me at my lowest and loved me just the same.

'Hey,' I said as Vanessa stepped inside, holding a large bag.

'You been crying?' Her eyes narrowed.

'No!' I protested a little too much. It was sort of true. It'd been a whole half an hour since my last tears which was a lifetime compared to this week's sob-fest.

'Oh, hon.' She wrapped her arms around me. 'It'll get easier. And in the meantime, I've brought your prescription.'

'Prescription?'

'Yep.' She loosened her arms from around my waist, then walked over to the kitchen area of my studio apartment.

Everything was open plan with wooden floors and a high ceiling. The kitchen area was to the left of the door, then there was a two-seater burgundy sofa, with a small TV opposite. There was a tiny bathroom with a shower, then my small double bed was by the window. Like I'd said to Jake, it wasn't much. It definitely wouldn't compare to the luxury mansion he was staying in right now.

Jake.

I wondered if I'd ever be able to go more than two minutes without thinking about him.

'I don't follow. I don't have any prescriptions.'

'Oh, yes, you do. Dr Vanessa is prescribing you wine, chocolate, doughnuts and ice cream to get you out of this funk,' she said, unpacking the contents of the bag. 'By the time we've devoured this, you'll feel much better.'

I'd already eaten enough chocolate and ice cream to sink the *Titanic* this week, but what the hell. It was the weekend and calories didn't count.

'Thank you. Maybe I should do your nails first though. Not sure how steady my hands will be after I've had wine.'

'Okay, sweetie,' she said, following me to the two-seater kitchen table. 'So. How are you doing?'

'Better. I miss him like crazy, but that will stop soon, right?'

'Hopefully,' she said. 'Normally, instead of chocolate, I'd suggest you go and find a guy to take your mind off Jake. But (a) I know that's not you, and (b) I'm not gonna lie, I haven't seen you fall this hard for someone before, so I have to keep it real and tell you, it's not gonna be easy.'

Great.

I was hoping that Vanessa of all people would reassure me that I'd forget about Jake soon.

'I've got a feeling that you're right.'

'But *better to have loved and lost than never to have loved at all*, right?'

'Look at you getting all philosophical and talking about love!' I laughed. 'You sure you're feeling okay?'

'Very funny!' She rolled her eyes. 'Just because love isn't *my* cup of tea, doesn't mean I can't understand when other people are head over heels. You don't regret it though, right?'

'God, no,' I said without hesitation. 'I mean, yeah, when Jake left, I was kicking myself, thinking I'd pushed too much too quickly. And maybe asking someone to move in with you after knowing them for a fortnight was moving too fast. But I've never felt like that before. It all just seemed so right. My gut told me to try, so I'm glad I did. If I didn't ask, I would've always wondered, *what if?*'

'Babe, I'm not sure if you realise it, but you've grown so much. Pre-California Halle would've been beating herself up about asking him to come here. Actually, what am I saying? Pre-California Halle never would've had the courage to sleep with him, never mind ask such a big question. But you did. When life gave you lemons, you didn't just make lemonade. You made limoncello, lemon drizzle cake *and* lemon sorbet! You pushed yourself out of your comfort zone and although it didn't work out how you wanted, you made the most of your time there. I'm so fucking proud of you!'

'Thanks,' I said, pride filling my chest.

She was right. I had come a long way in the last three weeks. I felt stronger.

Things hadn't lasted with Jake, but if it wasn't for him, I wouldn't believe in myself as much as I did right now. I wouldn't even be considering trying to pursue my dream career.

I was more determined than ever and I wasn't going to let that newfound ambition go to waste.

I would've preferred to have done that with Jake by my side, but it wasn't to be.

Although I knew I shouldn't, there was still a tiny part of me that hoped that in a year or two, once Jake was back on his feet properly, we could try again.

I'd had visions of me going to one of his concerts, him seeing me in the crowd and telling me that he'd never stopped loving me.

Was I crazy? Probably.

But as deluded as I sounded, I believed that Jake and I were meant to be together.

I'd laid my heart on the line. I'd done all that I could. And although I couldn't put my life on hold, there would always be a place in my heart for him.

46

JAKE

'This place is sweet!' Roger said as he stepped into the grand living room which had huge glass doors leading out to an even bigger swimming pool. 'Makes my apartment look like a matchbox!'

'It's cool,' I said.

'Cool? You're staying in freaking Liam Stone's mansion and you call it *cool*? If I was him, there's no way I'd leave this place, never mind rent it out.'

'He's in London. He doesn't use it.'

I was tempted to add the fact that he didn't live here any more because he'd found Mia, the love of his life, and decided that being with her was more important, but that shit felt way too close to home.

Objectively speaking, Roger was right. This place was more than just *cool*. And I couldn't even begin to put into words how grateful I was that he'd let me stay here. Without him, I might be on the streets right now.

Roger always said he'd never let that happen, but I knew that I couldn't stay with him forever.

Make no mistake, my lack of enthusiasm had nothing to do with the fact that I wasn't grateful. It was just that as incredible as this place was, without Halle, it felt cold and empty.

'I brought breakfast.' He held up a bag which I knew from the logo was filled with my favourite bagels.

'Thanks. Let's go to the kitchen and put the fancy coffee machine to use.'

Whilst I made coffee, Roger pulled up a stool at the glossy white marble island.

'So how are things?' he asked.

Roger had been busy with work and spending time with Cathy this week and we hadn't had time to catch up, so he'd offered to come over for breakfast.

'Wrote a couple of new songs this week,' I said, as I sat beside him.

'Amazing!'

'Yeah,' I said flatly. They hadn't flowed as easily as they did when I was at the hotel. *With Halle.* 'I called in a couple of favours and I should be able to get some studio time next week.'

'So why do you sound so goddamn miserable?'

I shrugged, knowing exactly why, but not wanting to say it out loud.

Ever since I'd walked out of that villa I'd felt like shit.

Halle put her heart on the line by asking me to move in with her and I'd crushed it. I'd walked away like a coward.

Okay, maybe that was harsh.

I didn't walk away because I was scared. I did it because I didn't think it was fair to ask her to be with me whilst my life was still such a mess.

But I'd regretted doing it ever since.

I should feel happy. I was staying in a multi-million-dollar mansion for at least another three weeks.

I had studio time next week.

Thanks to all the songs I'd written at the hotel and the others I'd managed to write I had almost ten tracks to record. The ones I'd written this week were pretty depressing and mainly focused on how much I missed Halle, but despite my sadness, I'd still forced myself to put pen to paper. I could never have dreamt of being in this position a few weeks ago.

So yeah, things were finally looking up on the career front.

But despite that, my life felt hollow. Like a shell. An empty cave.

I'd even listened to the playlist she'd made me and when I heard the songs, my heart swelled. The hateful tracks at the beginning when she assumed I was in love with myself made me laugh, but the later additions showed that she was into me, just like I was into her.

'You miss her, don't you?' Roger said, somehow reading my thoughts.

'Yeah,' I admitted. I couldn't bottle it up any longer. 'Like crazy. All of this,' I gestured around the room, 'and the songs and the possibilities don't mean shit without her.'

'What you gonna do about it?'

I stared at Roger as his question played on repeat in my brain.

He was right. I needed to do something.

Right now.

Without saying a word, I jumped off the stool, raced to the bedroom, opened my suitcase and pulled out the envelope Halle had given me.

Liam had arranged for the house to be stocked with groceries and all the essentials so I hadn't needed to spend a penny.

This cash was enough to buy me a plane ticket.

I'd said before that my life was in LA, but I was wrong.

My life was with Halle.

I needed to see her.

I needed to *be* with her.

When I was with her, I felt happier. Lighter. Like I could do anything.

I couldn't imagine a world without her.

I wanted her in my life.

Forever.

She was right when she said, *when you know, you know*.

I tossed some clothes in my suitcase, grabbed my wallet then sprinted back to the kitchen.

'Sorry, man, but I'm going to the airport,' I announced.

'Good for you,' Roger said, a wide smile spreading across his face. 'I'll give you a ride.' He patted my back as I locked up.

As I stepped outside, a mixture of nerves and excitement flooded my chest.

I was going to New York to see Halle.

Now I just needed to hope that it wasn't too late.

HALLE

I handed the customer his kale juice, then stifled a yawn. I must've had about four hours' sleep last night.

And this time it wasn't just because I was missing Jake.

Vanessa had arranged for me to come to her office after work to do a couple of her colleagues' nails, which was amazing. Especially as they both asked if I could do them again next week. I officially had my first two customers in New York!

I was buzzing so much when I got home after ten that I started trying to mock up a price list and leaflet for my services and I'd set up my Instagram page.

I wanted to post the photos I'd taken so far, but I'd fallen asleep. Which was something I felt dangerously close to doing again right now.

The lunchtime rush was over, my boss had gone on a break and there were no customers, so now was the perfect time to post them.

I opened the app, selected the first photo, added a caption and a few hashtags, then pressed the post button.

Excitement flooded my chest.

I'd done it!

One photo down. Several more to go.

I started typing out the caption for the second picture.

'Shouldn't you be serving customers instead of posting photos on social media?' A deep voice sounded.

Wait.

I recognised that voice.

My neck snapped up and as I saw who was in front of me, I swear my jaw dropped so far that it could've landed on a subway platform.

It was Jake.

He was here.

In New York.

My eyes popped and as I dragged my jaw back above ground, I attempted to speak.

'J-Jake?'

'That's me.' He flashed his gorgeous smile and my stomach flip-flopped.

'What are you doing here?'

'I came to order the InKrediKale.'

'Do they not sell kale juice in LA?' I teased, a smile tugging at my lips. I still couldn't believe he was here.

'They do, but I heard the server here was pretty cute, so I preferred to ask her to make it for me. And I kinda hoped that I could take her to lunch afterwards.'

'I don't think she gets a break for another twenty minutes,' I grinned, my pulse racing.

'I can wait. I waited my whole life to find her, so twenty minutes will feel like two seconds.' Jake stepped forward, reached over the counter and took my hands in his. 'Especially considering I want to spend forever with her. If she'll have me.'

My eyebrows shot up.

'You mean...' I couldn't even get the words out.

'Yep. I missed you. So much. I don't want to be without you. I want us to be together.'

'You do?'

'Yes! I want it *all* with you. I want forever. And one day we can have our own house with a huge garden and allotment we can both work on.'

'*Oooh*,' I groaned. 'That is *so* hot.'

Most people wouldn't think that a man saying he wanted a garden with them was attractive, but it was for me. I knew how much Jake loved gardening and I did too. But it was also what it represented: a long-term commitment. Spending our lives together.

'Weeds... plants... flowers... *soil*...' he growled in an overexaggerated sexy voice.

'Oh, Jake...' I panted dramatically. 'I love it when you talk dirty to me.'

We both tried so hard to keep up the act, but then burst out laughing.

'I mean it, Smiley. I'm ready to start a life with you. And if that means moving to New York, so be it. Hell, I'd move to the moon if it meant being with you. You're it for me, baby. I love you.'

A tear rolled down my cheek.

'I love you too,' I said.

'Yeah?' Jake grinned.

'Yeah. I've missed you like mad,' I added and Jake's face lit up. 'And there's no need to go to the moon. New York will be just fine!'

I raced from behind the counter and ran straight into Jake's arms.

He tilted my chin up, then pressed his lips onto mine.

As our mouths moulded together, wave upon wave of happiness, joy, relief and elation washed over me.

Jake had come to find me.

And best of all, he said he wanted forever.

Suddenly a round of applause filled the shop. When Jake and I sprang apart, I saw my co-workers and a customer I didn't see come in clapping and grinning.

Then I saw my boss, who had a face like thunder.

I should be worried about getting fired, especially seeing as Jake and I would need money to pay the bills, but I was too happy to care.

Somehow I knew that with Jake by my side and the love we had for each other, that would be enough. Together, we'd find a way to get through anything that the world threw at us.

'So I take it that's a yes, then? The offer to live with you still stands?' Jake asked, ignoring the commotion going on around us.

'No,' I said solemnly. 'It's not a yes. It's a *hell, yeah!*'

Jake picked me up and spun me around with such force that I almost kicked my boss in the crotch. I knew several of my co-workers would've said he deserved it, but it wasn't deliberate. *Honest.*

'Cut that shit out!' my boss spat. 'We don't allow canoodling on the premises.'

'I guess that means I better leave and canoodle outside then!' I untied my apron, dropped it on the counter, took Jake's hand and walked towards the door.

'Where are you going? Your break doesn't start for another ten minutes!'

'I'm going to follow my dreams, with the love of my life.' I took Jake's hand and led him out the door with my head held high.

I'd gone to the Love Hotel to find my soulmate, but I'd left with so much more.

I had a newfound confidence, self-belief, the chance of a new career and a romance that I knew was going to last a lifetime.

Jake wasn't just my Mr Right.

He was my Mr Forever.

And after waiting a lifetime to find a man like him, I didn't want to wait another second.

This time, there was no holding back.

My forever with Jake started right now.

EPILOGUE
HALLE

Nine months later

'You were amazing!' I said as Jake walked into his dressing room.

He'd just finished appearing on *The Graham Norton Show*.

Yep.

Jake was invited onto one of the UK's biggest talk shows and he'd knocked both the performance and the interview out of the park.

'Thanks.' He kissed me softly on the lips. 'It's all thanks to you.'

'Me? I wasn't the one who went out there and sang like an angel, or charmed the pants off every guest on the red sofa. I can't believe you got to meet Julia Roberts.'

'Yeah, she was great.'

'Did you tell her how much we enjoyed watching *Pretty Woman* on the beach?'

'I told her we were fans, but no, I spared her the details of what we got up to on that daybed whilst it was playing,' he smirked.

'Probably for the best,' I grinned.

'But seriously, if it wasn't for you, I would've never have written that song, had my first number one single in years or been invited on this show.'

Once Jake moved to New York, the songs kept flowing out of him. He managed to get some studio time, started recording some tracks and released them independently.

It took a while to get traction, but when it hit, it hit *big*. His streams went through the roof and all of those people in the industry that had turned their backs on him when he was at his lowest point suddenly started calling, begging to work with him. Record companies, agents and other musicians. Including my ex.

Yep. The gall of that guy.

When Brett called, not long after his wife caught him cheating (again) and their show got cancelled, Jake told him to call back in half an hour. I'd just got out of the shower and he asked me how I wanted to play it, suggesting that if I wanted to, I could use the opportunity to teach him a lesson.

So I did.

Brett called back, Jake put the call on loudspeaker. For ten straight minutes, Brett gushed about how much he loved Jake's music and wanted to work with him and how they could create magic together.

When he'd finished, Jake calmly said, 'Uh huh. Listen, I'm gonna hand you over to my manager and my amazing girlfriend, Halle Remington. Pretty sure you know her?'

Brett had gulped so loud it sounded like he'd just swallowed a watermelon.

'Oh, hi, Brett!' I'd said, acting all light and breezy. 'Remember me?'

'Look, Halle, I'm sorry about what happened before. I didn't mean to...'

'Don't be sorry! I'm not. You see, if you weren't such a lying, cheating arsehole, I never would've had the chance to meet a *real* man like Jake. And I never would've discovered what a real orgasm felt like. Such a relief to not have to fake it any more. Anyway, I think Jake will pass on working with you. Right, hon?' I'd said.

'Yep. No way I'd wanna work with a douchebag like you, man. Anything to add, baby?' Jake had asked.

'Nope! Karma's a bitch. Have a nice life, Brett!' I'd said, then hung up.

Was it petty? A little, but after what he'd done, I had to admit, it felt pretty good.

So, yeah, everyone wanted to work with Jake, but he'd stood his ground and was adamant that he wanted to do it on his terms. And it was paying off. His album would be dropping next week and he'd already been booked to appear on a host of American talk shows to promote it.

His career was going to be huge. And I couldn't be prouder.

As for me, my career was going brilliantly. Since I'd walked out of the juice bar, I hadn't looked back. I'd done the nails for Vanessa's colleagues and they'd told their friends, who'd told their friends and thanks to word of mouth, my customer list blew up.

And as much as it surprised me to say it, social media also helped.

I wasn't afraid of photos or the paps any more. Jake and I led a low-key life, which wasn't of great interest to them. We used social media to our advantage and didn't worry about the stuff we couldn't control. So far it was working.

As well as posting photos of my designs on Instagram and TikTok, I posted a couple of videos (they didn't show my face – I wasn't that brave) of me doing nails and when one of them went viral, things really took off. I got booked to do the nails on a magazine shoot which led to more recommendations.

Then, when we met up with Liam Stone and his partner Mia saw my nails, she asked me to do hers too and now, thanks to her very public endorsement, I've got more bookings than I can keep up with. Never in my wildest dreams did I think that would be possible.

There was someone who did though. And he was standing right in front of me. I was so glad that we found each other.

'I'm gonna get changed.' Jake whipped off his T-shirt and my eyes were immediately drawn to his chest. Not just because it looked as gorgeous as ever, but because on the right-hand side, just below his shoulder was a small red love-heart-shaped tattoo.

A tattoo that he'd got for me two months after we'd started living together.

At that point, he was still trying to keep me out of the public eye, so he didn't want to expose me by putting my name. He'd considered putting my initials, but HR sounded like he was in love with the Human Resources department.

So instead, he got my nickname, Smiley (which he knew I had grown to love) tattooed inside the heart instead.

I ran my hand over the tattoo and Jake groaned with pleasure. Just as he leant in for a kiss, the phone rang.

'I'm ignoring it,' he said. 'I don't know why I just switched it back on.'

'It's okay. See who it is. It could be important.'

'Okay,' he sighed, dragging it out of his pocket. 'Hey, Claude!' Jake put the phone on speaker.

'*Salut!*' Claude replied. 'Jake, I know you are a busy man, so as the British say, I will cut to the chase.'

'What's up?'

'We will finally be opening the Love Hotel in Paris in around two months and management would like to know if you would join us for the opening and perhaps to sing too?'

A wide smile spread across Jake's face and he looked at me, signalling with his eyes that he was keen to hear my thoughts. I nodded my approval.

'Sure, man. I'd love to.'

'You would?'

'Of course! How could I say no to the man and the organisation that helped bring me and my amazing lady together? If it wasn't for the Love Hotel, Sammie, you and all the other Romance Rockstars who worked their magic, I wouldn't have met the love of my life. I used to think your job titles were silly, but it's true: you guys rock! We'd love to be there.'

'*Fantastique!*' he shouted. 'I will send you the details and exact date once it has been confirmed and someone will of course be in touch to arrange everything.'

'Sounds great! I'm looking forward to seeing what the French Love Hotel looks like and having a ringside seat to watch the romances that blossom there.'

'I am sure you and Halle will love it. We have some very interesting guests who will be joining us from all over France and the UK too. And of course it's in Paris, so it is sure to be beautiful.'

'I bet. Speak soon, Claude. *Au revoir.*' Jake hung up. 'So what d'ya say, Smiley? Looking forward to spending some quality time together in Paris?'

'Visiting the most romantic city in the world with the most amazing man in the universe?' I said, wrapping my arms around him again as he leant in and gave me a long, slow kiss. 'Sign me up.'

* * *

MORE FROM OLIVIA SPRING

The next instalment in this gorgeously romantic, spicy series from Olivia Spring, is available to order now here:

https://mybook.to/LoveHotel5BackAd

ACKNOWLEDGEMENTS

I'd like to thank the following people for helping me to bring *Anyone But You* to life:

- **My amazing husband:** for the continued support and epic hugs.
- **My brilliant beta readers: Emma Grocott, Mum** and **Loz** for your fantastic feedback.
- **My publishing and editorial team: Megan Haslam** (editor), **Rachel Lawston** (cover designer), **Cecily Blench** (copyeditor), **Rachel Sargeant** (proofreader), **Niamh Wallace** (marketing) and everyone at Boldwood who helped to promote this book to a wider audience.
- The lovely **book bloggers, Bookstagrammers, ARC readers and BookTokers** for the wonderful reviews and gorgeous posts.
- And of course, to **YOU, dear reader.** Thank you for buying and reading this novel. I appreciate you SO much!

Looking forward to sharing book five in the Love Hotel series with you soon!

Lots of love,

Olivia x

ABOUT THE AUTHOR

Olivia Spring is a bestselling author of contemporary women's fiction and romantic comedies, now writing spicy romance for Boldwood.

Download your exclusive bonus content from Olivia Spring here:

Visit Olivia's website: www.oliviaspring.com

Follow Olivia on social media here:

- facebook.com/ospringauthor
- x.com/ospringauthor
- instagram.com/ospringauthor
- bookbub.com/authors/olivia-spring

ALSO BY OLIVIA SPRING

The Love Hotel Series

The One That Got Away

What Happens in Paradise

Too Hard to Resist

Anyone But You

Boldwood
EVER AFTER

X♡X♡

JOIN BOLDWOOD'S
**ROMANCE
COMMUNITY**
FOR SWEET AND
SPICY BOOK RECS
WITH ALL YOUR
FAVOURITE
TROPES!

SIGN UP TO OUR
NEWSLETTER

HTTPS://BIT.LY/BOLDWOODEVERAFTER

Boldwood

Boldwood Books is an award-winning fiction publishing company seeking out the best stories from around the world.

Find out more at www.boldwoodbooks.com

Join our reader community for brilliant books, competitions and offers!

Follow us
@BoldwoodBooks
@TheBoldBookClub

Sign up to our weekly
deals newsletter

https://bit.ly/BoldwoodBNewsletter

Printed in Dunstable, United Kingdom

76427227R00202